Digging Deep

Dexter Hutt

Published by New Generation Publishing in 2022

Copyright © Dexter Hutt 2022

First Edition

ISBN

Paperback	978-1-80369-669-0
Hardback	978-1-80369-670-6
eBook	978-1-80369-671-3

www.newgeneration-publishing.com

New Generation Publishing

Dexter Hutt spent his early childhood in Guyana. After graduating from Birmingham University, he pursued a career in secondary school improvement, during which he was knighted for services to education. He lives in Birmingham with his wife, Rosemary, and — from time to time — with his son's dog, Niuniu. Digging Deep is his first novel.

Contact: dexterhutt@hotmail.com

For Rose

Chapter 1

It had been hours since Walter's chance encounter with the girl. Staring at the single page of notes in his green moleskin notebook, he couldn't shake the sense of unease he'd felt since writing her words down. His study usually brought a sense of solace but having the notebook in his possession put him on edge – like it was a harmful, toxic thing. He knew it was irrational. It was the girl who was in danger, not him. But he decided to hide the notebook anyway.

Pacing up and down, he decided a run might help. He changed into his running clothes – his old green vest with the old school logo emblazoned across the chest, tracksuit bottom, trainers.

The side lights on the blue Audi flashed in the fading autumn light as he clicked the key to open the car. Reversing out of the drive, lost in thought as he headed out of the cul-de-sac, Walter, an active member of the local Neighbourhood Watch, would normally have noticed the white van parked in his street. But tonight, he had other things on his mind. So he didn't pay any attention to the white van, didn't see the two men sitting in it, the one in the passenger seat dropping his cigarette butt out of the window to join the three littering the tarmac, the one in the driver's seat munching a protein bar, trying to wave the cigarette smoke away with his other hand.

Walter headed towards the Bournville Community Centre running grounds, a ten-minute drive from his home. Usually, the familiar winding roads would relax him. But not tonight. He couldn't shake the girl from his mind.

The girl, Elira, had approached Walter hesitantly in the supermarket car park and asked him for money. She was in her early twenties, a good fifteen years younger than his much-loved daughter, but with the same mannerism of holding her head a little to one side as she spoke. Standing before him, looking about her skittishly, poised on the balls of her feet, he saw the fear in her eyes. But it was the overpowering sense of desperation that drew him in.

'Are you hungry?' Walter asked softly. 'I'm starving.'

He took her across the road to the café and bought her breakfast, watched and waited as she devoured the food, hardly pausing to breathe. When she had finished eating and taken her first sip from the mug of tea, he took a chance and asked her the obvious question. Elira did not reply straightaway. She had first taken a long look into his eyes, must have seen something there to make her trust him. She spoke quietly; he had to lean forward to hear her. She told him why she was in the car park, why she was asking strangers for money.

Walter's instinctive response was to take the girl to the police. But she was alarmed at this suggestion, sitting bolt upright and violently shaking her head. Her reaction surprised him. He saw the defiance in her flashing eyes, saw the strong-willed young woman she must have been before this. Waiting until she had lowered her head, taken another sip of tea, he said, 'Elira, you're not in Kosovo anymore. This is Birmingham, England.'

Putting the mug of tea down, she had raised her head and given him a look that was at first puzzled, and then scornful.

'You are a good man, Walter, but you don't know your own country. Swear to me you will not go to the police. You must promise if you want me to tell you more.'

He could not deny the urgency in her voice. So, he had promised.

The large community centre car park at the running club, set away from the main pavilion, was big enough to host a local market on Saturday mornings. It was almost empty at this time of the evening, but by habit Walter parked at the far end, his front bumper against the thick hedge that separated the car park from the path leading down to the lake.

Breathing deeply, he embraced the rapidly cooling evening air as he crossed the road to the oak tree that marked the start of the 5K and 10K routes. It was half past seven. Setting his watch to running mode, he started off, easing into a gentle ten-minute mile pace. He'd taken up running after his fortieth birthday, completed the London Marathon in three and a half hours when he was forty-two. But that was twenty-five years ago when he could run eight-minute miles. He kept up the running partly for his health, partly because he found the rhythm helped him to order his thoughts.

The girl would not say any more in the café. But from what she had already told him, he knew he had to do more than just give her money. She was in danger. Extreme danger. And she needed somewhere safe to stay. He'd phoned his friend who chaired the board of a women's refuge, managed to arrange a one-night emergency stay.

The room in the refuge was in dire need of a lick of paint. Elira had sat cross-legged on the single bed. Lifting the chair from behind the small table, Walter sat opposite her. He did not interrupt her as she finished telling him her story, even though the outpouring of anger and emotion made it sometimes hard to follow. But he understood enough. When she stopped, a long silence stretched between them. Then, standing up, he reached for the little bag that he always carried with him.

'You don't believe me.' She stared at him defiantly, her arms folded tightly across her body.

He took out his green moleskin notebook and searched his inside jacket pocket for a pen.

'I do believe you. Tell me again. But slowly this time. I must make notes if I'm going to help you.'

Those who worked with Walter during his long career would have described him as a calm person with an appetite for problem solving. But this was a problem beyond him; he had stumbled into a world that was both unfamiliar and dangerous. He knew he was out of his depth.

The 10K route was along paths that took him through three adjoining parks to a large duck pond marking the midpoint of the run. People out for the evening walk with their dogs made way for him; most nodded a greeting as he jogged past. Glancing at his watch as he rounded the duck pond, Walter saw that his pace was about right. Crossing the little wooden bridge that spanned the stream, he started the return leg. He wondered again if he should have kept his promise to her.

Returning home after leaving Elira to spend the night in the refuge, Walter had sat in his study, reading the notes he'd made. He didn't know who to turn to for help, if not the police. And then the idea had come to him. He found the phone number in his old address book, climbed the stairs up to his bedroom to make the call.

Walter had determined to say as little as possible on the phone, but his request for an urgent appointment was refused at first, a full diary given as the reason. Caught unaware by the refusal, he had to swallow hard to ease the knot in his stomach. Where else could he go for help? He ended up saying more than he had intended to but was rewarded with a swift change of heart when he mentioned the girl was from Kosovo. He now had an appointment for 8 a.m. tomorrow; he felt elated when he put the phone down. But then something was nagging at him, making him uneasy about the conversation. He was glad he'd hidden the notebook.

He was nearing the end of the 10K run now. The last three hundred metres were uphill to the oak tree; with head down and arms pumping, he finished with a spurt. Bending over, chest heaving, he breathed deeply.

Walter walked to the little gate at the end of the playing field. Elira would be safe where she was for the night. But what about after that? She'd been insistent they would be searching for her, would want to hunt her down. He worried she was right. She knew too much.

Pulling the metal gate shut behind him, he crossed the road to the car park. The moon moved from behind a cloud; he could see the car park was empty apart from his car and a white van that was also parked at the far end. He was reaching for the car doorhandle when he heard the voice.

'Walter Price?'

It was the accent that triggered Walter's reaction. The same accent as Elira's. Pivoting sharply, his elbow up and raised, he caught the man on his windpipe. There was an audible gasp and as the man staggered, Walter turned to run. But his path was blocked by a short, stocky man with the build of a gymnast. Grasping Walter around his waist with his left arm, holding him in close with a vice like grip, he worked the knife with his right hand. Walter felt the blade pierce his skin. Open mouthed, he looked down into the shorter man's upturned face, saw the glint in his eyes, felt the knife being dragged across his chest – and knew that he was going to die.

Chapter 2

The phone kept on ringing. Detective Chief Inspector Gavin Ross swore, rolled over, sat up in the bed. He reached for his mobile, stared at the screen, and swore again.

'Do you know what bloody time it is?'

'Sorry, sir. Order from Deputy Chief Constable Henderson. He told me to ring you. There's been a murder.'

That bastard. 'So what? This is Birmingham. Murders happen. Why can't the Duty Inspector handle it?'

'The Duty Inspector has been on the scene for the last hour, sir. But the Deputy was insistent that you should be the Senior Investigating Officer.'

Ross spoke through gritted teeth. 'Right. Let's have the details.'

Switching on the bedside lamp, he wrote the address down on the pad, the one his wife used to keep by her side of the bed. He went into the bathroom to rinse the smell of curry from his breath, then threw on yesterday's clothes. He'd returned home too late from visiting his mother in the Home to bother cooking. He got dressed. The remains of the takeaway lay open on the worktop in the kitchen, the spicy aroma lingering. Grabbing four sausage rolls out of the chest freezer, he zapped one in the microwave for thirty seconds and wrapped it in kitchen roll. The other three went into a sandwich bag to defrost in the car.

It was gone 2 a.m. There were very few cars about. He drove past the Activities centre that now occupied the old BSA motorbike site. An old couple were walking along the road, the man in front, unsteady on his feet, pausing to raise a can to his lips, the woman hanging on to a bottle of wine, staggering ten yards behind, mouthing at him. Ross wondered why the hell they weren't tucked up in bed.

He stopped at the traffic lights and took a bite of his sausage roll while he waited for red to turn green. Past the Central Mosque, he turned left at the roundabout, passing the graffiti strewn boarding where his old college used to be. The site was still waiting to be redeveloped; the college had long moved to the city centre, next to one of the university campuses.

Ross's time at the Further Education College was the only phase of his education he'd enjoyed. Good teachers who saw something in him. And said so. But he'd gone against their advice and joined the Police Force, refusing the university place that was on offer. Now he was surrounded by bloody graduates, smart arses who the Chief Constable spoke of as the guardians of the future of policing. Well, good luck to them; he would take his retirement in four weeks' time when he was fifty-five.

It was one year and one week since his wife had walked out – gone to live with a man he suspected she'd been seeing for some time. Well, sod her. Sod the lot of them. He would soon have his freedom. He could travel. He reached out to the passenger seat for the half-eaten sausage roll.

Ross was now driving through the part of Kings Norton that estate agents referred to as an established residential area. Three-bedroom or four-bedroom houses on either side, well-tended front gardens of the respectable middle class. All quiet and in darkness at this time of night. The cul-de-sac was off to the left, number 21 at the end, facing down the road. His headlights picked out the uniformed constable standing at the entrance to the short drive. Lowering his window as the constable approached, he flashed his ID.

'Ross. I'm the SIO. Where's the body?'

The constable was young. Narrow face with a prominent nose. He looked confused by Ross's question.

'It's not here, sir. The victim was stabbed in the car park at Bournville Community Centre. We were sent here to his home address. There was nobody in, but the house had been broken into. Forced entry at the front door. We informed the station.'

Ross swore softly. 'The idiot gave me this address.' He glared at the constable. 'Who's we?'

'Me and my partner, sir.' He turned his head toward the front door; Ross made out the outline of another uniformed constable. 'We were told not to go into the house.'

Ross got out of his car, straightened up, suddenly aware that the constable was taller than he was. He turned to look at the house, then turned back and stared at the constable suspiciously. 'So, you were told not to go inside. Why are the lights on, then?'

'Your inspector is inside, sir. Arrived twenty minutes ago.'

'My inspector?' Ross didn't wait for an answer. Turning on his heels, he marched towards the front door of the house.

Taking some overshoes from his pocket, he slipped them on, nodded as the other constable moved aside to let him pass. He found himself in a small hallway with wooden flooring that extended out into a corridor. At one end of the corridor, carpeted stairs led up to the bedrooms. The room in front of him had a wall made up of lead-lined panes of glass set in a white wooden frame. On the other side of the glass partition, he could see a mahogany dining table and chairs; a picture window ran along almost the entire width of the far wall. In the reflected light from the hallway, he could just make out what looked like a patio. He supposed there was a garden beyond that.

To his right was an open door, the entrance to a carpeted lounge. Two different sized sofas in red fabric, a large television in the corner, a freestanding wall display unit that housed books and ornaments. No signs of disturbance. Leaving the lounge, he went through to the kitchen at the end of the corridor. He turned around as he heard footsteps coming down the stairs.

She was above average height for a woman, about 5 foot 7 inches, he reckoned, a slim figure with short dark hair, a tanned complexion. He didn't recognise her.

'Ross, I'm the SIO. And you are?'

Her voice was firm. 'Inspector Angie Reeves, sir. Returning from an extended leave of absence. I've been assigned to work with you. I was told to meet you at this address.'

He ignored her outstretched hand. 'For me.'

'Sir?'

'You've been assigned to work *for* me. Not with me.'

She was silent. He remembered the phone call a fortnight before from the Deputy Chief Constable. He had been given the barest information about a Detective Inspector Angie Reeves – that she had been involved in an incident in the Middle East, had returned with PTSD nine months ago, would benefit from a quiet reintroduction.

'Ignore the rank,' Henderson had said. 'She's not joining you as a DI, just a member of the team. We want you to ease her in. It's a four-week trial.'

Ross let his silence speak for itself.

'And since your retirement is imminent,' the Deputy had added, not bothering to disguise the sneer in his voice before hanging up, 'see this as your last contribution to the force.'

Ross now looked at her more closely. He saw her eyes were red, as though she'd been crying. Wondered if he was going to have to babysit a returning wreck.

He was brusque, 'Syria, wasn't it?'

'No, sir. Iraq.' She was staring at his chin.

He nodded, felt the pastry crumbs, licked his lips with his tongue and wiped his mouth with the back of his hand to make sure.

'Well, what have we got?'

'I've checked the bedrooms, sir. No sign of anyone having gone up there.'

She followed him into the kitchen. Tidy black granite work tops with a matching table in the centre, chairs neatly pushed in. Two white painted wooden doors to the left, one presumably leading to the double garage Ross had parked in front of, the other one where one would expect a pantry to be. At the far end of the kitchen, glass double doors opened out on to a good-sized conservatory. Another set of glass double doors led from the conservatory to the patio. Nothing seemed out of place.

'They must have known where to look,' Ross said, 'for whatever they were after.' He switched off the kitchen light. 'We'll leave it to Forensics.

We need to get to the car park. Where they should have sent us in the first place.'

He headed back along the corridor. His hand was on the handle of the front door when she said, 'We haven't seen a study.'

Ross turned around, frowning. 'What?'

'We haven't seen a study.'

Ross shrugged. 'Not everyone is an avid reader.' He knew this to be true – his own reading these days was confined to the odd website and magazines in waiting rooms.

The determination in her voice caught him by surprise. 'But he was. He read voraciously. He would have a study.' She stared at Ross. 'We haven't looked at the garden.'

He understood what she meant. It was more common these days for people to fit out a garden shed, to turn into a comfortable personal space where they could work or read. Or write. Or just sit and think without being disturbed.

A question formed in Ross's mind: how did Reeves know the victim was an avid reader? But before he could ask, she was striding back along the corridor. Swearing under his breath, Ross stalked after her.

. Powerful security lights came on as they stepped on to the patio, revealing leylandii trees down the left side and along the back of the garden. What looked like a mixture of shrubs and fruit trees made up the line of demarcation on the right. It was a larger space than Ross had expected and very private, ideal for hosting a study at the bottom of the garden. But there was no study, only a fox lying in front of an arbour; he raised its head in the sudden light and fixed them with an unblinking gaze.

Ross said, 'We need to get to the body. I know the way to the car park. You can follow me.'

He waited in the kitchen, drumming his fingers on the black granite table while she locked the outer conservatory door. Turning around, as she glanced to the right, a puzzled look appeared on her face. She strode into the kitchen, up to the nearest white door on her right.

'That'll be the pantry,' Ross said, turning to go.

Only it wasn't. She turned the handle to reveal a box room that had been converted to a study. The picture window she had glimpsed overlooked the garden. The carpeted study was fitted out with light oak desk furniture along the back wall. The Apple computer and the swivel desk lamp were in place, the golf trophies on the top shelf undisturbed. But the rest of it was a mess. Three filing drawers housed on the left had been emptied, their contents strewn on the carpet. The same for the three desk drawers on the right. Books that had lined the two long shelves above the furniture lay scattered on top of the files. Two white cushions, pulled out from the small sofa, had been thrown against the radiator, their covers ripped off.

They stood in the doorway, Ross with his head to one side, trying to read the title of a book on top of the pile. 'Another do-gooder,' he muttered under his breath. Following his gaze, Angie read the title that had attracted his attention. *Crime and Punishment*.

'It's a novel,' she said. 'He liked the Russian classics.'

There was an awkward silence before Ross spoke, the sharpness in his voice making the accusation clear. 'You knew the victim.'

She looked away for a moment before turning to face him. He was taken back by the fierceness of her tone. 'His name was Walter Price. And yes, I knew him. I was at his school for seven years. He was my headteacher.'

Ross remembered her red eyes from earlier. He wondered what she was holding back. And if she would hold up.

***

Sitting in the darkness of her car, taking deep breaths, Angie exhaled slowly to relieve the tightness in her chest as she waited for Ross to finish his phone call. She'd been shocked when she switched on the bedroom light and been confronted with the framed photograph of Walter. It was one of him with the then Prime Minister who had visited the school. She'd collapsed on the bed, unable to move. Her heart was racing. She closed her eyes, waited for the psychiatrist's words to surface: '*You need emotional awareness and*

16

will power. Fear causes pain. Direct your attention somewhere else; where your attention goes, you go.'

Managing to get her phone out, she'd focused on the photograph. *'Find one that reminds you of happy times.'* Her chosen one was the first photograph she had ever taken – the one of her father on the beach in Majorca. He was smiling proudly at the sandcastle she'd just finished.

It had been a good five minutes before her breathing returned to normal. Sitting on the bed, she'd let the tears flow as she remembered Walter.

Walter Price had been more than a caring headteacher to her; he was the man who saved her father's life when his car overturned on the icy slip road as he came off the motorway. It was Walter who'd spotted the leaking petrol tank; it was Walter who'd forced the driver's door open and lifted her unconscious father out just before the car burst into flames.

Her aunt Peggy came to stay while her father recovered. And it was at the hospital Angie met Walter for the first time when he visited her father. She was eleven years old, had passed the 11 plus exam and been offered a place at one of the King Edward's grammar schools. But she got to know Walter during his regular visits to the hospital. When he told her he was a headteacher she told her father she wanted to go to his school. Her father had thought for a moment, then held her hand and told her it was her choice. But he'd seemed pleased.

Walter had made a difference to her life. And now he was dead.

Ross's question had caught her by surprise, but she'd instinctively not told him how much she was indebted to Walter. Officers with too strong an emotional attachment to the victim were usually taken off the murder enquiry team.

She knew what awaited her at the crime scene. She'd made steady progress with her PTSD, had been excited to return to active duty. But her reaction in the bedroom was a warning. She didn't think she was ready to see Walter's dead body. Or any dead body. Not yet. But she had no choice. She sat in the car, pressing her thumbnail hard into the palm of her left hand, winced as she felt the pain.

Coming out of the house, Ross slipped his phone back in his pocket, looked around for her. Angie flashed her headlights, got out of the car as he walked over.

'That was Armstrong, the Duty Inspector. Wondering why we hadn't arrived at the car park. He was livid when I told him we were both sent to this address. He sent the constables over here to inform the next of kin. That's how they discovered the break-in.'

'He's got a daughter,' Angie said, 'Roxanne. I think she's a GP somewhere in London.'

'Married?'

'I don't think so. Roxanne Price.'

'I'll head over to the car park now,' Ross said.

Angie nodded, got back in her car, was fastening her seat belt when she realised Ross hadn't moved. She lowered her window.

'Armstrong is one of the competent ones,' Ross said. 'The car park has been taped off; Forensics are at the scene. We'll arrange for the body to be moved after I've seen it. I'll get Armstrong's report. We'll have the first briefing at 7.30 a.m.'

She looked at him questioningly. He leant in through the window, so his eyes were level with hers. 'I didn't think you'd want to be staring at the dead body of someone you knew on your first day back. Go home. There's nothing more we can do tonight.'

His phone was ringing again. He motioned with his hand for Angie to go. Looking in the rear mirror as she moved off, she saw him staring after her as he put the phone to his ear.

***

Angie felt the tightness in her chest ease as she turned out of the cul-de-sac. She thought Ross was a strange mixture. Brusque to the point of rudeness, yet aware that she might not be ready to look at a dead body. She remembered seeing him once before, eleven years ago, when she was at the Police College. He was a newly appointed Chief Inspector, invited to give a talk on the work of a detective. He'd been brilliant. She was glad to be working with him. *For* him. All that mattered was that he found Walter's killer. She thought about what the constable at the front of the house, who had come from the car park, had told her. 'Looks to me like a carjacking that went badly wrong. They might have been drug crazed. Or had one too many. A case of the victim just being in the wrong place at the wrong time.'

There was little traffic. All the lights went her way, and she reached her destination in under twenty minutes. She'd been through an agency, rented a furnished two-bedroomed flat on the second floor of an apartment block on the Hagley Road. The owner lived in Majorca. It wasn't "home", but it was all that she needed for the time being.

Angie undressed, swallowed the medication that helped to dampen her body's hyperactive alarm systems and climbed into bed. It had been a long nine months recovering from PTSD. The flashbacks that always started with Wafaa's staring eyes, that woke her up screaming and unable to move, had gradually become less frequent. The last one had been two months ago. She thought she'd almost regained what the psychiatrist referred to as self-mastery. The depression was gone. She no longer woke up feeling irritable. Lying on her back, she waited for the medication to work its magic, her eyes growing heavy as she drifted off.

She woke up half an hour before her alarm, wondering why she was smiling. And then flashes of her dream came back. She could recall only some of it: herself as a twelve-year-old girl being told to report to the Head's office; Walter introducing her to Philip, a boy with red, curly hair, telling the two of them he would mentor them together; the hour-long meetings with them that Walter never missed; his end-of-term visits to her house to go through Angie's progress with her wheelchair-bound father; the competitive games of cribbage the two men would play that became part of every visit.

The psychiatrist had told her that when normal dreams came back, it would be an indication of her progress. She'd woken up from a normal dream.

And now, at last, she was back at work. Not the desk job they'd offered before finally agreeing to a trial on active duty without the normal responsibility of a DI. Just as a member of the team.

She was grateful Ross had excused her from seeing Walter's body. But now she worried he might think she was too fragile to contribute to the investigation. She stood in front of the bathroom mirror and stared back at herself. She would have to show him. Prove herself. She could do that.

Chapter 3

Ross had said the briefing was at 7.30 a.m. Angie had allowed time for the build-up of the rush hour traffic – she turned into the police car park at 7.15 a.m. The desk sergeant directed her to the incident room on the second floor of the station. She was surprised there were only four others there. Three detective constables – two men and a woman – were sat around the top end of a conference table that could have seated twelve. A detective sergeant sat at the desk next to it, below an electronic whiteboard on the wall. The chatting stopped as Angie took the nearest empty seat, next to an older man with a shaven head and the shoulders of an ex-rugby player who turned and introduced himself as DC Simpson. The sergeant stood up, came around the table to Angie, held out his hand.

'You must be DI Angie Reeves,' he said. 'DCI Ross will be along shortly. He told me you'd be joining us. I'm DS Bridges. Think of me as Ross's bagman.' Angie shook his hand, taking in the broad face, a nose that looked like it had been broken more than once, and a receding hairline that spoke of his age. But there was genuine warmth in his smile and in his eyes.

'I'll do the introductions,' Bridges said. 'You've met Simpson.' He pointed across the table. 'Washington and O'Byrne.' Washington nodded an acknowledgment. He looked to be in his mid-forties with a full head of black hair and a trimmed moustache. Angie guessed O'Byrne was ten years younger, blonde hair framing a round face. She gave a smile as Bridges called her name.

The door opened and Ross ambled in. He paused for a moment, looked down and brushed some crumbs off his front with the back of his hand, then took the seat at the far end of the conference table before nodding at Bridges, sitting at the desk with his laptop open. Bridges stood up. A picture of Walter appeared on the whiteboard.

'Walter Price,' Bridges said, 'a retired headteacher, aged sixty-seven. Went for a run last evening, returned to the car park where he had left his car and was stabbed to death.' Bridges moved back to the laptop. Angie guessed what was coming, stole a quick glance as an image of Walter taken by the police photographer appeared on the screen. She looked away.

He was lying on his back. They could see the black trainers, the black tracksuit bottoms, the short green sleeves of his running shirt. The front of the shirt had turned dark red, stained with blood. 'Jesus!' Simpson said softly. Angie felt the pounding of her heart, made herself breathe slowly and deeply until it receded.

'Two reasons for that amount of blood,' Bridges said. 'According to the pathologist, the knife used was unusual. It had a sharp point but also a finely serrated blade. In this case, the knife was plunged into his body, then dragged across his chest by someone with considerable strength.'

There was silence while they took that in. The visual image was powerful.

'What's the second reason?' asked Simpson.

'Warfarin. It's an anticoagulant that thins the blood; the downside is more bleeding takes place if there's a cut. Walter Price had been prescribed Warfarin because he suffered from atrial fibrillation.'

'Do we have an approximate time of death?' Washington asked.

'Two students returning from a party found the body and called 999. The call is recorded at 00:45. The pathologist has to do more tests, but her initial opinion is that the body had been lying in the car park for at least three hours. Joggers don't usually run that late so let's assume a two-hour window from 19:45.'

'And the motive?' O'Byrne's voice was surprisingly deep. 'Do we know of any reason why the headteacher would have been attacked?'

'Retired headteacher,' Bridges corrected her. 'There's been five carjackings in the community centre car park in the last six months. The most likely explanation is it was not Walter Price, but his car that was the target.' He brought another picture up on the whiteboard. The photographer had pulled back to get a wider view: this was a photograph that showed the body and the blue Audi. They could see the front of the car was against the hedge.

'Look at the position of the body in relation to the car,' Bridges said. 'The body is this side of the boot. Since the car was parked against the hedge, his only escape route was past the back of his car, further into the car park.'

'Surely he wouldn't run towards a man with a knife,' Washington said.

'Not knowingly. But if there were two of them, and one approached him from the side, he might have turned to run and found himself blocked by the second man.'

'Why not just let him run if it's the car they're after? And why didn't they take the car?' Simpson asked what they were all thinking.

'I don't know the answer to your first question but maybe they panicked. Didn't want to take the risk of his car being traced. None of the other carjackings were as violent as this; in two cases, knives were brandished but not used.'

Bridges raised his hand. 'There's something else to consider. The victim's house was broken into last night as well. In fact, both DCI Ross and DI Reeves were directed, or to put it more accurately, misdirected, to the house in the first instance.' He paused as he saw the shaking heads. 'As it turned out, this was not a typical break in.

No valuables were taken. The only room disturbed was the victim's study, which was ransacked. The conclusion is that the intruders were searching for a letter or document.'

'Are you saying the same people who killed Walter Price broke into his house searching for a specific document?' Simpson asked.

'Not necessarily,' Bridges said. 'We don't know that for sure. It might have been two separate incidents involving different people. A coincidence that they took place on the same evening. They might not be connected.'

Angie saw her scepticism reflected on the DCs faces. Bridges did too.

'The thing is,' he said, 'the front door of the house had been forced open, the lock was broken.' He paused to let that sink in then put the earlier photograph of Walter back on the screen. He pointed to an object slightly to one side of the body. 'That is the car key for the Audi. And on the same key ring is the key to the front door of Walter Price's house.' He waited for them to catch up. Angie got there first.

'So, if it were the same people, why would they have forced the door open? They could simply have used his key to unlock the front door.'

Bridges nodded at her and then looked down the table at Ross. They all turned expectantly to where Ross sat, arms folded. But he remained silent.

Bridges broke the silence, rapping the desk hard with his knuckles. They turned back, saw his grim-faced expression.

'Right,' he said. 'Enough speculation. We need to get out there, go door to door.' Coming forward from the whiteboard he stood at the head of the table. 'We'll work in pairs. DCI Ross and I have got the addresses of the two students who found the body; apparently, they were too drunk last night to give a statement. We've also arranged an interview with the manager of the community centre.'

He gestured to Angie and Simpson, 'You two focus on the break-in. Talk to the immediate neighbours, the other residents in the cul-de-sac. It's a Neighbourhood Watch area. Someone might have noticed strangers in the street. On foot or in a car.'

Then, turning to Washington and O'Byrne. 'You two find out if any of the residents around the community centre spotted any cars other than the blue Audi in the car park after 19.45 last night. Or any cars parked on the road outside, opposite the playing fields. The killers might have seen him finishing his run, followed him into the car park.' Bridges raised his hand as Washington and O'Byrne started to move. 'Look at this first.'

He projected a new photograph on the whiteboard, this one showing the far end of the car park where Walter had parked his car. 'You can see the front bumper of the Audi is up against a hedge. On the other side of that hedge is a narrow path leading down to a lake, and beyond it, further housing. That path is a dog walker's trail.' He paused. 'Either of you have a dog?' They both shook their heads. 'Most dog owners walk their dog morning and evening. Usually along the same trail. So, question anyone walking their dog along the path this morning. Find out if they were out last night at the relevant time, if they noticed anything unusual.'

He pointed to where the hedge ended. 'I used to be a member of the running club. It's a high hedge. From the path, the car park is only visible through this gap that allows access to the lake. So focus particularly on those walking *up* from the lake. They're the ones who could see into the car park.'

***

Simpson had to slide the passenger seat right back to fit his long legs into Angie's Peugeot. At 8.20 a.m., the rush hour traffic was still heavy, workers heading into the city centre, parents on the school run. They stopped at a pedestrian crossing to let a posse of school children cross, all wearing green blazers with a gold crest.

'You'll have gathered Ross and Bridges are a double act,' Simpson said. 'They were the force's crack team at one time. Ross was the ambitious one, a hotshot DCI; Bridges was just content to stay at his side.'

Angie told Simpson about Ross's talk at the Police College when he was the newly promoted DCI. 'But that was eleven years ago,' she said. 'What happened to his career?'

'He fell foul of the higher ups.'

Angie kept her foot on the brake pedal and turned her head to look at Simpson.

'There was a hit-and-run incident involving a politician. A young boy was badly injured. The case never made it to court. Ross accused Paul Henderson, the officer in charge, of a cover up. There was an internal inquiry. Henderson was cleared of any wrongdoing. He's now our Deputy Chief Constable. Competent enough but ambition can cloud his judgement sometimes.' Simpson gave Angie a knowing look. 'There's no love lost between him and Ross.'

The last of the school children had reached the other side. Angie put the car in gear; they made slow but steady progress until they joined the queue to turn right at the big Cotteridge roundabout.

'Ross is retiring in four weeks,' Simpson said. 'This is his last case.'

He saw the surprise on Angie's face.

'Yes,' Simpson said, 'Strange, isn't it? For Ross to be assigned to lead a murder investigation when he's leaving so soon. Apparently, it was the Deputy's doing.' Simpson smiled grimly. 'Henderson's parting shot.'

Angie gripped the steering wheel tightly. She stared straight ahead, her mind whirling. So, Ross was retiring in four weeks. How committed could he be to finding Walter's killer? Was he mentally winding down? Was that why he had played no part in the briefing? And was it because of the bad blood between the Deputy and Ross that the murder team was smaller than she'd expected? She knew what would happen if they hadn't found Walter's killer by the time Ross retired. A new murder team would have to start all over again. Without her.

She noticed too late that the car in front had stopped. Simpson was jerked forward as she stamped on the brakes. Glancing across, he saw the tension in her face and kept quiet.

The road was relatively clear after the roundabout; the traffic was in the opposite direction. Turning into the cul-de-sac, they saw the police car in front of Walter's house. A uniformed constable was removing the tape that ran across the drive. It was the same constable who had been there the previous evening. Angie asked him about the Scene of Crime Officers.

'SOCOs have been and gone,' he said. 'We've secured the front door. I'm just off back to the station.'

'Any neighbours enquiring?'

'Not yet. I think they're mostly retired folk. No one's been rushing off to work.'

An upstairs light was on in the house on their left. Simpson pointed with his chin.

Angie nodded, 'Let's start with that one.'

***

They sat in the station canteen with half an hour to kill before their appointment with the community centre manager. Bridges was silent, seemingly concentrating on slowly stirring his coffee. Ross saw his DS's clenched jaw and knew what that meant.

'Enough!' he said. 'Say what you want to say.'

Bridges looked up, holding Ross's gaze. 'Alright,' he said. 'But you're not going to like it.' He put the teaspoon down. 'I think the Deputy is playing you.'

Ross's eyes narrowed but he remained silent.

'Henderson doesn't forget or forgive,' Bridges said. 'He's a man who bears grudges. And he's bided his time ever since your accusation of a cover up resulted in him having to sit through an internal inquiry. We both know that's why you've had no substantial cases since he became Deputy Chief Constable eighteen months ago. And then suddenly, when you're four weeks from retirement, he hands you a murder case and a reduced team. Why do you think that is?'

Ross managed a bitter half-smile. 'It's because the bastard knows I'm winding down mentally.

And he wants to keep my nose to the grindstone right to the end.'

Bridges was nodding to himself. 'I wondered if that's what you were thinking. So you've decided to show him two fingers, to take a back seat over this investigation. That's why, for the first time, you didn't lead this morning's briefing, isn't it? You're minded to sit out the next four weeks and wait for the investigation to be handed to a new team.'

Ross pursed his lips. But he didn't answer.

'I thought so,' Bridges said. 'Have you considered Henderson was hoping you'd react that way?'

This time, Ross laughed openly. 'Why would he want that?'

Bridges took his time before answering, 'We've had a lot of success over the last sixteen years. But everyone will tell you it's your last case that remains freshest in your memory. And in the memory of others too. Failure in your last case can tarnish your reputation, your legacy. But more importantly it can tarnish your self-worth. Do you really want to end up in the proverbial rocking chair with the bitter taste of failure dominating your memory of your life's work?'

Sitting back, fingers interlocked, pressing his thumbs together, Ross stared at Bridges for a long moment. 'You're saying that's what Henderson really wants.'

Bridges held his old comrade's eyes, nodded slowly. 'I think the Deputy has shown you the bait. And you're in danger of swallowing the hook.'

Chapter 4

The front door opened before they reached it. A jet-black spaniel bounded out, tail wagging furiously, head held high as he sniffed the air. The man on the other end of the lead, locking the door, had his back towards them. He turned around as the dog barked. Looked to be in his late sixties, tall, thin, with a full head of grey hair.

He looked enquiringly at them, 'Can I help you?'

Angie showed him her ID. 'I'm Detective Inspector Reeves. This is Detective Constable Simpson. There's been a break-in next door. I wonder if we could have a word with you.'

The look of alarm on the man's face didn't show in his calm voice. 'I'm Tim Kendall,' he said. 'Is Walter, okay? Has the house been vandalised?'

'Could we talk inside?'

'Yes, of course.' He felt for his key, tightening the dog's lead as he turned back to unlock the door. But the spaniel planted his feet and strained at the lead, looking determinedly up the road.

'Nero looks forward to his morning walk,' Tim Kendall explained. Crouching down, he held the spaniel's head between his hands and spoke softly.

Angie shared a smile with Simpson as the dog relaxed, turned, and followed his master back into the house.

They were with Tim Kendall for twenty-five minutes. They explained Walter hadn't been in the house at the time of the break-in.

'Must have taken off to visit Roxanne – his daughter. He gets the urge to do that sometimes. He stays at her place overnight.'

'In London?' Angie asked.

'Oh no, he tried that once, but got stuck in traffic. It's since she moved to Milton Keynes about two years ago. She's a GP, a partner in a practice there. Walter says the drive to her house is only just over an hour.'

They asked him if he'd been out the previous evening, spotted any strangers or cars he didn't recognise in the cul-de-sac.

'Any specific time?'

'We think the break-in was between 8 p.m. and 11 p.m.'

'Too late for me,' he said. 'I took Nero out for his usual evening walk, but we were back by 7 p.m.'

'Did you see anything unusual?' Simpson asked. 'Any strangers loitering, any cars you didn't recognise?'

He shook his head. 'Nothing unusual.' He paused. 'Unless you count the plumber's van outside number 40.'

'Plumber's van?'

'Yes, a white Mercedes van. It wasn't there when we started out; I noticed it on the way back. We all use the same tradespeople in this cul-de-sac. Word of mouth recommendation when we find a good one. This wasn't our usual plumbers. But then the people in number 40 have only recently moved in – they probably don't know who we usually use. I'm just thinking the plumber might have noticed anyone hanging around.'

'Did you see if anyone was in the van?'

'No, I crossed the road behind the van – I was in a hurry to get back for the news on Channel 4. It's just that in my experience, workmen seem to spend a lot of time sitting in their van.'

'Do you remember the name of the company?'

'Oh, yes,' he said smiling. 'It was in large letters on the back. The same as my initials. "T K Plumbing".'

They thanked Tim Kendall, stood up to leave. 'One last thing,' Angie said. 'Have you got Walter's phone number?'

He shook his head. 'Not his current one. He was having trouble with his mobile; I think he's getting a new one. But if he's at Roxanne's, I've got her number – Walter gave it to me as an emergency contact.'

Nero was hovering by the front door as they left.

Angie phoned Ross. No, they hadn't tracked down the next of kin yet. She told him Roxanne had moved from London to Milton Keynes, gave him her mobile number.

***

They spent the next two hours knocking on doors. There was no answer at number 40. They spoke to the residents on either side and the houses opposite. No one had observed any strangers or strange vehicles in the cul-de-sac the previous evening. No one had needed a plumber. Or noticed a white Mercedes van parked outside.

'I thought this was supposed to be a Neighbourhood Watch area,' Simpson said when they were back in the car. 'Not a lot of watching going on.' They headed back to the station.

'I'll get in touch with the plumbing company,' Angie said. 'Maybe I can speak to the plumber they sent out.'

'Tim Kendall might have had a point,' Simpson said. 'Workmen do spend a lot of time sitting in their van. He might have seen something.'

Ross was halfway through a sausage roll when she looked through the glass panel of his office door. She loitered a little in front of the coffee machine before heading back. Looked through the panel again before knocking on his door. He was brushing the crumbs off his jacket.

'The Milton Keynes police have visited the daughter at her medical practice,' Ross said. 'I'm meeting her at the front of the hospital at 4 p.m. We need her to make a formal identification.' He paused. Angie waited with her heart thumping,

37

dreading that he would ask her to go to the identification with him. But all he said was 'Did the door to door throw up anything?' She felt the relief, reported on the interview with Tim Kendall.

'Probably too early in the evening for the plumber to have seen anything,' he said. 'But check it out just in case.'

She nodded, turned to go. 'I've called in a favour,' Ross said. 'Forensics are giving us priority, so we should have more from them for tomorrow's briefing. Same time – 7.30 a.m.'

Angie climbed the stairs to the open plan computer area with a spring in her step. Ross had just said 'I've called in a favour.' That didn't sound like he was just going through the motions. Maybe they *would* find Walter's killer before Ross retired in four weeks.

Sitting down at the bank of computers, she googled T K Plumbing. Three matches appeared on the screen: two in America, one in Western Australia. Swearing under her breath, she googled T K Plumbing, Birmingham and then T K Plumbing, West Midlands. There were no matches. She'd made a note of Tim Kendall's phone number. He answered on the third ring, confirmed the name on the back of the van was T K Plumbing. She tried Companies House without success. Simpson caught her sitting back in the chair, staring into space.

'Deep in thought?'

'I can't track down T K Plumbing.'

'Google it,' he said, then quickly put both hands up in mock surrender as he saw her face.

***

They went back to the cul-de-sac at 5.30, parked outside number 40. Simpson rang the bell. They heard someone coming down the stairs. The recent arrivals turned out to be a young black couple – Sam and Rachel Hunt – both lawyers in the same firm. Angie thought the wife was in the early stages of pregnancy. They sat in the lounge, accepted a cup of coffee. Angie explained there had been a break-in further down the cul-de-sac the previous evening and they were interviewing the residents in the street to see if they had noticed anything untoward.

'We understand there was a white Mercedes van belonging to a plumbing firm parked outside your house around 7 p.m. last night,' she said. 'Can you tell us how long the plumber was here for?'

The two young lawyers looked at each other, then at the two detectives. 'We weren't home at that time last night,' Rachel Hunt said. 'We both worked late, then had dinner at an Italian restaurant. It was just after 10 p.m. when we got home.'

'We don't have a need for a plumber,' her husband added. 'Everything's been working fine since we moved in.'

Rachel Hunt saw them out, said the baby was due in four months when Angie asked.

'We thought we'd found the perfect place to start a family,' she said. 'Quiet. Safe. Now, I'm not so sure.'

'Nowhere is perfectly safe, but you've chosen well.' Simpson was trying to be reassuring. 'A break-in like this is a relatively rare occurrence in a cul-de-sac.'

From where they sat in Angie's car, parked outside number 40, the hedge that bordered the front garden hid the front door of Walter's house. But the drive and the white double doors of the garage were visible.

'Looks like our man sat here waiting for Walter to leave,' Simpson said.

'Looks that way.'

They started back to the station, neither of them speaking. They were halfway there when Angie yanked the steering wheel and pulled into a side road. Simpson looked at her with raised eyebrows.

'What do you do when you're waiting in a car?'

'What?'

She repeated the question.

'I hate waiting in a car,' he said. 'I have to listen to a CD or the radio. Maybe play with my phone. Or read the paper.'

'You can't do the last two if you're watching a house. What else?'

Simpson took a moment before replying. 'Smoke,' he said. 'My wife doesn't like the car smelling of cigarettes, but I might have one or two with the window down.'

Angie nodded excitedly, 'That's what I thought. If our man was a smoker, he might have left cigarette stubs. We could run a DNA test.'

'Damn right!' Simpson said, catching her excitement. 'Let's go check it out.'

She took the next left, made a three-point turn. They drove back to the cul-de-sac, stopped the car in front of number 40. Facing Walter's house. She leapt out of the car, crouched down to inspect the tarmac by the driver's door. There was nothing there. Disappointed, she shook her head in response to Simpson's query and got back in the car.

Reaching for her seat belt, she had a sudden thought. Getting back out of the car, she strode around the front to Simpson's side, and crouched down by his passenger door. And there they were: four cigarette butts lying on the road in the space between the car and the kerb. Where they would be if someone had dropped them out of the passenger window. She felt the adrenaline rush, slapped the wing of the car and stood up grinning as Simpson lowered the passenger window. She told him to grab the tweezers and an evidence bag out of her glove compartment.

Back at the station, she stopped to let Simpson out. 'Find Ross and tell him what we've found before you head home.' She held up the evidence bag. 'I'll take this to Forensics.'

Simpson gave her a smile and a thumbs up. 'Nice work. See you in the morning.'

The forensics block was at the far end of the site with its own small car park. The lights were still on; three staff inside were visible through the glass window, but the door was locked when she tried it. She rapped on the window. A tall man in a turban looked up, came out of the room into the corridor and opened the door. Angie showed him her ID.

'You're working late,' she said.

'Bit of a rush job for DCI Ross. I think the boss must have a soft spot for him.'

'I'm part of Ross's team,' Angie said. 'I just wanted to check if you'd found any cigarette butts at the murder scene. In the community centre car park.'

He stepped aside to let Angie through the door.

'I'm Harpal Grewal. I was with the team at the car park. And yes, we found some cigarette butts. Why are you asking?'

Angie held up the evidence bag. 'I've got some more cigarette butts here. Can you test them as well? I need to know if there's a DNA match between these and the ones you found at the car park.'

He looked at her, kept his hands at his side.

'It could be important,' Angie said. 'Please.'

He took the evidence bag from her. 'I suppose you want the result in time for Ross's morning briefing.'

'That would be great.'

'No promises,' Harpal Grewal said as he closed the door behind her.

Chapter 5

Walking away from the forensics block, Angie's stomach growled. Hunger gnawed at her – she hadn't eaten since the early morning scrambled eggs. The lasagne waiting in the fridge would assuage her hunger. But not, she realised with a quickening pulse, the need she was now feeling for human company.

She started her car with a growing reluctance to go straight home to her empty flat. Simpson, recently remarried, had rushed off to be with his new stepdaughter. 'She's a shy ten-year-old girl. The three of us having dinner together helps with the bonding.'

Angie envied him.

After they'd flown her home from Iraq to her aunt Peggy's bungalow in Devon, she'd been overtaken by a sense of futility, becoming withdrawn and prone to outbursts of temper. She shunned social interaction. Peggy was the only one she would talk to. She was close to her aunt. It was Peggy who had come to stay for a while when her sister died giving birth to Angie, and who had returned when her father was in hospital. Peggy had sent her a home-baked, three coloured birthday cake, every year, and Angie spent two weeks of every school summer holiday with her aunt in Devon.

Peggy welcomed Angie with open arms after the incident in Iraq. She met with the psychiatrist to be briefed on Angie's likely behaviour and needs as she fought to recover. She was told about the likely flashbacks and the sudden mood swings. And that Angie would need her personal space, would find it hard to relate to friends or groups of people. But that she needed to gradually rebuild her capacity for an emotional attachment.

'Do you have a dog?' the psychiatrist had asked.

So Peggy had gone to the dogs' home and Angie had been presented with Nikki, the brown and white dog her aunt said was a Cojack – a mixture of Corgi and Jack Russell. The little dog sensed her vulnerability; she adopted Angie at first sight and insisted on sleeping on her bed. Angie's weekly sessions with the psychiatrist had helped. But so had her long walks in the Devon countryside with Nikki.

She reflected on her day, remembered the psychiatrist's words when she told him she was returning to active duty: *'Developing relationships and a sense of community is central to restoring your well-being.'* Having avoided other humans for so long, she'd turned up for that morning's briefing unsure how she would respond. But she'd felt excited to be part of a team again, and she'd enjoyed interacting with Simpson during the day.

Waiting at the traffic lights, her eye was drawn to the neon sign of a Chinese restaurant, set back off the main road. Making up her mind as the lights turned green, she signalled left and parked in the cutaway. The restaurant was having a good night; large circular tables encouraged the buzz of conversation. The waiter showed Angie to a small table set in an alcove. She sipped a glass of the house white and perused the menu. She was still buzzing from the find in the cul-de-sac. When the waiter came for her order, she treated herself to a second glass of wine. It was the first time she had been in a restaurant in the last nine months; the first time she had put herself in a social setting. She sat back and soaked in the atmosphere while she waited for her lemon chicken.

***

Angie slept through the night. No flashbacks.

It was raining heavily in the morning; even with the wipers at full speed and the heater on full blast, the windscreen still misted up. The slow flow of traffic came to a standstill a mile from the station.

Sitting impatiently in the Friday morning traffic jam, turning the radio on and off, she wondered what this morning's briefing would throw up. Her head was still full of the same questions. Was Walter just the victim of a random killing? If it was a carjacking, why didn't they take the car? Why kill him if he was trying to run away? Did the same people break into his house, or was it a coincidence? What were they searching for? And she was still confused by Ross's behaviour: he'd appeared disinterested in the briefing but then he'd called in a favour from Forensics. How committed was he to finding Walter's killer?

The traffic began to move. She crawled along until a traffic officer in his high visibility jacket waved her through. Leaning forward, Angie wiped the misted-up windscreen with her hand and looked to her right as she went past. A black SUV faced the wrong way on the central reservation, the passenger side against the trunk of a silver birch; she guessed it had tried to change lanes in front of the mini that was lying on its roof, half on the road and half on the reservation. It didn't look good for the occupants of the mini, but the ambulances had been and gone; the only positive for the injured would have been that the hospital was only a ten-minute drive away. It was the same hospital her father had been taken to, the one where she had met Walter.

She'd left the flat early, intending to go straight to the forensics block, to find Harpal Grewal before the briefing. But it was too late now. She'd be just in time for the briefing.

There was one parking space left in the station car park. Grabbing her keys she ran through the rain to the entrance to the station, up the two flights of stairs and along the corridor to the incident room. The others were sitting around the conference table; Bridges was at the desk. He looked up as she burst into the room, observed she was breathing heavily.

'Alarm not working then?'

Holding up her hand in apology and ignoring Washington's amused look, she took the seat next to Simpson.

'Did you catch Ross last night?'

'Only just. He was about to drive out of the car park. I told him about the cigarette butts, told him you had taken them to Forensics.'

'And?'

'And nothing. If anything, he looked annoyed. He just nodded and drove off.'

Simpson leant in closer, about to say something else, but before he could speak, the door opened and Ross strode in, holding a folder in his left hand. Angie noticed the plaster on his chin.

'Someone's cut himself shaving,' Simpson said under his breath.

Ross, standing at the desk next to Bridges, extracted a single sheet of paper from the folder. 'The report from Forensics,' he said. 'What they've found so far.' He reached into the inside pocket of his jacket for his reading glasses.

'We knew the murder weapon was a knife. But according to the pathologist, it wasn't just a stab wound. The victim was stabbed and then the knife drawn across, tearing at his insides. That takes considerable strength. The stab wound on its own would have been fatal; the extra force suggests a sadist who gets a kick out of what he can do with a knife.'

Simpson broke the moment of silence. 'That doesn't sound like the attacker panicked and killed him accidentally. More like deliberate murder.'

Ross didn't respond, just read from further down the page of the report.

'No sign they entered the car. The glove compartment was still locked. Forensics found only the victim's fingerprints on the driver's door handle.'

'What about DNA from inside the car?' Washington said.

'They analysed hair from the two front seats. The driver's seat had the victim's hair, which is no surprise. Evidence from the passenger seat points to a woman with blonde hair; fibres they found suggest she might have been wearing a thick, green, wool jumper.'

'What was in the glove compartment?' Simpson asked. 'Did they find his mobile phone?'

Ross looked at the report again. 'No mention of a mobile phone. Just the manual for the car and the service record. The car had one previous owner.' He took off his reading glasses, motioned to Angie.

'You need to talk to his daughter. Find out what she knows about her father's personal life. A botched carjacking looks the most likely cause but we can't rule out a jealous partner or husband. And ask her about his mobile phone.'

'What about the break in?' Simpson said.

'Nothing that's going to help us much,' Ross said. 'The front door was forced with a crowbar. But whoever broke in must have been wearing gloves and overshoes. The only fingerprints in the study belong to the victim.' He folded the report, replaced it in the folder. 'That's all Forensics have got so far.'

Simpson and Angie exchanged glances, Simpson shaking his head, showing his disappointment that there was no mention of the cigarette butts Angie had left with Harpal Grewal. Angie shifted in her seat, tried not to show her own disappointment, but she felt deflated.

Bridges said, 'The two girls who found the body are both second year language students at the university. They were on their way back from a party, took the shortcut across the car park. They'd both had too much to drink but still had enough about them to call 999.' He paused, then added, 'Nice girls. Still in a state of shock when we saw them. The blue Audi was the only car in the car park. They didn't see any other vehicle. Or anyone else.'

'We interviewed the manager of the community centre as well,' Ross said. 'She left at 7 p.m., earlier than usual because a Zumba class had been cancelled. After the recent car jackings, the centre's management committee wanted to improve security, but a limited budget meant they had to choose between installing CCTV or floodlights. They voted for floodlights. But they're still waiting for planning permission – the residents in the house adjoining the car park have objected.'

'She's an angry woman,' Ross continued. 'She believes this wouldn't have happened if the floodlights were up. She knew Walter Price, confirmed he was a long-standing member of the running club. Described him as one of the nicest people you could meet. But she was surprised he was running on a Wednesday night as the club usually meets on Mondays and Thursdays. She wondered whether Walter had missed last Monday and was trying to make up for it.'

Leaving the folder on the desk, Ross came forward to the head of the table. A drop of blood escaped the plaster on his chin. No one commented.

'Well?' he said. 'What did we get from the door to door?' His nodded at Angie and Simpson. 'Let's get the break-in out of the way first.'

Angie told him about the white plumber's van with T K Plumbing on the back, but that they couldn't find a company with that name. And that Walter's house was clearly visible from where the van had been parked.

'Maybe they went bankrupt, changed the name of the company. It happens.'

'No one on the street had called for a plumber.'

They agreed it was probably a stolen vehicle, the signage added to give reassurance when it was parked in a residential street.

'What time was the van there?'

'We know it was there at 7 p.m.,' Simpson said. 'That's when Walter Price's neighbour noticed it. We don't know how long the van stayed there. No one else noticed it. Whoever was in the van would have waited until he saw Walter Price drive off.'

Ross nodded at Simpson, 'Okay. We'll check the CCTV in the surrounding streets. A license plate would be useful.' He looked back at Angie. 'Anything else?'

Angie felt Simpson's glance upon her, knew he was willing her to speak up.

'Well?' Ross said impatiently.

Angie sat up straight, pressed her back against the chair, held Ross's gaze. 'Yes. There is one other thing. We found some cigarette butts in the cul-de-sac, handed them into Forensics last night to check if there was a DNA match with the ones from the car park. It should have been in their report.'

'I told you about it when you were leaving the car park last night,' Simpson added.

'Ah! The cigarette butts,' Ross said, focusing on Angie. 'I wondered if you would bring that up. There was no mention in the report from Forensics.' His voice hardened. 'I appreciate you might feel a need to demonstrate you can use your initiative, but you should have talked it over with me first. Most modern cars don't have cigarette lighters or ashtrays. It's against the law to litter, but most drivers who smoke still drop their cigarette butts out of the window. The cigarette butts you found in the cul-de-sac could have been dropped by anyone. They could have been laying there for days, blown by the wind.' He paused to let his words sink in. 'Forensics are understaffed and always under pressure. They depend on us not wasting their time and their resources.'

Angie continued to hold his gaze but had to swallow hard to combat the dryness in her throat. *Ross was reminding her that she was on trial.* The report he submitted after four weeks would determine her future in the force. Whether she could return permanently to active duty. And if so, whether she could keep her rank as Detective Inspector.

Ross was still staring at her. 'It's not just initiative that makes a good officer. It's also judgement based on the balance of probability.'

There was silence in the room. Angie knew the others were watching her. She felt the burning in her cheeks.

Another drop of blood escaped from the plaster on Ross's chin. He turned away abruptly. 'Washington and O'Byrne. You two were door to door at the murder scene. What have you got for me?'

Chapter 6

Ross now had his back towards her, but Angie was aware that Bridges was still watching her, no doubt waiting to see how she responded to the telling off. Simpson was sitting on her right. Angie knew he would be feeling bad that she'd borne the brunt of the criticism, would be wanting to catch her eye. Moving her tongue around to loosen her jaw muscles, she forced herself to concentrate on the report Washington and O'Byrne were giving.

'It's the Jacksons who live in the house immediately next to the car park,' O'Byrne said. 'An elderly couple. Mrs Jackson is the one objecting to the floodlights. She's worried they'll shine into their upstairs back bedroom. But she was shaken by the murder, and we got the feeling she might withdraw her objection.'

'Any sightings of the car park?'

'Two sightings, both around the right time.' She looked down at her notebook. 'Mr and Mrs Rankin took their dog for a walk around 7.40 p.m., walked down to the lake, up to the community centre, and back around the lake. Then up the path to get back to their house.' She looked up. 'They were back in their house at 8.10 – they reckon they were walking past the gap in the hedge ten minutes earlier, at 8 p.m.'

'Did they see Walter's car?'

'Yes. They saw a blue Audi, and they caught sight of a white van that had just entered the car park. But no idea of the model or where it parked.'

'What about the second sighting?'

'Mr Wheatley. who lives two houses down from the Rankins. Same walk with his dog, but about fifteen minutes later. He was walking past the gap in the hedge about 8.15, noticed a white van parked facing out into the car park, with its rear bumper against the hedge.'

'If he was fifteen minutes later, it was even darker,' Ross said. 'How could he be sure of the colour?'

'We asked him that very question, but he was adamant it was a white van. He said it was a full moon that night. The moon had been hidden behind a cloud, but it came out as he was on the path.'

'Where was the van parked in relation to Walter's Audi?'

'He didn't see any other car – we think the Audi was hidden by the height of the van.'

They were silent for a moment. Simpson exchanged a look with Angie, then looked across the table at O'Byrne.

'Did he say if there was any signage on the van? On the side or on the back?'

'Nothing was written on the side. He wouldn't have seen the back with the van parked against the hedge.'

Bridges was making notes. Ross sat back in his chair for a moment before continuing. 'What about the residents at the back of the lake?'

Washington answered. 'Quite a few dog walkers from the houses beyond the lake. Most of them too early in the evening to be relevant, but we think we can pinpoint a time slot when Walter Price started his run.'

Bridges stopped writing in his notebook and looked up.

'One of the dog walkers passing the gap in the hedge at approximately 7.25 said the car park was empty. Seemed very sure of that. But two others who passed between 7.35 and 7.45 spotted a blue Audi.'

Washington waited for them to work it out. They agreed Walter Price must have entered the car park in the ten minutes between 7.25 and 7.35 and started his run shortly afterwards.

'If we knew how long he was running we could work out what time he returned to the car park, and what time the attack took place.'

Bridges closed his notebook and joined them at the conference table. 'The club has got 5K and 10K routes mapped out; the manager told us Walter usually ran with the 10K group.'

'So how long would that take him?'

'He was a sixty-seven-year-old man,' Bridges said, 'running rather than racing. He'd probably aim for ten-minute miles, a bit quicker on a good day. I'd estimate between fifty-five- and sixty-five-minutes running time.'

They worked it out. Walter Price had probably been killed between 8.30 and 8.45.

'There isn't any CCTV in the car park or the road that runs past the centre,' O'Byrne said. 'We haven't checked the approach roads yet.'

They heard a phone ringing, looked at each other, realised the noise was coming from the chair by the desk where Ross had slung his jacket. Retrieving the phone, he glanced at the screen, and turned away from them to take the call.

He listened, his back towards them, didn't speak, then ended the call. He put his phone back in his jacket and stood still for a long moment before turning to face them. 'That was Harpal Grewal from Forensics.' He nodded at Simpson, then spoke directly to Angie. 'DI Reeves, I was wrong. On this occasion you made the right judgement call. Forensics found a DNA match between the cigarette butts you handed in and the cigarette butts they collected from the murder scene. The same person who was waiting in the plumber's van was also in the car park.'

Angie felt a mixture of relief and excitement flooding through her. This time she looked at Simpson. He gave her a broad smile and a wink.

The others were quiet as they took a moment to work through the implications of the DNA match.

'Just one thing,' Bridges said. 'Walter Price was trying to run away when he was murdered, and we're pretty sure he was attacked by at least two people. Wasn't the driver waiting in the plumber's van on his own?'

'No,' Angie answered firmly. 'There were two of them waiting in the van. They parked facing Walter Price's house, so the driver's side was roadside. The cigarette butts were dropped kerbside by someone sitting in the passenger seat.'

So now they knew it was not a coincidence; the same two people who had killed Walter had also searched his house.

'Something still doesn't fit,' Bridges persisted. 'We're back to the question of why they forced the front door when they could have used the key. They must have seen the house key when Walter dropped the key ring with his car key. Why not take it if they intended to search the house?'

A silence stretched out before Ross spoke. 'Maybe we've got it back to front. Perhaps they searched the house first, after they saw him leave. Then drove to the car park and waited for him to return from his run.'

Bridges pulled a face. 'How would they know where he was going? That he'd left his car in the community centre car park?'

'Maybe they followed him before. Knew where he started his runs from.'

Bridges pulled another face. Ross stroked his forehead to keep his irritation at bay. The others were quiet.

'Would they have searched the underside of the Audi?' Angie said.

Ross stopped stroking his forehead, let the irritation out, 'What?!'

Angie took a breath. 'Sorry, I meant Forensics. Would they have inspected the underside of Walter's car?'

A moment passed before he understood what she was getting at. Before they all did.

'There's no mention of an underside inspection in their report,' Ross said, his tone back on an even keel. 'I'd better check with Harpal Grewal.' He fished his telephone back out of his jacket, made the call. They heard him ask, saw him shake his head, heard his response.

'Do it now!' he said. 'It won't take you long.'

They waited. Harpal Grewal rang back after ten minutes. Ross listened, ended the call with a grim expression on his face.

'Forensics found a magnetic tracker under the front left wheel arch. That's how the bastards followed him to the car park.'

He waited until the buzz had quietened down. 'So now we know we're not dealing with a botched carjack. This was deliberate murder. They searched the house first and then decided Walter Price had to die. We need to find out why.'

They waited for his instructions. 'We'll start with CCTV. O'Byrne and Washington, you two look at the most likely route the van would take to get from the house to the car park. Simpson, you look at CCTV too, but focus on where the van went after it left the car park around 8.45 p. m. It could've turned right to take it to the Pershore Road or left to take it to the Bristol Road. Both are arterial roads with ANPR cameras. Check the approach roads as well. Get me that van's license plate. Or better still, get me a face.'

Angie had remained seated. Ross walked over to her, waited until she made eye contact so she wouldn't miss his nod of acknowledgement. 'You did well. Good detective work.'

Angie glowed as Ross continued. 'Talk to the daughter. Roseanne. Find out if she can think of any enemies her father had. And check his movements on the previous two or three days. Something happened that resulted in his murder. She might be able to give us a lead.'

Angie nodded. 'It's *Roxanne.*' She got up and started moving. Bridges followed her out, caught up with her in the corridor.

'Ross told me you about your PTSD,' he said quietly. 'My younger brother did two tours of Afghanistan. I've got some idea what you're coping with. I know it can result in self-doubt.'

Angie came to a halt, turned to meet his eyes.

'Ross can be a funny bugger,' Bridges said. 'But there aren't many better coppers around. And he knows a good 'un when he sees one.'

Chapter 7

The farm was in Mid Wales, past Machynlleth and just after the village of Pennal. Bujare often thought that she and Pavel could be happy there: she loved the Welsh countryside dotted with sheep, the darkness, and the quiet at night. And the locals they met, when they drove to the weekly street market in Machynlleth, were welcoming. The market reminded her of the one her mother used to take her to, when she was a child in the village in Albania.

It was the fishmonger, who on Bujare's third visit to the street market, when there was no one waiting behind her, asked if she knew the history of the farm. She smiled and shook her head.

Cradling a cup of tea, the fishmonger told her the farm had been owned and worked by the same family for generations, but the last farmer was the only surviving child. And he himself had been childless, his wife having died of a heart attack not long after they married. Wanting the farm to stay in his family as a working farm, he left it in his will to a nephew who made that promise, but promptly sold it to a rich man in London. The story was that the new owner wanted to invite his friends from

London to grouse shooting weekends. But that had never happened.

'Instead,' the fishmonger said, giving Bujare a wide smile, 'a couple came to look after the farmhouse. They were here for just over a year before the man died from a heart attack. Then you and your husband took their place as the housekeepers.

'Yes,' Bujare said, returning his smile. 'Pavel and I are the housekeepers.'

'Tell me,' the fishmonger said, lowering his voice, leaning forward across the fish on ice in front of him. 'Is it true that the owner is a rich investment banker?'

'I don't know,' Bujare said. 'I've never met him. We were hired by an agency. Their representatives visit us to check that everything is in order.'

***

Bujare and Pavel had been told what to say to the questions the locals might ask. Some of it was true. It was true Bujare didn't know who the owner was. And true that they'd been told they would be the housekeepers. But when she saw the punishment block and it became clear their duties included keeping people locked up, she'd wanted to give it up. Pavel had dissuaded her. 'I don't know what would happen to us if we left,' he said. 'They have my passport. And I'm worried that they might harm my mother. They know her village outside Tirana. We have to make the best of it. It's only for three years. Then they've promised us a little bar in Tirana. We'll run it together.'

Running a little bar in Tirana with Pavel was Bujare's dream. So, they'd stayed. Sometimes there was no one in the punishment block – it was just the two of them in the farmhouse. That was when she was happy. She looked forward to the evenings with Pavel on the sofa in the lounge – he would open a bottle of wine and they would watch television together.

But there were other times when the representatives came. The punishment block, formerly a grain storage room forty yards behind the main farmhouse, had been converted into four single cells off a corridor. Each windowless cell was nine feet square, the floor covered with linoleum. Into that space was squeezed a single bed, a toilet, a small sink and a fold down shelf that could be used as a table. The sliding hatch on the door of each cell could only be opened from the outside when the bolt was pulled back; Bujare passed the trays of food through the hatch.

The two representatives, Rumesh and Erag, would come from Birmingham with anyone who had caused trouble, usually by trying to run away or agitating amongst the other workers. The penalty was a week in the punishment block, sometimes longer. But not before Erag, the one who Pavel said was a former gymnast, had his fun.

He would go into the cell, goad the man into attacking him, threatening to arrange for his sister or his mother to be raped if he didn't respond.

Once, when the other man had landed a blow, Erag had beaten him unconscious, then peed on his face. Pavel told Bujare that when Erag unzipped himself and leant forward, his T-shirt had ridden up, and Pavel had seen the knife strapped to the back of his waist.

They'd come early on Thursday morning. The blonde girl was still drowsy from the drug they'd given her, still in the sleeping bag with her hands tied and a gag in her mouth. Bujare saw Erag fondle the girl's breasts as they pulled her out of the sleeping bag and lay her on the bed in the punishment block.

Before they left, they parked the white van in the shed next to the two SUVs and covered it with a dust sheet. Then they told Pavel to fetch the keys to the red SUV. Bujare stood with Pavel and watched them drive off, down the farm track that led to the road to Machynlleth.

'Erag makes me shiver,' she said. 'There is a gleam in his eyes that isn't normal.'

'We're not to use the white van,' Pavel said. 'They've left us with only the old green SUV. And that one badly needs a new clutch.'

65

Chapter 8

Angie rang the number Tim Kendall had given her for Roxanne. She told Roxanne her name, explained she was a Detective Inspector on the team investigating Walter's death and asked if it would be convenient to visit her.

'Yes, your Chief Inspector explained someone would be around to interview me,' Roxanne said. 'It's just I've got someone with me at the moment. Could you come in about an hour's time?'

Angie put her phone down, wondering if Roxanne would recognise her. They'd met briefly twice over the years. Walter had brought her to the school's Christmas play once when she'd been home from medical school. He'd called Angie over during the interval.

'So, you're the Angie I've heard about,' Roxanne had said, giving her an engaging smile. 'It's good to be able to put a face to the name.'

The second time had been just after she'd become the youngest DI in the force. Shopping in the Bullring, she'd entered Selfridges just as Walter and Roxanne were leaving the sushi counter. Smiling broadly on seeing her, Walter wanted to know if she was still happy with her career choice. He congratulated her warmly when she told him about her recent promotion to Detective Inspector.

'Thank you, sir.'

He'd laughed. 'Please call me Walter.'

She'd nodded but realised she couldn't. Not to his face.

***

There were two cars on the drive – a red Saab and a blue Toyota. Angie parked on the road outside. The door had had a temporary repair; she could still see signs of the forced entry. Roxanne answered the bell straight away, managed a welcoming smile.

'I thought it might be you,' she said. 'Your name came back to me as soon as our call ended.' She took a step forward and hugged Angie before stepping back. Angie saw the puffiness around her eyes.

'It comes and goes,' Roxanne said. 'I think I'm okay and then the tears suddenly come.'

Angie squeezed her hand.

'I'm glad it's you,' Roxanne said. 'I know how determined you'll be to find the carjackers who killed Dad.'

Angie followed her into the lounge. A tall, slim man with curly red hair sprang up from the sofa as they entered. Angie moved from behind Roxanne to introduce herself, and his face came into view.

Angie froze, then felt a rush of excitement. Her spine tingled. 'Philip?'

'Roxanne said she thought it might be you,' he said, a delighted grin on his face. 'I couldn't believe it!'

Angie stared at him, open mouthed. 'I didn't realise you were in Birmingham!'

'I wasn't until a year ago. I work at the FE College in the city centre now.' He examined her more closely. 'And I hear you're a Detective Inspector!'

'Yes.' Angie's smile dimmed. 'That's why I'm here. I'm afraid this isn't a social call.'

'Roxanne explained you're part of the investigation team.' He picked up his jacket from the back of the sofa. 'I saw what had happened on the local news, so I came around to see Roxanne. I'll leave you two alone now.' His eyes met Angie's. 'Maybe we can catch up over the next week?'

'I'd like that.'

They exchanged phone numbers. Roxanne showed him out. Looking out the lounge window, Angie watched Philip as he got into his car. Her mind was whirling.

'I didn't realise you knew Philip,' she said when Roxanne came back in.

Roxanne gave her a surprised look. 'He lived here for the last five months of the sixth form. After his mother died, Dad took him in to prevent him from being taken into care. He had the old au pair's room.' She looked at Angie with her head to one side. 'I'm surprised you didn't know that. Dad always said you two were very close.'

'Philip became a recluse after his mother died,' Angie said. 'He came and went, didn't mix at all with his usual friends – including me. We hardly spoke in the months after his mother died.' She remembered with a sad smile, then caught herself. 'Anyway, that's in the past.'

Roxanne was looking at her speculatively. 'If you say so. But you should have seen his face when I realised it was you who was coming to see me. He couldn't hide his excitement.'

Angie felt the tingle in her spine again. She turned away, not wanting to meet Roxanne's eyes.

'Let's go into the kitchen,' Roxanne said. 'You can ask your questions there. I need to have some lunch. I didn't feel like breakfast this morning so all I had was a cup of black coffee.' Angie followed her into the kitchen. Roxanne took a box of eggs out of the fridge, turned around and saw Angie staring at the closed door of the study.

'I've cleared it all up,' she said. 'He would have hated it being in that mess – it was his home within a home.' She opened the egg box, paused, closed it, and put it back in the fridge.

'I'm famished. And I could really do with getting out of this house for a while. Is there any chance we can do this in a restaurant? I'm sure we'll find a quiet table at this time of day where we can talk.'

They drove in Angie's car so that Roxanne could have a drink if she wanted one. Angie, following Roxanne's directions, realised they were heading for the Acocks Green area; they would pass close to her old school.

So Philip had been excited to see her. He was slimmer than she remembered, and the boyishness had faded from his face. The spark in his eyes she remembered so well was no longer as bright. But the wide grin remained the same. She wondered if he was in a relationship. Or married. But she hadn't noticed a ring on his finger. An old hurt, buried deep, was trying to surface. The past was the past. She pushed it back, was glad when Roxanne spoke.

'Take the next right. It's the local Italian off the main roundabout in Acocks Green – a family run business. Dad always said it was the best Italian restaurant in Birmingham. He became friendly with Luigi, the owner.'

The few parking spaces on the roundabout itself were taken, but Angie found a space in a side street, and they walked back to the restaurant. It was the beginning of lunchtime, but three tables were already occupied.

The waiter standing behind the bar looked up as they entered the restaurant, spoke over his shoulder to someone. A short, barrel-chested man wearing an apron emerged from the kitchen with a smile and an expression on his face that managed to make him appear both welcoming and sad. Angie hung back as he came up to them and embraced Roxanne, holding her close and speaking quietly in her ear before stepping back.

'Thank you, Luigi,' Roxanne said.

She gestured towards Angie, kept her voice down to avoid being overheard. 'This is Detective Inspector Reeves. We were hoping for a table where we can have some privacy.'

Luigi nodded at Angie, turned back to Roxanne. 'Come with me. You can use the private dining room. I'll lay a table for two.' He ushered them into a small room to the right of the bar.

'Are you driving?'

Roxanne shook her head.

'Just sparkling water for me,' Angie said.

With the water, Luigi brought a bottle of Chablis in an ice bucket. He opened the bottle, poured a glass for Roxanne, and waited for their order.

Angie asked for spaghetti carbonara. Luigi exchanged looks with Roxanne, then went out, closing the door quietly behind him.

'I always have the Filetto Stroganoff,' Roxanne explained. She looked down, concentrating on tracing small circles on the tablecloth with the index finger of her left hand.

'I can't believe this has happened. To have his life ended like that. Why did they have to stab him? He wouldn't have fought over a stupid car.' There was a moment of silence while she allowed the anger to fade, then she raised the glass of wine as she looked up. 'Sorry. You wanted to ask me some questions?'

Taking a deep breath, Angie spoke slowly, tried to keep her voice level. 'Roxanne, there's been a development in our investigation. We don't believe anymore that this was a botched carjacking. Or that Walter was killed by accident. We believe that Walter was followed to the car park by the men who killed him.'

Roxanne put her glass down. She stared at Angie, wide eyed, her mouth open. She tried to speak but no words came out. Angie reached across the table and held her hand, tried to answer the questions that hadn't been asked.

'We don't know why. We think two men were watching the house and broke into the study when Walter left to go running. Whatever they found in the study caused them to follow Walter to the car park and wait for him to return from his run. We don't know who these men are or what they were looking for. Not yet. But it is an ongoing investigation, and we're determined to get those answers.'

'Thank you for telling me,' Roxanne said through tear-filled eyes, still struggling to regain her composure. 'What were those questions that you had?'

'Just some background on Walter would be helpful. Do you know of any enemies he might have made when he was Head of Longlands? Anyone who might have left with a grudge?'

Roxanne shook her head, 'He tried very hard to avoid that, regarded it as a failure. He said if anyone left with a grudge, their attitude to school would probably be passed on to their own children.' She paused. 'There was one boy he said he'd failed with. I can't quite remember his name. Jason… something.'

'Cave,' Angie said. 'Jason Cave. We were in the same primary school class. Walter expelled him when he was in year 10. He's currently serving a ten-year stretch for armed robbery.'

Roxanne went back to tracing small circles on the tablecloth.

'What about since he retired? How did he spend his time?'

'Golf three days a week for the first two years,' Roxanne said. 'He'd played as a youngster but didn't have the time when he was working. He was determined to get down to a single figure handicap.'

'Did he?'

'Yes. To a nine handicap. He took me out to dinner to celebrate, framed the certificate, and put it on the top shelf of his study.' She smiled at the memory. 'It didn't last though; the last time I asked, he was back up to twelve.' The waiter came with the food. Roxanne refilled her glass, and they ate in silence for a while.

'What about relationships?' Angie said. 'Was Walter seeing someone?'

'Probably. He enjoyed the company of women and they found him attractive. But no serious relationship as far as I know.' She looked up at Angie. 'Why do you ask?'

'We found hair belonging to several women on the passenger side of the car. Mainly brunette, but some blonde.'

'The last two had dark hair. Maybe he met somebody new.' Roxanne drained her wine glass and reached for the bottle. She was slurring her words a bit; Angie recalled her saying she had skipped breakfast. She waited while Roxanne stared into space.

'We didn't always get on, you know,' Roxanne said suddenly. 'We hardly talked in the year after my mother died. I was so angry with him.' Angie kept quiet, made a show of refilling her own glass with sparkling water.

'He started a series of casual relationships with different women. The first one was only three months after Mum died. I didn't expect that. I felt so hurt and angry with him I wouldn't take his calls or see him. And then, after a year, he persuaded me to go to Majorca with him on a walking holiday. We stayed in Sant Elmo, a little village on the southwest tip of the island and we walked every day: along the coast, through pine woods, and even

74

up a local mountain. He told me things about him I never knew.' She paused and poured the last of the wine into her glass.

'His father – my grandfather – had been diagnosed with early dementia when he was fifty-five. And his elder brother, my uncle Tom, had the same diagnosis when he was fifty-three. Both had spent their last few years in a home. Dad said he assumed it was genetic, that he would go the same way in his early fifties. He said it was terrifying. He felt he was on borrowed time, living with a ticking time bomb.'

'But he didn't suffer from early dementia,' Angie said.

'No. His consultant persuaded him to take the newly developed long-term test that gives you your likely risk factor for dementia. He turned out to be low risk.'

They talked some more, Roxanne sharing more memories of her father. The waiter came in with the Tiramisu they'd asked for. Roxanne waited until he had gone, shook her head. 'I don't understand why he was in the car park on Wednesday night,' she said. 'He liked his routines – Mondays and Thursdays were his running nights. He said running helped him think through issues. He must have had something on his mind to go running on a Wednesday evening.'

'What did he normally do on Wednesdays?'

'Oh, Wednesdays was food bank day,' Roxanne said. 'They're open from 11.30. He would go to the Aldi in Selly Oak, fill the boot of the car with bags of non-perishables and take them to the food bank in Cotteridge.'

Angie nodded. 'What about his mobile phone? We didn't find it in the glove compartment. We assumed it was where he would leave it when he went on his run.'

Roxanne grimaced. 'That bloody mobile phone! He was a bit of a technophobe, took me ages to persuade him to get one, and then he kept dropping it. This one was broken. I offered to buy him a new one, but he wouldn't hear of it. Said he'd heard you could get a reconditioned one. I told him to get a protective cover this time. So, he probably didn't have one when…' Her voice tailed off.

Angie could see Roxanne was feeling the effect of the wine on an empty stomach. They ordered a black coffee for her. Luigi came out of the kitchen to say goodbye, embraced Roxanne again, waved away the payment she offered.

They drove back to the house in silence, Roxanne with her eyes closed until Angie turned into the drive. Then she said, 'He thought most people underachieved. He hated that. That's why he was determined to take over a failing school and show what was possible.'

'He certainly did that,' Angie said. 'And I was one of the ones to benefit.'

'He was worried I might resent the time he spent with his students,' Roxanne said. 'But I never did.

I understood his motivation. And I felt secure in our own father/daughter relationship.'

She undid her seatbelt and turned to look at Angie. 'He believed in the Gordonstoun motto "*Plus est en vous*" – translated as "There is more in you".' She held Angie's gaze. 'That's where your own school motto, "Dig Deep," came from. He wanted something simple to express the same sentiment.'

'It worked,' Angie said. 'Students understood what it meant. And parents liked it.'

She didn't tell Roxanne she had both mottos, inscribed front and back, on a red marble block. Walter had presented it to her after her A level results. It had stood by her bedside during her nine months in Devon. When she'd had to dig deep.

Chapter 9

Back at the station, Angie found Ross and Bridges in the canteen with cups of tea in front of them. Ross caught her eye, raised a hand, and stood up to pull another chair over. Angie hid her surprise at the warm welcome. She had the feeling they had been discussing her. She went to the counter, then took her tea over to them.

'How did it go with the daughter?' Bridges asked.

'No real leads,' Angie said. 'No valuables missing as far as she can tell. There was still a lot of her mother's jewellery in the main bedroom if they had gone upstairs.'

She told them about the broken mobile phone. 'Roxanne thinks he was waiting for a reconditioned one.'

'What about the study?'

'She's tidied it up. But it was her father's private place. She doesn't know what they could have been searching for. Or what might have been taken. We agreed she'd phone me if she thinks of anything.'

'What about potential enemies?'

Angie shook her head. 'She said he led a pretty ordered life. Female friends but not married ones. Playing golf, reading, and his running took up most of his week.'

'Nothing out of ordinary in the days before the murder?'

'Only she was surprised he went for a run on the Wednesday evening. She confirmed Mondays and Thursdays were his usual running nights. She said he liked his routines.'

'Maybe something happened earlier in the day to throw him out of his routine,' Bridges said.

'According to Roxanne, he used to take a carload of stuff to the food bank in Cotteridge every Wednesday morning. They're closed over the weekend. I thought I'd pay them a visit on Monday morning, check he was there last Wednesday, and that nothing untoward happened.'

Ross nodded. 'How's the daughter herself? How does she seem to be coping?'

'Roxanne is in shock. She doesn't understand why anyone would want to murder her father. She asked if we could keep her informed as our investigation progresses.'

Ross and Bridges exchanged a glance. Then Ross said, 'She's not the only one. Our Deputy Chief Constable phoned about an hour ago to find out how much progress we had made. He wants to be kept informed.'

It dawned on Angie that Ross was taking her into his confidence. Treating her like a Detective

Inspector. She said, 'He must have been surprised to find out it wasn't a botched carjacking. That Walter was a targeted victim.'

'He wasn't at all surprised,' Ross said, 'because I didn't tell him.'

Angie almost spilt her tea. She looked from one to the other to see if they were being serious. There was no semblance of a smile on either man's face. She stared at them, not understanding. There was no one sitting at the adjoining tables, but Bridges still leant forward and lowered his voice.

'Paul Henderson is a slippery customer. We were suspicious as to why he assigned us to this case in the first place when he knows Ross is about to retire. And now we're speculating why he's taking a special interest in this case – it's very early on for him to be asking about progress.'

Bridges leaned back in his chair. Angie looked at the two older men across the table, saw the anger and resentment in their faces.

'Is the Deputy Chief Constable the reason you're taking early retirement?' she asked Ross.

Ross didn't answer straightaway, and Angie wondered if she'd overstepped the mark. But then Ross raised his head and looked at her.

'He's not the only reason. But he tips the balance. Our current Chief Constable retires in eighteen months. The new Chief Constable will be appointed by the Police and Crime Commissioner and Henderson has ensured he's well in with the PCC. He's the favourite for the post.' Ross shook his head slowly. 'I wouldn't want to be in the force when that happens.'

Bridges leant forward again so Angie could hear him. 'A friendly warning. We know it was the Deputy who finally approved your trial return to active duty with us. I don't know what the agreement is about your rank, after your trial return, but just be wary. He sent around a memo about cost cutting recently. He might be keen to reduce the number of Detective Inspectors.'

In the silence that followed, Angie sipped her tea and thought about what they'd said. She was desperate to get back on permanent active duty as a Detective Inspector. Not as a constable – her ambition was to become a Detective Chief Inspector. Like Ross. So that she could lead her own murder team. It was what she'd always wanted.

Bridges drank the last of his tea, put the cup down. 'We've made some progress with the van,' he said. 'The cameras picked it up. On the route from the house to the car park and after it left the car park. In both cases, the timing fits what we thought. We got a clear shot of the rear license plate.' He saw the expectant look on her face and shook his head. 'No images of the occupants. And we lost the van after it crossed the Pershore Road and disappeared into the side streets. O'Byrne and Washington are still looking at CCTV within a two-mile radius.'

'What about the license plate?'

'They kept the license plate, but the van has had a respray and the signage has been changed. A green Mercedes Sprinter van with that license plate was stolen from a builder's yard in Aberystwyth two months ago. We've been in touch with the Dyfed-Powys police. The license plate has moved to their priority list now they know the van is linked to a murder investigation.'

Angie finished her tea. Ross pushed his chair back. 'We've got to find that van. It's the only real lead we've got.'

***

The flush of the toilet sounded unnaturally loud in the confined space. Coming out of the cubicle, Deputy Chief Constable Paul Henderson glanced at his watch. He would be in a box at the Millennium Stadium this time tomorrow, watching England battling Wales in the Six Nations Championship. Rugby was still a passion.

He stood over the sink washing his hands. There was no one else in the men's room. Looking up, he studied himself in the mirror, was pleased with what looked back at him. He was a big man, on the right side of six feet and broad shouldered. His head was large, but he thought it proportionate to the width of his shoulders. His complexion was one that burned rather than tanned, but he could still boast a head of sandy hair, with the first signs of a receding hairline only just appearing. He could have done with darker eyebrows, but his nose was straight. He thought his strong jawline gave him an authoritative look. His regular medical check-ups confirmed he would always have to nurse the shoulder injury from his rugby playing days, but apart from that, he was in good condition. He aimed to go to the gym twice a week.

Back in his office, he asked for a cup of coffee. His PA brought it in – black with no sugar.

'The PCC phoned. I've made an appointment for 6 pm on Monday.'

The Deputy pulled a face.

'I think it's about that carjacking that went wrong,' she said, 'the one where the headteacher was stabbed. He wants an update.'

'I gave him an update earlier this afternoon. There was nothing new to report.'

His PA sounded sympathetic. 'I know. But I think he wants another one.'

The Deputy nodded, tried not to show his irritation, waited until his PA had closed the door behind her. Then he leant back in his chair, deep in thought. He knew he'd held a grudge against Ross for the last twelve years. But he felt it was justified. After all, the man had made a formal complaint against him, had threatened his career. So, as he climbed higher up the slippery pole, Paul Henderson had used every opportunity he had to make Ross pay. He didn't really expect Ross to solve the case; he just wanted him to end his career in failure. He'd appoint a new SIO after Ross retired. Phoning Ross earlier, he'd allowed himself a smile when Ross had very little to report.

But he was surprised the Police and Crime Commissioner was showing such an interest in the case. The first phone call had come yesterday, the PCC reminding the Deputy that one of his election pledges had been to tackle the spate of carjackings. The PCC had been non-committal when the Deputy had reported the lack of progress.

Paul Henderson regarded himself as an ambitious man. He did not consider himself a corrupt man. Admittedly, he had strayed from the true path once – twelve years ago – but that had been an aberration. He considered himself to be a man of integrity. He would make a fine Chief Constable, would have a good ten years in the post and would leave a legacy to be proud of. He reminded himself that it was the Police and Crime Commissioner who would appoint the next Chief Constable. He had to be the PCC's preferred candidate when the vacancy came up.

His phone buzzed. 'Your next appointment is here,' his PA said.

'Give me five minutes.' Paul Henderson sat back in his chair, reflected on his relationship with the PCC. He had worked assiduously to establish one that went beyond working hours and he thought he'd succeeded. Certainly, the PCC seemed to enjoy his company.

The Deputy had particularly enjoyed his weekend in Monaco the previous May, watching the Grand Prix from the yacht moored in the harbour. He had enjoyed the champagne on ice, and the food prepared by a Michelin starred chef. The invitation had come from the PCC. Apparently, the owner of the yacht was a close friend of his who had intended to host them but couldn't make it at the last minute. 'Unexpected business problem,' the PCC explained. 'He's sorry not to be joining us, but he wants us to enjoy ourselves. In fact, I am under strict orders to see that you have a good time.'

The Deputy had found standing on the yacht in the middle of the harbour, watching the formula one cars racing along the side, to be a truly amazing experience, one he would have liked to have shared with his wife. He had married late, only five years ago, to a woman fifteen years his junior. He loved her, and he vowed to stay faithful to her. And so far, he thought he had.

He regarded his behaviour in Monaco as an aberration. After the race he at first wanted to cry off, pleading stomach cramps, when the two girls who looked like they had been brought in specifically for that evening's entertainment, appeared. But the PCC was insistent, told him that the owner would be offended if his hospitality was refused. So, he gave in.

The PCC paired up with the blonde girl, leaving the Deputy with the tall brunette who told him she was originally from Kosovo. He'd had a sensational evening. Dinner in a Michelin restaurant, champagne in a night club, the return to the yacht and the luxurious bedrooms with four-poster beds and strategically placed mirrors. Taking the lead, the brunette from Kosovo had given him an unforgettable evening.

The Deputy was still smiling at the memory when his PA buzzed again. 'Show him in,' Paul Henderson said, 'and get Ross on the phone later. Make an appointment for 3 p.m. on Monday. I need his latest update before I see the PCC.'

Chapter 10

Washington and O'Byrne were off for the weekend. When Angie went in, Simpson was already in the incident room, watching the CCTV footage, looking at the glimpses of the white van on its journey from the cul-de-sac to the community centre car park. Angie took the chair next to him. 'I hear we got the license plate. And that the van was stolen from a builder's yard in Aberystwyth.'

'Yes.' He leant back in his chair, rubbing his eyes. 'If only we could find an image of the occupants.'

'Show me.'

Simpson played the CCTV back, frame by frame. The first sighting of the white van was when it turned in to Wychall Lane. The second sighting was the van waiting behind a Range Rover at the traffic lights at the end of Camp Lane. They saw the van turn left, go straight across the roundabout. They hadn't noticed Bridges standing behind them, were startled when he spoke. 'You're missing a good four to five minutes.'

Angie turned around. 'What do you mean?'

'Freeze the CCTV at the first sighting.' He pointed. 'It's showing 20.49. Now freeze it at the Camp Lane traffic lights.'

'Look at the time now,' Bridges said. 'It's showing 20.57. It shouldn't take eight minutes to get from the first sighting to the second one. Three or four minutes would be my guess.'

'You're thinking they must have stopped somewhere.'

'Looks that way.'

'There's a petrol station just before the traffic lights.'

'The problem there,' Bridges said, 'is that it's only the exit on Camp Lane. The entrance to the petrol station is on the Pershore Road; they would have to turn right along the dual carriageway and double back. But we can see the van turned left, towards the Cotteridge roundabout.'

They stared at the screen. 'There's been the odd occasion when I've entered a petrol station through the exit – when there's been little or no traffic,' Simpson said. 'Maybe that's what they did.'

The other two nodded. 'Worth a try,' Bridges said.

Their visit to the petrol station turned out to be straightforward. Parked by the air pump, they watched a steady trickle of cars entering from the Pershore Road, not all filling up with petrol – some just stopping to use the grocery store or the cash point.

In the shop there were two people serving behind the counter: a middle-aged man and a younger woman who was in charge. Waiting until there was a break in the queue, Angie showed her ID and explained what they wanted. Ushering them into a small room at the back, she set up the CCTV for the Wednesday evening and left them to it.

They let it play from 20.45. At 20.53, they saw the white van turn into the exit, drive past the petrol pumps and park by the air pump. The passenger door opened; a man wearing a black anorak with the hood up, got out of the car and strode towards the entrance to the shop. Angie judged him to be just under six feet, slim build. He was third in the queue in the shop, but the loose-fitting hood prevented them getting an unobstructed view of his face. Money changed hands; he left with a packet of cigarettes in his hand and headed back to the car. Halfway across the forecourt, he stopped by the bin next to one of the petrol pumps, looked down as he fiddled with the packet of cigarettes.

'He's having trouble finding the end to unwrap the cellophane,' Simpson said.

The hooded figure finally unwrapped the cellophane, took the foil out of the packet, and reached for the bin. The cellophane had clung to his fingers; it fluttered to the ground. He bent down to pick it up and as he straightened up, the camera monitoring the adjoining row of petrol pumps picked up a side image of his face.

'We've got one of the bastards!' Simpson said.

Angie felt the adrenaline rush. 'Yes, we have!' They continued to watch as the white van reversed, skirted the perimeter of the forecourt, took the exit and turned right towards the traffic lights on Camp Lane.

***

Back at the station, they headed straight to Ross's office. Angie looked through the glass panel. Bridges was with him, the two of them poring over what turned out to be a large road map of America spread across Ross's desk. They knocked and entered without waiting for a reply. Bridges, looking somewhat embarrassed, started to fold the map up.

Ross smiled. 'We're planning Bridges's holiday. He's got some daft idea of driving America coast to coast.'

'It's been my wife's dream,' Bridges said. 'Ever since she first heard that Simon and Garfunkel song – "America".'

'I remember that song,' Simpson said. He glanced at Angie, smiled condescendingly. 'Before your time, I'm afraid.'

Ross and Bridges nodded in agreement. Angie saw their smug faces, stared at them for a moment. Then she breathed deeply, sang the lyrics softly:

'It took me four days to hitchhike from Saginaw… I've gone to look for America…'

All three of them were staring at her in disbelief. She grinned, enjoying the moment. 'It's from the album, "Bookends". "America" was one of my dad's favourite tracks.'

Bridges, laughing, still trying to fold up the road map, stopped as he remembered where they'd been. 'No luck at the petrol station, then?'

'Just a bit. You were right about them stopping. They drove into the petrol station through the exit. We picked the van up on the CCTV. The one in the passenger seat was after some cigarettes.'

'And?'

Angie took the flash drive out of her pocket, held it up. 'He had his hood up. But we've got a side image.'

Ross and Bridges exchanged glances; she heard the note of excitement in Ross's voice. 'Show me. I've got to see this. Set it up on one of the computers in the incident room. We'll be along in a minute.' He opened the bottom drawer of his desk, took out one of his sandwich bags. Bridges was still struggling with the road map; Ross was taking the first bite of his sausage roll as they closed the door behind them.

***

They spent the rest of the weekend door knocking again. Some houses were ones they had visited before, but others they were seeing for the first time – the residents had been away or at work during their first round of door to door. Showing the side profile of the hooded man in the black anorak, they asked them if they could recall seeing anyone like that on the Wednesday evening. They were nearing the end when an elderly woman said she had seen a hooded man in a black anorak when she was walking her dog.

'He came out from behind a bush at the side of the path,' she said. 'I'm pretty sure he'd been having a pee.' She said she was embarrassed, kept her head down, didn't see his face. She thought that was probably just after 8.15 – which fitted when the van was in the car park, the men waiting for Walter to return from his run.

They went back to the cul-de-sac. Tim Kendall, Walter's neighbour, also recognised the CCTV image. He'd seen a man dressed like that walking out of Walter's drive with a stack of leaflets in his hand. 'I didn't think it was anything out of the ordinary. We often get leaflets pushed through our letter box. Mostly from the local takeaways, or self-employed offering their gardening or handyman services.'

'What time was that?'

'Oh, dead on 7 p.m. Like I told you before, Nero and I were rushing back to be in time for the news on Channel 4.'

'Did you see his face?'

'Sorry, I was just focused on getting back in the house.'

'Did the man put a leaflet through your letter box?'

Tim Kendall regarded them thoughtfully. 'No,' he said finally. 'Not that I can recall.'

None of the other residents in the cul-de-sac remembered a leaflet being put through their door on that Wednesday evening. So now they knew when the tracker was placed on Walter's car.

Chapter 11

On Monday morning, Angie decided to stop and breakfast at Starbucks on her way to the station. She took two croissants and a latte to a table at the back, eating the croissants while they were still warm, savouring the buttery taste, remembering the ones she used to share with her father on Sunday mornings.

Her thoughts were once again invaded by Philip. She remembered when they were both taking the English Literature A level paper. From where she was seated, she could see the back of his head, ahead of her, and two rows to the right. Finishing the exam with five minutes to spare, she saw that he too had finished. Gazing at the mass of curly red hair, she had waited for him to glance to the side, to acknowledge her with a smile, but he hadn't looked around. He disappeared at the end of the exam. And he hadn't come in on results day. That was fifteen years ago, but the hurt was still there.

She was back in her car, fastening her seat belt, when her mobile rang. Glancing at the screen, she saw it was Roxanne. Letting go of the seatbelt, she picked up the phone.

'Good morning,' Roxanne said. 'I know it's early, and this might be nothing, but you did say to let you know if I thought of anything missing from the study.'

'You're not too early,' Angie said. 'And we never know what can help. Tell me.'

'Well, believe it or not, I went straight to bed after you dropped me back home on Friday and slept through until the next morning. And I've spent most of the weekend sleeping.'

'That should have done you a power of good.'

'Anyway, the thing is, I think my subconscious must have been in overdrive while I was sleeping. Because the thought popped into my head as soon as I opened my eyes this morning. Only it might be nothing important and I didn't want to waste your time.'

Angie waited, her heart beating quicker.

'It's his notebook,' Roxanne said. 'His green moleskin notebook. He was an inveterate note taker. He loved his green moleskin notebook; he took it everywhere and made notes all the time. We used to joke it would be his chosen luxury if he was ever on Desert Island Discs.' Angie heard the catch in her voice, stayed silent as Roxanne gathered herself. 'I can't find it in his study or anywhere in the house. It seems crazy but I think the people who searched his study might have taken it. You asked me what was missing. That's the only thing I can think of.'

'I'm glad you told me,' Angie said. 'Let me think about that. Okay?'

'Okay,' Roxanne said. Then she added, 'Thanks again for listening to me in the restaurant. I know I unburdened myself a bit, but it helped. And it felt good when you said Dad made a difference to your life.' She rang off before Angie could say anything.

Angie sat in her car, staring straight ahead, her hands on the steering wheel, pondering what Roxanne had just told her. Trying to make sense of it. She pounded the steering wheel in her excitement as the breakthrough came. She drove to the station, took the stairs to Ross's office two at a time. He was talking to Bridges. Ross caught sight of her and waved her in. She took a moment to catch her breath then told him what Roxanne had said.

'You think they were after the notebook?'

'Yes!'

Ross's reaction was downbeat. 'Well, if they got what they were after, why wait for him in the car park? Why kill him?'

'It could be because of what he had written in his notebook,' Angie said. 'Which meant he had knowledge that was dangerous to them. That's why I think they killed him.'

Ross drummed his fingers against the top of his desk, looked at her sceptically.

'Murder is a big step to take. It would have to have been something big. Not the sort of business you would expect a retired headteacher to get involved in.'

Deflated by Ross's response, she wandered over to the large glass window behind Ross's desk. Bridges joined her. From there, they could see the boating pool across the road from the station. It was too early for any of the remote-controlled boats to be out. This early in the morning, it was mainly dog walkers, and students in uniform making their way to school.

Angie turned away from the window. 'What if he wasn't involved in any kind of business? What if he just stumbled into it? If he came across the information that killed him by accident?'

Ross still had that sceptical look. 'What would you expect a normal, law-abiding citizen to do if they stumbled across what they realised was dangerous information?'

'Tell us. Tell the police.'

'Exactly. But he didn't do that. We have no record of your headteacher contacting us. And we are the nearest station to where he lived.'

Angie looked at Bridges, knowing she needed his support. 'Maybe he didn't have time,' Bridges said. 'Maybe he was going to contact us. Maybe they killed him before he could do so.'

Ross spoke dismissively, 'That's a lot of maybes.' He stood up. 'We're still searching for the van. The only other lead we've got is the CCTV passenger image from the garage. There's no immediate match on our system.' He looked at

Bridges. 'Let's clean up the side image and circulate it more widely. See if anyone recognises our chain smoker.' He turned to Angie. 'If your theory is correct, if Walter Price stumbled onto dangerous information, he wouldn't have sat on it. We still need to double check his movements over the last two days before he died.'

Angie nodded, 'I was planning to start with a visit to the food bank – they aren't open until later this morning.'

***

Bridges told her Simpson's stepdaughter had been rushed into hospital with a perforated appendix. Ross had deployed Washington and O'Byrne to continue with the door to door, mopping up any residents who had been out or away during the weekend. Angie was on her own.

She'd decided to retrace Walter's journey on the day he was murdered. She would start from the supermarket and follow the route to the food bank that the satnav gave her.

Looking at the food bank's website brought back a memory: Every year, before his accident, her father would load his car with bags of foodstuffs and deliver them to their local church the week before Christmas. And he would take the young Angie with him. She knew there were well over a thousand foodbanks in the country now. And that they met a need throughout the year, not just at Christmas. It was why Walter had gone every Wednesday.

She found a space in the Aldi car park, fished out a pound coin, and walked over to the bank of empty trollies chained together. The woman standing to one side with copies of *The Big Issue* gave her an enquiring look and held out a copy of the street newspaper. She looked to be in her forties, undernourished with a thin face, a long brown coat drawn tightly around her. Her head was covered by a black scarf tied under her chin. Angie handed her a five-pound note, indicated she didn't want any change.

'Which country are you from?'

'I am from Kosovo.' She gave Angie a broad smile. 'Thank you.'

Starting at the aisle nearest the entrance, Angie went up and down, selecting food stuffs that were on the food bank's recommended list: rice, pasta, long life milk, tinned meat and fish, baked beans, cereals, tinned fruit... At the checkout, she needed eight carrier bags. Pushing the trolley out of the supermarket, she noticed *The Big Issue* seller handing over a black scarf along with the newspaper.

The food bank was in the community hall, next to the church in Cotteridge. The small car park was empty. Seated behind a trestle table, two middle aged women greeted Angie as she entered the building. Behind them four circular tables gave the appearance of a mini café; the elderly men and women around them were engaged in conversation, the inevitable tea and biscuits on the tables. Food for those in need and a social meeting point for the volunteers running the food bank.

One of the men came out to the car and helped her take the shopping bags to a storeroom off the corridor. Angie accepted a cup of tea, showed them her ID, and asked about Walter Price. They all knew him. She could see they were genuinely shocked by what had happened.

'Every Wednesday without fail,' the elder of the two women seated at the trestle table said. 'Ten full bags. Sometimes he would stay for a cup of tea and a chat.'

'Did Walter make his usual visit last Wednesday?'

'Yes, he did. I helped him bring the bags of food in.' She held out her hand. 'By the way, I'm Margaret.'

Angie shook Margaret's hand. 'And did Walter seem his usual self? Did he stay for a cup of tea afterwards?'

'He didn't want a cup of tea,' Margaret said. 'He must have got held up somewhere because he was an hour later than normal – he didn't get here until after 1.30. He seemed calm enough, but he said he was in a hurry. He had to take the girl with him somewhere.'

'Which girl was that? Someone who you knew?'

Margaret looked thoughtful. 'No,' she said slowly. 'I didn't recognise her from the church. I wondered if she was his niece or some other relative. I thought he might introduce us. But he didn't.'

'What did the girl look like?' Angie asked.

'I'd say she was in her twenties. Striking good looks – bright blonde hair, symmetrical face, prominent cheekbones. Reminded me of my nephew's fiancé. She's Croatian.'

Angie took out her notebook. 'Can you tell me what she was wearing?'

'Just her top,' Margaret said. 'A green jumper. She was sitting in the passenger seat, so I couldn't see what else she was wearing. The green jumper made a striking contrast with her blonde hair. Before she put the headscarf on.'

'She was wearing a headscarf?'

'Not the first time I went out. But I made two trips to get the bags from the boot and the second time I walked past, she'd covered her head with a black scarf which hid most of her hair. I remember thinking it was a bit strange.'

'Okay, Margaret,' Angie said, turning to a fresh page in her notebook. 'It would be really helpful if you can think back and give me as good a description of this girl as you can.'

'I can do better than that,' Margaret said eagerly. 'I used to be a portrait painter. Still do the odd one for friends and family. I can do a portrait of the girl for you if you like. With scarf or without scarf?'

Angie knew how to ride her luck. 'Both,' she said. 'If that's okay with you?'

Margaret's smile lit up her face. 'Absolutely! Like I said, I've done portraits for friends and family. And obviously for my paying clients. But never one for the police. This will be a first for me!'

Chapter 12

Margaret didn't want Angie looking over her shoulder – she removed herself to one of the meeting rooms behind the mini café and said she would be about a half hour. Angie turned down the offer of another cup of tea, decided she could do with some fresh air. Opposite the church, set back from the main road, a row of small shops included a fish and chip take away. Angie asked for a cone of chips.

She crossed back over, walked past the church and community hall. Rows of shops ran along both sides of the road; the pavements on both sides carried a flow of pedestrians. She looked for a bin, eventually spied one on the opposite side of the road, outside a Co-op supermarket. A white van stopped, waiting to turn into the supermarket car park. There was no signage on the back, but as her eyes followed the van, she noticed a woman holding out copies of *The Big Issue*.

It was the black headscarf covering her hair that caught Angie's eye. As she watched, a woman pushing a full trolley stopped as she came level with the seller of the street newspaper. After a brief conversation, money appeared to change hands.

The seller glanced around surreptitiously, reached down to unzip the blue bag beside her and handed the woman a black scarf. As she straightened up, she spied Angie watching her. She looked afraid, moved so the blue bag was hidden behind her and held out a copy of *The Big Issue* as Angie approached her. Angie smiled at the woman and shook her head. She pointed at the blue bag. 'I want to buy a scarf.'

Margaret was waiting for her when she got back to the community centre. She took Angie into the side room and showed her the two portraits she had sketched. First the one without the headscarf, laid flat on the trestle table she had worked on. Angie looked at it with surprise: at the symmetrical face, cheekbones that she thought would be described as Slavic, eyes that looked defiant. Margaret pointed to the short, cropped hair. 'Sorry, I only worked in pencil. You have to imagine her hair is a bright blonde.'

'Incredible!' Angie said. 'You've done this from memory? From only seeing her once?'

'Twice. I saw her twice. And yes, I've always had a photographic memory. Since I was at primary school.' She giggled, seeming almost embarrassed by the gift she'd been given.

'Can you show me the one with the scarf?'

Margaret reached down for the second sheet of A3 paper, turned it over, and laid it out on the trestle table. 'It does make a difference, doesn't it?'

'Yes, it does.' Angie untied the black scarf from around her waist, handed it to Margaret. 'Does this look like the headscarf?'

'Yes, it does!' Margaret said. 'Where on earth did that spring from?'

'From *The Big Issue*,' Angie said, then seeing the look of confusion appearing, she explained.

'Well, I think I'll get one of those,' Margaret said. 'They're always useful for funerals. And at my age that's becoming a more frequent outing.'

'No need. You can have this one. It's the least I can do as a thank you.'

'You're welcome,' Margaret said, clutching the scarf to her chest. 'It's a privilege to be able to help our police. And exciting to be part of the team!' She giggled as she handed Angie a third sheet of paper. 'A little surprise for you.'

***

Angie drove back to Aldi. Walter must have met the mysterious girl there if she was with him when he arrived at the food bank. But if the girl was worried about being recognised, she would not have gone into the supermarket with Walter. Who was she? Why was she wary of being recognised?

The Big Issue seller wasn't in her usual place. Spying a café on the other side of the road, Angie crossed over, peered in through the window and recognised the brown coat and the black headscarf of the woman sitting with her back to the window.

She was the only one in the café apart from the young waitress behind the counter examining her nails. Angie went back to her car for the two rolled up A3 sheets.

The woman had her head down, looking at her phone, a half-finished cup of coffee and a plate with only crumbs left on the table in front of her. A small pile of the street newspaper lay on the chair next to her, but Angie was more interested in the blue zipped up canvas bag resting on the floor.

She pulled out a chair, sat opposite the woman, caught the startled look as she raised her head. Angie smiled reassuringly – the woman's face slowly relaxed as she recognised her from before. Angie pointed at the blue carrier bag and raised her hands as if covering her head. The woman nodded her understanding, reached down, and handed Angie a black scarf. It was identical to the one she'd left with Margaret, the same as the one the blonde girl in Walter's car had been wearing.

Angie ordered a latte, took her first sip before showing the woman her warrant card. She looked terrified. 'It's okay,' Angie said, holding her hands up and shaking her head. 'Not a problem. This is not about the scarves. I just need to ask you some questions. Let me get you a fresh cup of coffee first.' She smiled at the woman, waited until the fear had gone from her face, 'What is your name?'

The woman's name was Irina. Her hand flew to her mouth in surprise when Angie unrolled the sheet of A3, revealing the portrait of the girl. Then the second sheet with the girl wearing the scarf. 'Did you sell a scarf to this girl?' Angie asked.

Irina stared at Angie, swallowed hard, tried to speak. Then she turned around, raised her voice, spoke to the waitress behind the bar in what Angie recognised as Italian. The waitress came from behind the counter, released the latch on the door and turned the 'open' sign around before coming back to their table.

'Irina understands some English, but she can only speak a few words. Her Italian is much better, and I speak Italian. Would you like me to help?'

Angie nodded. 'Please.'

'Irina says you are from the police, and you want to ask her questions. She thought you were going to arrest her because she is selling scarves. A market trader brings her the scarves. She is not the only one. The women know they shouldn't be doing it, but he lets them keep £1 for every scarf they sell.' The waitress shrugged. 'They need the money.'

Angie pointed at Margaret's portraits. 'I need help with something else. Ask her if she sold a scarf to this girl.'

Through Gina, the waitress, Irina said a man had bought a scarf for the girl in the portrait. Angie opened her wallet, took the folded photograph of Walter that she'd cut out of the local newspaper and showed it to Irina. She saw the smile that accompanied the look of recognition.

'Yes, she says that was the man.'

Irina was clear in her account. She had been working outside the supermarket for three months now. She recognised Walter because he came to the supermarket every Wednesday, always came out with a full trolley and always gave her £5 for a copy of *The Big Issue*.

'The man's name is Walter,' Angie said. 'Ask her about last Wednesday. Was the girl with Walter when he went into the supermarket?'

Irina seemed to understand the question – Angie could see her shaking her head before Gina asked her. Angie waited, listening to Irina's voice rising and falling as she became animated, using her hands to emphasise her words. She shook her head vigorously in response to a question Gina asked.

'Irina says the girl did not come to the supermarket with Walter. It was only when he was getting into his car that the blonde girl approached him.'

'Does Irina know the blonde girl?'

'No,' Gina said. 'I asked her that. That morning was the first time she'd seen the girl. But she says the girl had been there since early morning, only approaching shoppers when they were walking back to their car with the £1 coin from the returned trolley in their hand. Some had waved her away; some had given her the coin.'

Angie pointed at Walter's photograph. 'What did he do?'

'Irina says he talked with the girl. Then he took her into this café.'

Angie stared at Gina who shook her head. 'Sorry, I don't work Wednesdays.'

'Okay. Can you ask Irina if she saw what they did afterwards?'

'They were in here for about a half hour. Then when they returned to the car park, Walter brought the girl over to where Irina was and bought a scarf. The girl was sitting in the front passenger seat of Walter's car when he drove out of the car park.'

'What was Irina getting excited about when she was shaking her head.'

'Sorry, that was me playing detective. I asked her if she thought the man meant the girl any harm. She was adamant he's not that kind of man.'

'Ask her why she thinks the girl went off with Walter. And if she seemed nervous.'

Angie waited while Irina responded to Gina.

'Irina says the girl was always looking around, glancing over her shoulder in the car park. She thinks the girl hasn't been on the streets long, thinks maybe she's run away from someone.'

'Why does she think the girl went off with Walter?'

'She thinks he offered to help her.'

***

Driving back to the station, Angie tried to make sense of what she'd learnt. So, Walter had befriended a girl on his way to the food bank. A girl who might have been running away. Why was she running away? Who was she running from? And even if the people looking for the girl had found her, had got her back, why would they deliberately kill Walter? Just for helping her? It didn't make any sense... Perhaps the girl had nothing to do with Walter's death.

She took the stairs to Ross's office, looked through the glass panel. He wasn't at his desk, but Bridges was standing by the window, his back towards her as he looked out over the boating lake. He turned around as she knocked and opened the door; she noticed he was holding a folder in one hand. He saw her questioning look.

'Ross should be back soon. He's gone to see his mother. The Home phoned to say she'd had a bad night.' Angie was still looking at him, so Bridges elaborated. 'Ross is an only child and after his dad ran off, it was just him and his mum. She brought him up. He feels guilty that she's in a Home, visits her three times a week.'

Bridges held up the folder. 'From Forensics. Confirmation of the verbal report. Same DNA from the cigarettes in the cul-de-sac and the community car park. And a magnetic tracker under the front left wheel arch.' He put the report down. 'I've circulated the CCTV image of the chain smoker that you got from the garage. Nothing back yet. Although I have to admit it's not the best image.' He gazed at Angie. 'You've got that look again. Tell me about your trip to the food bank.'

She'd just started when Ross came into the room. She paused, but he took one of the chairs and waved a hand to indicate she should continue. They listened attentively, Ross with his head still and his eyes focused on her face. When she'd finished, he pointed to the rolls of paper she was holding. 'Are those the portraits?'

'Yes.'

There was a cork board on the wall by the round table. She pinned the two sheets of A3. They stood and looked at the portraits of the blonde girl that Margaret had done. Ross scratched his head. 'Impressive. We can circulate copies of these,' he said, but she heard the hesitancy in his voice. 'If you're convinced that they're accurate.' He looked at the third rolled-up sheet of A3 Angie was still holding. 'What's that one?'

Smiling, Angie unrolled the third sheet and pinned it to the cork board. 'Margaret had this one ready for me when I got back from my walk. A little surprise she called it. She said we might need the reassurance.'

They gazed with unbelieving eyes at Margaret's portrait of Angie. 'Clever Margaret,' Bridges said, shaking his head. 'Case proven. We'll get both portraits of the girl circulated.'

Ross stood up. 'I'm off to see the Deputy now. He won't be expecting us to have made any progress. Let me take a copy of the girl's portrait with me. I'll enjoy showing it to him.'

'Good luck with the Deputy,' Bridges said with a wry smile.

Ross snorted. 'I'll let you know how it goes at our briefing tomorrow morning.'

Chapter 13

Philip had suggested to Angie they meet at the café in Brindley Place at 7.30 p.m. and then decide on a restaurant. He got the cross-city train in from Redditch; it was then only a ten-minute walk from the station to Brindley Place.

He'd kept away from Birmingham for twelve years, buried himself in London – a combination of having no remaining family expecting him to visit and memories he wanted to forget. Needed to forget. All push and no pull. But on his thirtieth birthday, he decided that his conscience could take no more; he felt he was slowly drowning in a sea of depression. His birthday present to himself had been a series of counselling sessions. The advice offered came as no surprise. Return to Birmingham. He took up his post at the FE College three months later. He was now in his second year at the college as an Assistant Principal.

Birmingham had continued its path of change in the intervening years. Brindley Place was at the heart of it. Its centrepiece, a raised central walkway, was framed along its length by fountains on either side. The only other building in the plaza itself was a small café with some outside seating.

Philip saw Angie at the same moment as she raised her head and saw him approaching. He took a good look at her as they got closer. She put her coffee down and stood up to embrace him. They were both grinning as they sat down.

'You look great,' he said. 'I can still see the old Angie.'

'Thanks.' Her face was as he remembered it. Glowing skin that always suggested the remaining hint of a summer tan. Smiling eyes that looked at you directly although now there was something else there. Something to represent the years that had gone by.

'I can't believe it's fifteen years,' Angie said. 'Would you like a coffee here first?'

'Yes,' he said. Not particularly wanting a coffee, but not wanting to break the mood.

So, they talked, probing gently, trying to find out about each other, but backing off when the hint was given. They'd been friends since their first year at secondary school when Walter chose them as his two to mentor together during their seven years at his school. They became best friends, supporting each other through the ups and downs of school life. In the sixth form, Philip had desperately wanted to be more than her friend but didn't know how to ask without putting their friendship at risk. Before he could work up the courage, his mother had died. And then Angie had started going out with Ian Gill.

'Did you and Ian go to the same university?'

'Oh, no. The day we got our results and went out to celebrate was the day we broke up. What was funny was that neither of us felt too bad about it. I think we both recognised a new phase beckoned. We went to different universities. I think Ian is in America now.'

He nodded. Knowing that she was waiting to hear why he hadn't turned up for his results or been at the celebration that evening.

But all he said softly was 'Things happened. I just needed to be on my own.'

Her hands were in front of her on the table, fingers interlocked. Philip realised he was twiddling his thumbs. He stood up. 'Let's take a walk along the canals, maybe walk through by Symphony Hall. Then we can choose a restaurant.'

They took the few steps up to the narrow, raised walkway, water from the spouting fountains on either side.

'Not the safest place for a boisterous stag do,' Philip said.

'Or a hen party. They seem to want to outdo the lads these days.'

As they exited the plaza, the frontages of the buildings closed in more. Restaurants offering a variety of cuisines lined both sides, some acknowledging the cool autumn air with outside heaters for the alfresco diners. Reaching the canal, they climbed the steps to the hump-backed bridge with the ornamental black and gold metal railings, stood and looked. The canal ran into the distance whether they looked straight ahead or behind them; couples or groups of friends strolled along the paved banks on either side.

'So much for the old, grimy, industrial Birmingham,' Philip said. 'The city has got new clothes.'

'As predicted by Walter. Remember?'

'Yes. As Munich is to Germany, Barcelona to Spain, Lyon to France, so Birmingham will be to England.' They laughed, sharing the memory of Walter's assembly, showing them pictures of Birmingham's past with Matthew Boulton and James Watt, and then the city council's plans as the new century dawned.

Philip chuckled, 'No longer the Birmingham of *Peaky Blinders*.'

Angie turned and gazed at him thoughtfully. 'Not as we know it,' she said.

They left the bridge, taking the steps down to the entrance to the Convention Centre that housed Symphony Hall. The glass doors slid open automatically; they took the escalator up to the ground level, walked past the concert hall, and came out on to Broad Street. Angie's eye was caught by a ten-storey building on their left, the golden, silver and glass facade covered by a filigree pattern of interlocking metal rings. It was a standout, unmissable building, no concession made to blending in with its surroundings. Angie wondered what it said about the personality of the architect.

'It's the new public library,' Philip said. 'You either love it or hate it.'

'I love it.'

'Me too.'

They walked up Broad Street, past the pubs and restaurants, feeling the buzz of the city's awakening night life that would grow in intensity until the clubs closed their doors in the early hours.

Philip stopped outside a restaurant with a wide glass frontage. 'This one only opened last year, describing itself as a contemporary Indian restaurant. People at work say it's a different atmosphere to the traditional Indian, and the food is good. Want to try it?'

'Sure.'

A smiling waiter held the glass door open as they entered. Angie asked for a table at the back section of the dining area, away from the others. Seated at the table, they ordered two Cobra beers, scanned the menu, and agreed on the five-dish banquet for two.

They kept to their unspoken agreement not to probe too deeply into the last fifteen years. Not tonight, anyway. When the beers arrived in ice cold glasses, Philip raised his glass.

'What should we toast to?'

Angie raised her glass. 'A renewed friendship?'

'Yes,' he said, as their eyes met. 'A renewed friendship.'

Philip raised his glass again. 'And to our old headteacher. To Walter Price, to whom we both owe so much.' But this time Angie did not raise her glass. He saw her expression and put down his glass.

She looked directly at him and spoke slowly, her eyes never leaving his face. 'I can't do it,' she said. 'It feels wrong. I need to know why he was murdered. When I have the answer, when we've got the man who killed him – that's when I'll raise a glass to Walter's memory.'

He heard the determination in her voice, saw the clenched jaw and the steely look in her eyes, stayed silent until her face relaxed.

'Angie, it was a terrible way for Walter to die, stabbed to death in a car park. A botched carjacking. The papers say it's the fifth carjacking in that car park in the last few months. Why didn't they just take the car? I can't believe he would have fought them over it.' He leant forward, waited until she was looking at him, lowered his voice. 'But it was a random event, Angie. It could happen to any of us. I too, want the murderer to be caught. But don't beat yourself up looking for a reason. Walter was just in the wrong place at the wrong time.'

They ordered two more beers. Their waiter arrived, pushing a trolley loaded with their five-dish banquet; he leant over to make room on the table, transferring the dishes from the trolley. Angie was grateful for the time to think. How much should she tell Philip? She had deliberately kept her feelings hidden from Ross, still worried he would take her off the investigation if he thought she was too personally involved.

She'd been persistent, but she had tried to stay calm, stay professional, not show her emotions. She had to stay on the case until she found Walter's killer. But the tension was building up inside her. She could feel it. She needed an outlet, needed to confide in someone she could trust. She gazed at Philip, remembered the confidences they had shared as they moved through adolescence. She'd trusted him then. She could trust him now.

Angie waited until the waiter brought the coffees. Philip reached for the sugar bowl.

'There's something I think you should know,' she said. 'But it has to be in the strictest confidence.'

'Ah! A secret from your wicked past.' He stopped stirring his coffee, looked up, saw she was being serious.

'You can trust me.'

She nodded, 'I know.'

He waited expectantly. Angie was silent for a moment, then she spoke in a quiet voice, leaning forward to make sure he could hear her.

'Philip, Walter was not the victim of a random carjacking that went wrong. He was followed to that car park and deliberately murdered.'

He stared at her in astonishment. 'Walter deliberately murdered? Why would anyone want to do that?'

'We don't know why. We're still trying to find out what the motive was. But it looks like the same people who broke into his house killed him.'

Philip was quiet. He picked up the teaspoon, stirred his coffee. He put the spoon down but didn't pick up the cup. Angie waited.

'I know you,' he said finally. 'I'm sure you're good at your job. You wouldn't make a statement like that without reason, so you must have evidence. Can you share that with me?'

She took him through the investigation. She told him about the van parked in the cul-de-sac, the non-existent plumbing company, the break in and only the study being searched, the DNA match between the cigarettes in the cul-de-sac and the car park, the van being captured on CCTV, and the tracker on Walter's car.

When she stopped talking, he was silent. Looking up, she saw that he had the white napkin in his hand, attempting to wipe the tears running down his cheeks. Angie felt the release as her own tears began to flow. She used her napkin. Philip held her hand and squeezed it. They smiled at each other through their tears before leaving the table to wash their faces. Philip was already back in his seat when Angie returned. He waited until she was sitting and looking across the table at him.

'I appreciate I'm not a police officer, and I can't play an active part in your investigation. But if there is anything I can do – if it would help to talk things through without compromising your own position, then please call on me. I would be grateful if I had the chance to help.'

'You've helped me already. Just being able to share my feelings is a big help. Thank you.'

Philip insisted on paying the bill. They parted outside the restaurant. Angie headed back across the plaza to the multi-storey car park. Philip walked in the opposite direction to New Street station and checked the departure board – the last train to Redditch was in an hour's time. The pub in Temple Street, opposite the station, was just down the road from the pitch where he'd stood with his hot dog cart. That thought brought back a bad memory. He took a bottle of red wine and a glass over to a table in the lounge bar. Thought about what Angie had told him and what he'd told her. And what he *hadn't* told her.

Chapter 14

Ross was kept waiting for fifteen minutes before the Deputy's PA told him to go through. A circular glass table and soft chairs were available, but Henderson sat in his black leather chair behind his desk and indicated that Ross should sit in the hard plastic chair opposite him.

He listened to Ross's report on the investigation with an impassive face. But inside he was seething. He'd looked forward to the meeting, looked forward to seeing Ross squirm as he admitted his lack of progress. And the meeting had started well with Ross's statement that Walter Price had not been the victim of a botched carjacking; he had been deliberately murdered. The Deputy had stared at him for a moment, then decided to play along and let Ross condemn himself as he sought to justify his absurd claim.

'Interesting,' he said, keeping the inward smile off his face. 'What evidence have you got to support that statement?'

And then he'd had to sit and listen as Ross told him about men in a van, a DNA match and the tracker found on Walter Price's car.

'We believe Walter Price befriended a girl who had run away from someone,' Ross said. 'We don't yet know why, but we believe it was that act of kindness that got him killed.'

The Deputy sensed a weakness. 'And who is this mystery girl? Do we even have any idea what she looks like?'

Ross had allowed the question to hang in the air, unanswered, while he held the Deputy's gaze. But then he unfurled the roll of paper he was holding and placed the portrait in front of the Deputy. 'We don't know yet know who she is, but this is what she looks like.'

The Deputy noted Ross had used the word "yet" twice. *The bastard thinks there is a chance he might solve this case. Retire in a blaze of glory.* Deciding to bring the meeting to an end, he reached forward, rolled up the portrait and held on to it. 'Thank you for your report. I need some time to reflect on what you've told me. The PCC has taken a personal interest in this case and has requested regular updates. I'm meeting him later this evening. I'll get back to you after I have seen him.' He stood up to indicate the meeting was over. He couldn't bring himself to look Ross in the face, didn't want to see the smirk he knew Ross wouldn't bother to hide.

***

The Deputy was shown into the Police and Crime Commissioner's office promptly at 6 p.m. The PCC came out from behind his desk, greeted him with a handshake. They sat in the soft leather seats.

'Well, Paul, you will have gathered I have a personal interest in this case,' the PCC said. 'The victim was a former colleague. How is the investigation going?'

The Deputy began by telling him Ross believed Walter Price had been deliberately murdered. The PCC sat up and stared at him. 'We both thought this was a botched carjacking. And now you're telling me that Ross thinks this is something different.'

'Yes, it does seem rather fanciful. But he thinks he's got evidence to support that claim.'

'What evidence?'

The Deputy told him about the DNA match, the tracker, the missing green notebook. And that Ross thought it might all be connected to a girl that Walter Price had befriended.

'Ross is now looking for the girl.' He took the sheet of paper out of his briefcase and handed it to the PCC. 'This is the girl who Ross thinks might be somehow involved in the murder.'

Glancing at the portrait, the PCC turned away quickly, his body racked by a coughing fit. He poured himself a glass of water from the jug on his desk, sipped it before turning back.

'What have you said to Ross?'

'I said I'd get back to him this evening after I'd spoken to you.'

The PCC thought for a moment. 'Right. I've got another appointment now. Give me some time to think about this so-called evidence. I'll get back to you before 8 p.m. You can ring Ross after we've spoken.'

Remaining seated after the Deputy had gone, the PCC gently massaged his temples and waited for his heartbeat to slow. The girl in the portrait was the special girl Albert had promised him, the blonde bitch who had run out of the hotel room almost a week ago while he was having a shower. The PCC always had a long, hot shower before sex; the almost scalding temperature of the water turned his skin pinkish, left him tingling all over and seemed to make his nerve endings more receptive to the pleasures that awaited him.

Albert had phoned in the middle of his shower – the Deputy's hands were wet and soapy, so he'd put the phone on speaker. The girl had come out of the bed to the bathroom door, overheard their conversation, and run off.

There had been a long silence at the other end of the phone when he told Albert what had happened. The PCC had waited, swallowing hard, his throat dry, his heart pounding. He'd thought he felt a pain in his chest. When Albert had eventually spoken, the lack of emotion in his voice was menacing. The PCC's throat went dry again as he remembered. But since then, Albert had told him they'd found the girl. That she was no longer a danger to their plans.

And now he would have to ring Albert again. His heart rate wasn't back to normal, but he could wait no longer. He had to make the call. He sipped some more water, used the special mobile phone. He told Albert about his meeting with the Deputy.

'It's your mess,' Albert said, the vicious quietness of his voice making the Police and Crime Commissioner shiver. 'You clear it up. Phone me back when you've done so.' He rang off.

The PCC remained seated at his desk for a while, bent over, his head in his hands. The pain in his chest had returned. When it subsided, he poured himself a glass of water, sipped it slowly while he thought long and hard about what the Deputy had told him. After thirty minutes, he rang the Deputy and gave him his response to Ross's report.

'Phone me back when you've spoken to Ross,' he said. 'I should be free at 9 p.m.' He put the phone down and felt his breast; his heart rate was almost back to normal. He knew he could count on the ambitious Deputy – after all he held the man's future in the palm of his hand.

***

At 9 p.m., the Police and Crime Commissioner rolled over and reached for one of the few cigarettes he allowed himself. He didn't really consider himself a smoker, not like in the past when he was a regular twenty a day man. But the truth was he enjoyed smoking, and after these occasions, he ignored the no smoking signs in the hotel room and succumbed to temptation.

The young, blonde girl lying next to him was a smoker. Not so bright with the conversation, but with a body that more than made up for that. Just what he had asked for. And she was willing to do everything he wanted. The girl finished her cigarette, leaned over and dropped it in the glass half filled with water. She turned back to the PCC, showed him the tip of her tongue. He had just leaned in towards her when his phone rang. With a curse, he pushed her aside. He looked at the screen, saw the call was the one he had been waiting for. He took the phone out with him to the small balcony.

'Did you speak to Ross?'

'Yes,' the Deputy said. 'I did as you suggested and talked him through it.'

'How did he respond?'

'Let's just say he wasn't impressed.' The PCC heard the chuckle in the other man's voice. 'But he'll do as he's told.'

'Good.' The PCC rang off, then smiled to himself. It was a smile of relief.

He went back into the bedroom from the balcony. The girl was still lying naked on the bed, smoking another cigarette, looking bored. She pursed her lips.

'Get dressed,' he said.

She looked at him in surprise and pouted.

'Go! I have business to attend to.'

He waited impatiently while she dressed. When she closed the door behind her, he lit another cigarette and smoked it out on the balcony. Then he dialled Albert's number. The phone was answered immediately.

'Have you cleared up your mess?'

'Yes.'

'Tell me what you have done.'

The Police and Crime Commissioner told him.

'Good. Was Henderson a problem?'

'No, not at all. If anything, he seemed pleased. I think there is some history between him and Ross. And he wants to be Chief Constable.'

'We want that, too,' Albert said, the menace in his tone no longer discernible. 'It's good we still have the video in reserve. I watch my copy from time to time. It is both stimulating and illuminating!'

'I do too,' the PCC said. 'Maybe I could meet up with that brunette at the Grand Prix next year. You know I prefer blondes, but for her I would make an exception.'

'Something to look forward to,' Albert said, ending the conversation.

The video under discussion was the one taken in Monaco by the hidden camera in the yacht's bedroom. It featured the Deputy with the tall brunette who had entertained him. Watching her in action the PCC had regretted choosing her blond companion. The Deputy was unaware of the video's existence.

***

The two-starred Michelin restaurant was close to the Barbican. Sitting in the private dining room, Albert, a short, wiry, well-groomed man with wavy grey hair, who favoured bespoke suits and handmade Italian ties, put the mobile phone back in his leather shoulder bag, and signalled to the waiter, hovering discreetly outside the open door.

Albert kept five mobile phones in his shoulder bag – three had red dots and were numbered 1 to 3. The ones with the red dots he used to call Birmingham; the other two with blue dots numbered 1 and 2 were used when he called Aberdeen. He changed the phones every week.

His father had been a professor of philosophy at the University in Tirana and an admirer of Albert Schweitzer. When the great man was awarded the Nobel Peace Prize in 1952, his father was elated. When his son was born on 4 September 1965, the same day Albert Schweitzer died, his father took it as an omen and named the baby after him. The young Albert was a good student who studied Economics at universities in France and Germany, but the academic life his father had hoped for was not for him. He had headed to England to make his fortune.

The waiter appeared with the fourth course of the tasting menu. He was followed by the sommelier; Albert listened attentively to his discourse on the wine that accompanied the Loch Duart salmon, wild horseradish and Arenkha caviar. He ate his way slowly through two more courses, savouring the flavours of the food and the accompanying wines, thinking all the time about the situation in Birmingham and what other measures he might have to take.

Satisfied, his mind turned to Aberdeen. Signalling to the waiter to delay the next course, he used the number 2 phone with the blue dot. When it was answered he asked one question and listened intently to the answer before ringing off. Indicating to the waiter, he put the phone back in his shoulder bag and sat back with a smile on his face.

Chapter 15

The early morning sky was an unpromising, uniform grey. It wasn't raining as Philip stepped out of the apartment block, but it hadn't long stopped; he could tell from the wet pavement, and the drops of water on the broad leaves of the shrub with the purple flowers.

He considered himself a morning person, but today he felt drained. It wasn't because of the beer and the bottle of red wine from the previous evening – the two paracetamol with a glass of water would have taken care of that. It was the tossing and turning and lack of sleep. Angie's revelation that Walter had been followed and deliberately murdered had shaken Philip to the core. He had returned to Birmingham to atone, had finally worked up the courage to face Walter. And now the opportunity to ask for forgiveness had been taken from him. Would Walter have forgiven him? He would now never know. And Walter would never know the price that Philip had paid for his act of betrayal, would never know of his years of living with depression that had culminated in his breakdown. He had wanted him to know.

The daily train journey from Redditch to the city centre took thirty-six minutes. He enjoyed going in by train – Redditch was where the train started from, so he was always assured of a window seat, away from the aisle that would get crowded as the train made its nine stops before New Street. It was a ten-minute walk from New Street station to the FE College. Getting the 6.57 from Redditch meant he would normally sit down at his desk on the fourth floor of the college by 7.50.

·As he went in through the automatic doors that fronted the college, the security guard, looked him up and down. 'Rough night?'

'You could say that, Daniel. Did Dave get off okay?'

'Yep! Flew out yesterday. California, here we come!' Daniel's son had landed a football coaching job in the Los Angeles area. His first full time paid job after graduating with a sports degree. There had been some hold up over the contract, some worrying delay about whether it was going to work out.

'That's splendid news, Daniel. Give him a year to settle down and you can go visiting.'

Daniel's grin widened. 'That's the plan.' He held up his hand. 'Thanks for all the encouragement you gave him. He might have given up trying if it wasn't for you.'

Philip took the offered high five, walked to the lift and pushed the button for the fourth floor.

Peggy, the cleaner whose parents he had discovered were part of the Windrush generation of Jamaican immigrants, was just coming out of his office. Her warm smile turned to one of concern. 'You don't look so good today, Mr Maddox. Would you like a coffee?'

When she brought the coffee, he said, 'Thanks, Peggy. I just had a bit of a rough night.' She giggled then. He wondered what she was thinking.

His ten o'clock appointment was with the HR director of an engineering company to discuss the number of apprentices the company would take the following year. The meeting went well. Philip decided on another cup of coffee, wanting to give himself five minutes thinking about Angie Reeves. But Becky, his secretary, put her head around the door. 'Anna phoned. She wanted to see you as soon as your meeting was over.'

Philip made a face. 'What about?'

'I don't know, but she sounded a little tense. And she phoned herself, rather than getting Jackie to put something in the diary.'

'Right. Phone Jackie and ask her if Anna is free now. If she is, tell her I'm on my way.'

Grabbing his jacket from the back of the chair, he went through to the outer office where Becky had her desk.

'Is Anna free?'

'Yes, she's expecting you,' Becky said, looking up. Philip noticed the bruising on her cheek under the makeup.

'Are you okay?'

She saw where he was looking. 'Oh that! Just one of those stupid accidents,' she said brightly.

Philip nodded, made his way to the lift, remembered it wasn't the first time Becky had come to work with a bruised face.

***

The principal's office and those of the other members of the college's executive team were clustered on the eighth floor, which was as high as the building went. From there the view was of the city centre – old landmarks like the iconic Rotunda building and the telecoms tower, cheek by jowl with the newer skyscraper office blocks.

Coming out of the lift, he raised his hand in silent greeting to Tom as he went past the Deputy Principal's office. Tom was leaving at Easter to be the principal of a college up north. Anna had told Philip about her conversation with the Chair of the Board; no promises, but they would welcome an application from Philip.

Anna's office was at the far end of the corridor. Jackie, the principal's PA, looked up as Philip came around the corner. 'Go right in. She's waiting for you.'

Philip knocked at the door lightly. Anna had left her desk, taken a seat at the long table they used for meetings. She sat with her back to the interior of the office, so she was looking out through the window, with a view of the Birmingham skyline.

'You look rough,' she said, beckoning Philip to sit opposite her. Jackie appeared, took their order, returned almost immediately with two coffees.

'That was quick,' Philip said.

She smiled, 'Preparation. I had the coffee waiting in the cups, the kettle already boiled.'

Anna waited until Jackie had closed the door behind her. Then she sat up, pressed her back against the chair, regarded Philip with steady eyes. 'We've got trouble.'

Seven students had received certificates through the post for courses they had never enrolled on. 'They haven't attended a class or completed an assignment, but the college has claimed and received funding for these students,' Anna said. 'We only found out because three of the students contacted us. We don't know how many other students are involved.'

Philip wondered why Anna was telling him this, wondered if it was her way of preparing him for the wider responsibilities that a Deputy Principal's role would carry.

'How are you going to handle it?'

'The first thing I did was to contact the Funding Agency. And that's when the shit hit the fan. They've got a new chief executive – the last one resigned after being mauled by a Parliamentary Select Committee and this one intends to make his mark. Zero tolerance of any fraud. An end to press articles berating the public sector.'

'But fraud at this college? We don't do fraud,' Philip said. 'A mistake might have happened, someone might have messed up somewhere, but it won't be deliberate.' He repeated, 'We don't do fraud.'

'You know that. And I know that. But it's public money and the Funding Agency are charged with being the guardians of it.'

Philip took a moment, digested what she had said, thought he understood why she was sharing this information with him.

'I guess we need to run an internal investigation. Carry out an internal audit and report to the Agency.' He thought she wanted him to lead the investigation.

'No,' Anna said, 'we won't be doing that. There will be an investigation, but we won't be leading it. The Funding Agency are sending in their own team to carry out the investigation. What they want from us is a list of all staff involved and access to all relevant files. They will also look at the email history of all relevant staff. And they want their work mobile phones.'

Anna was looking down, playing with her fountain pen, pulling the cap off, then pushing it back on. Philip, watching her, waiting for her to speak, felt a sense of foreboding. He swallowed to take away the sudden dryness in his mouth.

Anna put the fountain pen down on the table. 'The thing is Philip, these courses are in construction. They're in the curriculum area you're responsible for.'

'You're not suggesting…'

'I'm not suggesting anything. Of course not. But the Funding Agency need to carry out their investigation. Surely you can see that.'

He nodded. 'What do you want me to do?'

She picked up the pen again, played with the cap. 'I had a phone call from the chief executive of the Funding Agency first thing this morning. He wants his team to have a completely free hand while they interview individuals, so he wants our senior person with responsibility for the department out of the way. Seems to think your presence in the building could make a difference.'

'They want me suspended?'

'Yes.' She put the pen down. 'He requested I suspend you while his team carry out their investigation. And I've agreed to his request.'

Pushing his chair back, Philip stood up and turned to face the window. The autumn sun had finally come through; the rays falling on the golf ball facade of the Rotunda created a striking effect. He felt quite calm – he always went that way when faced with difficult situations. Anna came around the table and stood by him, looking out.

'I can see it makes sense from their point of view,' he said. 'I can see that. When does the suspension start? And until when?'

'It starts tomorrow morning. Two weeks. That's how long they think it will take them to complete their investigation. They'll almost certainly want to interview you in the first few days. I'll be in touch.'

'Okay. I guess I'd better tidy up my office before I leave. I'll get Becky to cancel any appointments in the diary over the next two weeks.'

He headed for the door, stopped and turned around as he heard Anna clear her throat. She managed a half smile. 'Just one more thing. I've discussed this situation with the Chair. He said to make sure you know he would still welcome an application for the Deputy's job from you. Once the investigation team has reported.'

'Thank him for me,' Philip said. He understood what the Chair meant.

Chapter 16

Arriving for the morning briefing, Angie was surprised to find Simpson on his own in the incident room. 'Good morning,' she said brightly. 'Where are the others?'

He sat up and shrugged. 'I came straight from the hospital, been here fifteen minutes and no one else has been in. Not even Bridges.'

Angie saw the dark smudges under his eyes. 'How is your stepdaughter?'

'Rachel had a perforated appendix. They operated on her last night. She'll be in the hospital for the next ten days.'

'Is she going to be okay?'

He nodded. 'Yes. They were worried about Sepsis, but the crisis seems to be over.' He pushed the chair back, stood up and stretched with his arms above his head, fingers interlocked. 'What have you been up to? Any progress?'

Angie told him about her visit to the food bank and the mysterious blond girl that Walter had picked up. And about Margaret's portraits.

Simpson whistled. 'That's some gift! Very helpful too if you are assuming this blonde girl is linked with Walter's murder.'

Angie took a moment before replying. 'Walter had his routine: food bank on a Wednesday morning, and Roxanne says he either read or occasionally went to Bridge Club on a Wednesday evening. Running with the other members of the club was on Mondays and Thursdays. But the Wednesday he picks up the girl, he changes his routine and runs in the evening. Something triggered the change in his routine and that something might be to do with the girl. It's just an instinctive feeling.'

Simpson looked at her speculatively. 'You made Detective Inspector at such a young age because you've got the mind of a natural detective. I think Ross has recognised that. And that includes having the right instincts, so don't dismiss it if that's what your gut is telling you.'

She told him about the phone call from Roxanne.

'So you're wondering if it's Walter's notebook they were searching for when they ransacked his study?'

'It's the only thing that seems to be missing.'

Angie waited in silence while Simpson mulled it over. He stretched again, sat down in the chair and looked at Angie, who had taken the seat opposite him. 'You're thinking they found out he'd made notes in his notebook and wanted to know what he'd written down. And when they read his notes, they decided he knew too much. He had to die. You believe that somehow, this is all linked with the blonde girl he picked up at the supermarket.'

'Yes!' She felt elated she was not alone in her thinking. It made sense to Simpson. But she still had to convince Ross.

'We need to find out what he wrote in the notebook.'

'We need to find out who they are – who killed Walter.'

The door opened and Bridges came in. There was no greeting; his face didn't invite one.

'We're meeting in Ross's office.'

Simpson shot Angie a look as they followed Bridges. Ross was sitting at his desk. A white crumpled paper bag had missed the bin and was lying on the floor. Pastry crumbs were stuck to the front of his shirt; he made no attempt to brush them off. They filed in silently. Bridges took the chair at the side; Angie and Simpson took the only other two chairs in the room. They looked at each other, shared the same thought: where was O'Byrne and Washington?

Ross spoke to Simpson first. 'How is your stepdaughter?'

'Rachel's had a tough time, but she's pulling through.'

'Good.' He stared at them for a while longer. Angie noticed that the plaster had gone from his chin.

'According to our Deputy, our Police and Crime Commissioner is taking a personal interest in the murder of Walter Price,' Ross said. He spoke quietly but they heard the anger. 'Which is why that bastard has kept pestering me for updates.' He looked down, showed his irritation at the crumbs on his shirt, and made a half-hearted attempt to brush them away.

'I saw Henderson yesterday afternoon in his office and took him through what we had so far.' Ross looked at Angie. 'I told him about your visit to the food bank and showed him the portrait of the blonde girl your friend had done. I said we thought she might be a run-away who Walter Price had tried to help. And that we were looking for her.' Ross paused. Angie saw him deliberately trying to relax his jaw muscles before he continued. 'Henderson made very little comment. But he kept the portrait of the girl. He said he wanted to reflect on my report before his scheduled meeting with the PCC later in the evening. He would phone me after he had seen the Police and Crime Commissioner.'

Reaching down, Ross opened the bottom drawer of his desk, came up with another white paper bag and extracted a sausage roll.

'The Deputy phoned me last night after a good dose of Dutch courage,' Ross said, his voice dripping with contempt. 'He started by saying they were dealing with an emergency. They'd received information about an impending terrorist threat, and they needed O'Byrne and Washington to help with the surveillance. He's taken them off the case.'

'Now you know why there was no one else in the incident room,' Bridges said.

'What did he say about the progress we've made?' Angie asked.

Ross took a vicious bite of his sausage roll, ate it while they waited. Angie glanced across at Bridges, saw that he was looking down at his feet, chewing the inside of his mouth.

Ross's voice was much calmer when he continued. 'The Deputy said he had been reflecting on the evidence in my report. He said the conclusions we had drawn were highly questionable. He wondered if we were trying to disguise our lack of progress by making a fanciful tale out of what he saw as simply an attempted carjacking gone wrong.'

Angie's stomach was churning. She felt the anger rising, felt herself getting hot.

Ross was still speaking. 'He said carjackers could be burglars too and all the DNA showed was that the van had been parked in the cul-de-sac. It didn't prove they were focused on Walter's house, because they are other, more substantial properties in the street they might have been more interested in.'

Ross paused. 'Tell them about the tracker,' Bridges said.

'The Deputy pointed out the car was ten months old when Walter bought it. The tracker might have been placed there by a jealous wife who thought her husband was playing away. Or if it had been a company car, by a business rival.'

'That's rubbish!' Angie burst out. She turned away, annoyed at herself for losing control. Anger was no good. She had to stay calm and professional.

'It probably is,' Bridges said quietly. 'But it's theoretically possible.'

'The Deputy also said it was clutching at straws to think Walter helping the blonde girl has anything to do with him being killed during a botched carjacking.'

Ross took another bite of his sausage roll. 'The bottom line from Henderson is that if we don't make what he considers to be credible and significant progress by time he gets the next update, the case will be passed to another team. He mentioned the carjacking team that was formed a year ago after the public outcry.'

'How long have we got?' Angie asked.

'Two days,' Ross said. 'He wants to see me at 6 p.m. on Thursday. Pointed out we will have had a full week by then. And apparently, it's the day of Walter Price's funeral.'

'I've told you I think the Deputy is just winding you up,' Bridges said. 'If Henderson was going to take us off the case, it would have to go to another murder investigation team, not the carjacking team.'

'That's for sure,' Simpson said. 'And certainly not with Rogers leading the carjacking team.'

They waited while Ross ate the last of his sausage roll. Simpson looked at Angie, 'When is Walter Price's funeral?'

'Thursday at 11.30. I had a text from Roxanne.'

'We need to track down the smoker from the van. And the girl,' Bridges said. 'Or at least one of them.'

'The girl,' Angie said. 'I think the girl told Walter something he wrote in his notebook and that's what got him killed. Find the girl and we'll find out why Walter was killed. And who killed him.' She looked at Ross to see his response, but he was bending down to pick up the crumpled white paper bag.

***

The girl had refused to speak the first time Bujare took her the tray of food. Pulling the bolt back, Bujare had opened the sliding hatch and placed the tray on the small drop-down shelf on the other side of the hatch. The girl sat on the bed, staring at her. She didn't get up.

'What is your name?' Bujare asked.

The girl had continued staring at her, her eyes flashing anger. Then she turned over and lay on the bed, face down. 'You need to eat,' Bujare said, trying to speak in a kind voice. 'I will bring you a tray of food once every day. Eat or you will lose your strength.'

She waited five minutes, but the girl didn't move, didn't speak. When Bujare came back an hour later, the tray of food was untouched on the shelf. The girl was sleeping. Bujare watched her for a few moments before taking the tray of cold food back to the farmhouse. Pavel was watching TV, a glass of red wine in his hand. He reached for the bottle to pour her a glass, saw the worried look on her face as she sat next to him.

'What's the matter?'

'It's the blonde girl they brought from Birmingham. She won't eat.'

Pavel shrugged. 'She will eat when she gets hungry.'

Picking up the remote control, Bujare pressed the pause button. 'Why is she here? Why have they put the girl in the punishment block?'

Pavel sighed. 'They didn't tell me. She must be one of the girls they use. Maybe she tried to run away like the other one they brought two months ago.'

'How long are they going to keep her here?'

'They didn't tell me that either.' Pavel reached for the remote control and went back to his programme. Bujare didn't ask him any more questions.

The girl did not eat on the second day. But on the third day when Bujare slid the hatch back, the girl was waiting. She took the tray of food to the fold down shelf against the back wall of the cell, then turned around and stared defiantly at Bujare. When Bujare came back later, the food had been eaten, the tray left on the shelf inside the hatch. The next day Bujare waited but the girl wouldn't eat while she was being watched. And she wouldn't speak. 'Well, at least she's eating,' Bujare said to Pavel.

Pavel nodded. 'I told you she would. And she'll talk too, when she is ready. You just have to give her time.'

Chapter 17

They were still sitting in Ross's office, reviewing the case, trying to decide on their next steps. The CCTV image of the chain-smoker in the white van hadn't turned out to be as good as they first thought in their excitement. The side profile was probably good enough for him to be recognised by someone who knew him well, but they were not the people likely to come forward. Bridges had put the image on the force intranet, categorised it as a suspect wanted for questioning in a murder enquiry. Police officers across the country could view it. Ross wasn't hopeful.

'You never know,' Bridges said. 'Stranger things have happened. Do you remember the police sergeant who recognised the side profile of a bank robber? It turned out their young sons played in the same Sunday morning football team. Their dads stood on the same touchline, so the sergeant had a view of the bank robber's side profile during every match. He spotted him straight away.'

Bridges had also circulated both of Margaret's pencil portraits of the girl. 'She has a striking face. Somebody might well remember seeing her.'

'The girl might not still be in Birmingham,' Simpson said. 'We know Walter was trying to help her, but we don't know how. Maybe he gave her some money and put her on a train. Or took her to the coach station in Digbeth. She could be anywhere. If she's still in Birmingham, she's almost certainly on the run, and they will try to hunt her down. If we're right in thinking Walter was killed because of the information she gave him, then she is an obvious danger to them.'

'She won't turn herself into us,' Ross said. 'She could have done that in the first place rather than end up living on the streets and begging in car parks.'

'Walter wouldn't have left her to go back on the streets,' Angie said. 'He would find her a safe place.'

'There is another possibility,' Bridges said. 'They might have already found her. If that's what has happened, she'll be hidden away somewhere.' He paused before continuing. 'Or they've killed her. We might be looking for a body.'

Ross stood up. 'Bridges and I will follow up on Walter's car and check whether a tracker could have been in place when he bought the car. We'll revisit our Tech people. See if there's anything they can do to enhance the CCTV image of our chain smoker.'

Angie and Simpson were looking at Ross, waiting for his direction. 'You two take the girl's portraits with you. Start with the three train stations – New Street, Moor Street and Snow Hill, and the coach station at Digbeth. See if anyone remembers seeing the girl. And then the supermarket car parks. Show her portraits to people selling *The Big Issue* outside the supermarkets – they stand there most of the day.' He focused on Angie. 'You've already had help from that source. Lightning might strike twice.' He patted his jacket, feeling for his phone. 'I've got the daughter's number; she'll know whether her father bought the car privately or from a dealer.' He glanced at Angie. 'It's Roseanne, isn't it?'

'*Roxanne*,' Angie said, shaking her head in frustration. 'Her name is *Roxanne*.'

Ross nodded. 'You two get off now. I'll ring Roxanne.'

When Roxanne answered, he explained who he was, reassured her they were working hard to find the man who had stabbed her father.

'I still can't understand why they killed him,' she said.

Ross waited a decent moment. 'It's the car I wanted to ask you about. We're pursuing a line of enquiry, trying to cover all angles. Did your father buy the Audi privately or from a garage?'

'Oh no, not privately. He always bought his cars from a dealer. This one was from a dealer in Milton Keynes where I live. I found it for him online and I went with him to see it in their showroom.'

'Can you tell me which dealer it was?'

'It was the Audi dealer. I've still got their card but I'm afraid it's in my other handbag, back in my house in Milton Keynes.'

'No problem. Can you remember the name of the dealer?'

She told him the name of the dealer. He asked her if she remembered the name of the salesman, but she said no, it was on the card in her handbag. Ross thanked her and ended the call.

He googled the name of the Audi dealer in Milton Keynes, found their phone number, rang, and asked to speak to the Sales Manager. The receptionist said he was with a customer. Ross explained who he was, told her it was urgent. She took his number and said she would give the message to the Sales Manager straight away.

The Sales Manager rang back ten minutes later. Ross explained this was part of an ongoing investigation.

He gave him Walter's name, the registration of the car, and told him what he wanted to know.

'A tracker?' the Sales Manager said incredulously. 'You're asking if there was a tracker on the car when it left our showroom?'

'Yes. A small magnetic tracker under the front left wheel arch. You would have noticed it if you did any work under the car.'

'The car was less than a year old, still under warranty. We always do a full-service check before releasing a car to the customer. I'll check with the salesman and the service team and phone you back.'

'Thank you,' Ross said. 'I'd appreciate it if you could be as quick as you can.'

***

They had their coffees seated at a table in the back corner of the canteen while they waited to hear from the Sales Manager. Staring into the distance Bridges sighed. 'It's starting to hit home. You'll be gone in three weeks. I don't know who I'll be working with, and I've still got five years to go.' He paused and looked at Ross. 'The job doesn't have the same excitement for me it once did. It cost me my first marriage. I won't let it happen twice. What I'm really looking forward to is my next holiday travelling across America with Meryl.'

Ross knew what he was talking about. Bridges's first marriage to the girl he'd met at the running club had started well, but he was devoted to the job, worked all the hours. She'd finally given up on him and walked away after fifteen years. Bridges had never said a bad word about her. Four years ago, he'd joined the Ramblers and bumped into his current wife, Meryl, on a weekend trek. They had a quiet wedding at the Registry Office in the city centre. Ross and his wife – she hadn't left him then – had been the witnesses.

They sat in silence, mulling over the demands of the job. Then Ross said, 'Let's focus on this case. I've decided we ought to run with Reeve's theory that Walter Price stumbled across some dangerous knowledge, and he was killed before he could share that knowledge.'

'I agree. But let's talk about DI Reeves for a minute,' Bridges said. 'You were down on her at the start. But you seem to have reconsidered after the second briefing. What do you make of her now?'

'I thought she was one of Henderson's last digs at me,' Ross said. 'Getting me to babysit someone who he implied was a broken officer. That's why she's here on a four-week trial. He gave me the impression they were just going through the motions of their duty of care responsibility: they expected her to leave the force.'

'He couldn't have got her more wrong,' Bridges said. 'When we were in our heyday, we would have been the ones to pick up on those cigarette butts she found that gave us the DNA match. We would have thought about the tracker too. DI Angie Reeves is smart. And as dogged as they come.'

'Yes, she is,' Ross said. 'You can spot a good one when you work with them. Mind you, she probably thinks we're a pair of old farts.'

'Maybe. But she told me while she was at the Police College, she heard you give a talk just after you'd been made DCI. She said you were inspirational.'

Ross stared hard at Bridges but said nothing.

'The other thing puzzling me is the role of our Police and Crime Commissioner,' Bridges said. 'We know that Henderson will lick his boots because he wants to be the next Chief Constable. And you've said he needs the updates because he told you the PCC is taking a personal interest in this investigation. I wonder if the PCC understands the situation – whether he is aware the Deputy is planning to pull the rug out from under our feet?'

Ross shrugged, was about to respond, when his phone buzzed. It was the Sales Manager phoning him back. Ross listened, thanked the Sales Manager, put the phone back in his pocket.

'As we thought,' he said. 'Our Deputy is talking out of his ass. The Sales Manager had some difficulty tracking down the salesman who sold Walter his car – it was his day off. But he remembered Walter and knew which of the mechanics had done the full-service check. When they had the car up on a ramp, they noticed a nail in the side of the front left tyre. So, they put a new tyre on, under the wheel arch where we found the magnet. The mechanic says there's no way he wouldn't have noticed if there was what he called "a foreign body" on the wheel arch.'

'One for you to feedback to the Deputy when you see him.' Bridges pushed his chair under the table, picked up the cups. 'They're short staffed today,' he explained, heading for the counter. Ross waited, then they started up the stairs together.

'Anyway,' Bridges said, 'you haven't told me what you've got planned for your retirement. I'm assuming you do have a plan?'

'I might do some travelling. Join a group of retirees, tour South America. I've always had a hankering to see the Amazon.'

'Talking about hankering, I think Helen Jackson might be hankering after you.'

Ross came to a halt. 'Helen Jackson? The pathologist?'

'The very same. For some time, I'd say. Have you never wondered why the turn around on the pathology reports for you is so quick, compared to what others have to put up with?'

Ross thought about that for a moment. 'I had no idea.' He patted his paunch. 'Even with this?'

Bridges chuckled. 'Even with that. But maybe the hankering would step up a gear without that. Might even lead to the two of you seeing the Amazon together.'

Back in Ross's office, they tried the tech department again. She said they should come up to the fifth floor with the CCTV image.

Chapter 18

Angie ate at the Chinese restaurant before going back to her flat. She was exhausted. She and Simpson had spent the entire day showing people the portraits of the girl. They'd started with the train stations, then to the Aldi supermarket in Selly Oak where Walter picked up the girl. Irina was there with her copies of *The Big Issue*, and her bag of black scarves. She recognised Angie, greeted her with a big smile. But, no, the girl hadn't been back.

They spent the rest of the day going to the supermarket car parks on the south side of the city, showing the portraits to every seller of *The Big Issue* they saw. But no-one recognised the girl. They decided the next day they'd concentrate on the north side of the city.

It was dark when she climbed the stairs to her flat. The light on the landing outside her door was flickering. Reaching up on tiptoes, she rapped the glass casing, saw she would need a small screwdriver to change the bulb. There was a small screwdriver in the kitchen drawer; she made a mental note to buy a bulb the next day.

Once inside her flat, she phoned Philip. He sounded pleased to hear her voice when he answered.

'Nice surprise,' he said. 'I was just thinking about you.'

'I expect you already know that Walter's funeral is the day after tomorrow?'

'Yes. It's at 11.30 at the church in Kings Heath. Roxanne has asked me to be a pallbearer.'

'That's thoughtful of her. Walter would've liked that.'

Philip didn't reply for a moment, then she heard the quiver in his voice as he struggled to get the words out, 'I hope so.'

Angie felt herself choking up.

'I take it you're going to be there,' Philip said. 'Maybe we can meet up at the reception afterwards.'

'Maybe,' Angie said. 'I'm not sure I'm going to make it to the reception.'

'Right.' She heard the disappointment in his voice. 'How's the investigation going? Any further progress?'

She paused, 'Not what you'd call a breakthrough.' She remembered what she'd told him in the restaurant. 'Don't say anything to Roxanne about the investigation. She knows it wasn't a botched carjacking. That we believe Walter was a targeted victim. But I haven't given her any details. The speculation won't do her any good.'

'I won't say a thing to her. I know what you told me was in the strictest confidence.'

'Right.'

She was about to ring off when Philip said, 'I've been suspended.'

'What? Why?'

'I've been suspended from work for two weeks. There's been an allegation of fraud in the department I'm responsible for. They're bringing in external investigators and they don't want me on the premises while they carry out their investigation.'

'Are you worried?'

'A little,' he said. 'I know I've done nothing wrong. But mud sticks. I just hope they can get to the bottom of it.'

'I'm sorry to hear that.'

'There *is* an upside to it,' he said. 'It does mean I can be completely at your disposal over the next two weeks. So, call on me if there's anything I can do to help.'

'Alright, I will.' She ended the call.

Angie undressed, took her medication and lay on the bed. The clock radio, unplugged, was next to her on the bedside table. She stared at it for a long moment, then got out of bed and plugged it in. The news programme was starting. She'd stopped watching the news on TV or listening to the radio during her recovery period. There was almost always an item about the Middle East; the psychiatrist had warned her reports of car bombs and suicide bombers could trigger her flashbacks. He'd said it would be a good indicator of her recovery when she could listen to the news and respond normally. She stared at the radio again. Made her decision. Turned it on and set the timer for it to turn itself off after an hour.

***

Angie's sleep was undisturbed. She was in Ross's office the next morning in time for the 7.30 briefing. 'Let's start with you two,' Ross said, looking at Angie and Simpson. They told him where they had been – to the train stations, the coach station and then the supermarket car parks on the south side of the city.

'No sightings?' Bridges said. 'Not even one of those "I can't be sure but…" sightings.'

'No.' Angie said.

'But we did have a moment,' Simpson said, smiling.

They had indeed had a tense moment when the man in the ticket office at the coach station – an obese man with a goatee beard – asked to see the portrait of the girl without the shawl again. He took another long look while Angie and Simpson waited. Angie had seen Simpson's glance, felt her pulse rate quickening. Then the man had smiled, nodded to himself and handed the portrait back.

'What a beautiful girl,' he said. 'She looks just like my first girlfriend. The one I should have married.'

Bridges chuckled. 'What a prat!'

They told Ross they were going to spend the day covering the supermarket car parks and *The Big Issue* sellers in the north of the city.

'What about the hostels?' Bridges asked Angie. 'The ones for waifs and strays run by Barnardo's and The Salvation Army.'

'We didn't think Walter would take her there. He wouldn't see them as safe. They're the obvious places the people hunting her down would look.'

'Fair point, but they have soup kitchens, too. She might have turned up just to get something to eat.'

'We'll check them out.'

Ross told them about the tracker and what the Sales Manager had told him.

Simpson smiled. 'I'd love to be a fly on the wall when you tell the Deputy his theory was nonsense.'

'The tech department helped with the CCTV image of our smoker,' Ross said. 'They've got rid of some of the glare so there's a sharper contrast. But it's not that much better. I've put the improved version on the force intranet, but I wouldn't hold your breath.'

'What about the white van?' Simpson asked. 'ANPR cameras not picked up anything?'

'Nothing. The van has vanished. They won't be using it. Probably in a lockup garage somewhere.'

Bridges glanced at Ross, 'Why don't the two of us take Barnardo's and The Salvation Army? I know the people there.'

Ross nodded. 'Fine.' He caught their eye as Angie and Simpson stood up. 'That'll free you two to just focus on the north of the city.'

'And if we get the time,' Bridges added, 'I'm tempted to visit our obese friend in the ticket office at the coach station and threaten to arrest him for wasting police time.'

***

The men slept in bunks, packed into the two downstairs rooms of the house. One of the upstairs rooms hosted a flat screen TV and chairs; they brought in extra chairs when a football match was on. The other upstairs room, made larger by knocking together two bedrooms, offered a fold away table tennis table, a small pool table, a table football machine, and a card table. They often moved the card table into the TV room.

The supervisors came in the minibus in the mornings and took them to the house or houses – sometimes they were working on two or three adjacent houses – and brought them back in the evening. They did their own cooking, but they were not allowed to go to the shops; Rumesh and Erag did the shopping and brought it to them.

The men were paid £50 a week each, in tokens; they could exchange tokens back for cigarettes and cheap beer or they could use them for their card games. They were told money was also sent to their families in Kosovo or Albania, but they didn't know if that was true. It was a life better than the prison life they had come from, where they'd often been locked up for twenty-three hours a day. And if they broke the rules, or agitated, they'd heard of a punishment block on a farm in Wales and the beating that went with it. But they were also told the next supervisor would be chosen from among them.

Erag had a different background – he was sometimes referred to as The Gymnast because of his prowess on the rings. He'd won many competitions before he joined the gangs in Kosovo and quickly established a reputation as someone who was fearless and enjoyed using a knife.

Albert heard of him and flew to Kosovo to seek him out. He told Erag his talents were wasted in Kosovo, that he could flourish beyond his wildest dreams if he came to work for him in England. Erag was flattered but told him he wasn't sure he would like England. Albert offered him a week's holiday in London at his expense and said he would personally show him the delights of the big city. And true to his word, he did just that.

He took him around all the major tourist attractions and on a river cruise. Erag posed for a photograph standing in front of the famous revolving sign outside New Scotland Yard. At the end of the week, Albert said. 'So do you want to work for me?'

'Yes!'

'I'm not getting any younger. I'm looking for a younger man I can trust.'

'You can trust me.'

'I'll set you a test. If you pass it, I'll know I can rely on you.'

Albert told him he had business interests in Aberdeen, but there was a rival who was making life difficult. 'I want you to kill him. Can you do that?'

Taking the eight-hour train journey from Kings Cross to Aberdeen, Erag found the big house at the address in Old Aberdeen that Albert had given him, along with a photograph of his rival. He watched the house for two days, saw that the man walked his dog in the nearby park twice a day, early in the morning and in the late evening, when it was dark. The dog was not a young dog, but the man was patient; he allowed the dog to walk at his own pace and was content to have a cigarette when the dog stopped to sniff. He was a big man, taller than Erag and just as broad.

On the third day, Erag, who had never smoked, bought a pack of cigarettes. In the evening, just after 9, he followed the man and his dog to the park. When the dog stopped and the man lit a cigarette, Erag approached the man with his open pack in his left hand and asked him for a light. As the man looked down, feeling for his lighter, Erag's right hand moved rapidly in an upward motion. The knife went deep into the man's chest. Erag felt his biceps tighten as he moved the blade across.

While the man lay dying on the grass, the dog licked his face and made crying sounds. Patting the old dog, Erag held his head still as he drew the knife slowly across his throat. He was in time for the last train leaving Aberdeen that night; it was a slow overnight train with four changes.

Albert sent him to Birmingham. 'I will put you with a man called Rumesh. I want you to be his driver and do what he tells you. But you will be my eyes and ears. Be patient and your time will come.'

He gave him a mobile phone. 'Only use this phone to call me if you think there is anything I need to know. I will text you a different number to use every week. And I will phone you on this phone if I have any special instructions for you.'

So, Erag arrived in Birmingham. He drove the car, and he did what Rumesh told him to do. But he despised Rumesh. He was proud of his body; he hated the cigarette smoke Rumesh constantly blew his way.

Chapter 19

Angie had agreed to meet Simpson at Starbucks in Northfield at 9 a.m. He was already there, nursing a coffee.

'I'm going to get myself two croissants,' she said. 'What can I get you?'

Simpson held his hand up. 'Nothing, thanks. I had breakfast before I left the house. But you go right ahead. I can't say I'm eager to rush off if it's going to be another day like yesterday.'

Angie came back with the croissants and a latte, noticed Simpson was still nursing his coffee, deep in thought. She finished the croissants, wiped the pastry crumbs away and took a sip of her coffee. Simpson's cup was still half full.

'What's up?' she asked him. 'Something's bothering you.'

He picked up the cold cup of coffee. 'Oh, I'm just wondering. Probably barking up the wrong tree.'

'Tell me.'

Replacing his cup on the table, Simpson sat up with his fingers interlocked. She thought he was going to twiddle his thumbs, but he looked down, pressed his thumbs against each other, then looked up at her. 'You've not been back long enough to have picked up on the internal politics of our force. But you'll soon see it. Or the way things are going you might even feel it.'

Angie waited, eyebrows raised.

'Take Ross's meeting with the Deputy. Ross said he'd threatened to take us off the case, hand it over to the carjacking team.' He laughed. 'He could give the case to another murder investigation team. But the carjacking team?!'

'What do you know of the Deputy?' Angie asked.

'Henderson and I played in the same police rugby team for a while when I first joined the force,' Simpson said. 'We shared a few drinking sessions. He was a newly appointed inspector then and I was a constable, but rugby is a great leveller. Inevitably some of the conversation was about work. I could see he was ambitious, so I've followed his career with interest. Like I've said before, he's competent but his ambition has resulted in several questionable judgements. He tends to hold a grudge as well. But he's a good networker and he's kept climbing the greasy pole.'

Angie noticed Simpson had started twiddling his thumbs.

'Now the question is,' he said, 'Is the Deputy making a serious threat? Or is he just jerking Ross's chain?'

'What do you think?'

'That's what I've been pondering,' Simpson said. 'It could be either. Ross and Henderson have been at loggerheads for years. Ever since Ross accused him of a cover up in that hit-and-run accident.'

Angie nodded, 'The one you told me about, the one in which a ten-year-old boy was badly injured.'

'But the point here is that since then, the Deputy has known Ross despises him. I'd say the feeling is mutual. He's certainly taken every chance to make Ross's life difficult. Particularly since he's been Deputy.'

'So that's why you're wondering if he's just jerking his chain. Because it's an opportunity to humiliate Ross, to show him the power he has over him. First, he assigns him the case when he knows Ross is mentally counting the weeks to his retirement, then when Ross gets interested and we might be getting somewhere, he threatens to take the case off him.'

'Spot on. Maybe he's waiting for Ross to plead with him. He'd enjoy that.'

'What about your other thought? Suppose the Deputy was serious when he threatened to hand the case over to the carjacking team?'

'I'll have another coffee now,' Simpson said. 'The last one went cold.'

'I'm okay,' Angie said.

Simpson got his coffee, drank half of it straight away.

'The carjacking team was formed a year ago,' he said. 'It was one of the election pledges of our PCC. Car crime had got out of hand. It wasn't only car jackings in dark car parks late at night. There were several cases of mums taking their children to the park during the day and being forced to hand their keys over at knife point when they returned to their cars. The media dined out on it and there was a public outcry. The force needed to be seen to respond. So, they formed a carjacking team.'

'Were they successful?'

Simpson laughed mockingly. 'They're a useless lot. I think they've made three arrests since they were formed.'

'So, it wouldn't make sense for them to be handed our investigation into Walter's death.'

'They're not a murder investigation team. It wouldn't be normal practice, but it's possible. We're the only ones who know Walter was murdered. His death was logged initially as a carjacking, albeit a botched one. They might decide to hand them the case – make them look like they're earning their keep.'

'But you're saying they're unlikely to find out who killed Walter?'

'I'm saying more than that,' Simpson said. 'I'm saying there's not a cat's chance in hell they would find out who killed your headteacher. Not with Rogers leading the team.'

'What's so wrong with Rogers?'

Simpson paused, seeming to give the matter serious consideration before answering. 'I guess he made the wrong decision a long time ago.'

'What do you mean?'

Simpson wasn't smiling. 'He should have stuck to Cluedo.'

***

Angie and Simpson spent the day in the north side of the city, doing what they had done the previous day on the south side – checking supermarket car parks, showing the girl's portraits to *The Big Issue* sellers. They went back to the two train stations and to the coach station, recognising different staff might be on duty. The obese man with the goatee beard wasn't in the ticket office at the coach station; the woman who was there couldn't remember seeing the girl.

There was no one in Ross's office when they got back so they went down to the canteen. Bridges found them fifteen minutes later, looked at them questioningly. They shook their heads. He told them they had been to Barnardo's and The Salvation Army hostels. 'No joy there either.'

'Has our Deputy been in touch?' Simpson asked Bridges.

'Not personally, but his PA just phoned. Ross is taking the call in his office.'

'What do you think about the Deputy's threat to turn the investigation over to the carjacking team?'

Bridges didn't hesitate. 'That would be an idiotic thing to do, but he's got form for making strange decisions.'

'He might just be winding Ross up, given their history.'

'That would be the lesser of two evils,' Bridges said.

Ross came into the canteen, saw the questioning look on all three faces. 'Henderson wants to see me at six pm tomorrow,' he said. 'Aren't I the lucky one?'

His gaze settled on Angie. 'You'll be wanting to go to Walter's funeral.' And then with a glance at his watch and a nod to Bridges, 'I said I'd be at the Home at five thirty.'

***

Turning off the minor road into the drive, Ross heard the crunching sound of his car wheels on the gravel. He visited his mother at least three times a week; it was a promise made to himself, and he kept it. The matron knew what his job was, agreed he could visit outside the normal hours.

It was almost half-past five – mealtime. Signing the reception book, he walked along the corridor to the dining room. The residents were sitting at small tables in ones and twos, the food on trays in front of them. A few were in wheelchairs with their food on a pull-out tray, like the ones on aeroplanes. Some were eating slowly, taking time to raise a forkful of food to their mouth, chewing methodically and thoroughly before swallowing. Others sat with their heads to one side, half asleep with their food untouched.

He looked for his mother, couldn't see her until one of the uniformed staff moved to the side, and he glimpsed her sitting at a table by herself. She was looking straight at him, but her glasses had slipped off – he knew she couldn't see him at that distance. Ross said, 'Hello Mum,' and kissed the top of her head. He put her glasses on properly. She raised her head, smiled brightly at him, 'Hello Gavin.' Moving a chair around to sit next to her, he took both her hands in his, held them while they looked at each other. She smiled again. He kissed her gently on both cheeks.

Today it was fish, with mash and cabbage. Cutting the food into small pieces, he offered her a forkful at a time. Afterwards, she had a bowl of stewed apple and custard, taking small sips of water between spoonfuls. When she had finished, he walked by her side, letting her use the Zimmer frame as they made their way to the lift. Her room was on the first floor; it overlooked the garden and caught the morning sun. Sitting side by side on the sofa, they looked through photographs Ross had put together for her. Today's chosen album was the one covering Ross's early childhood. He was again amazed at the sharpness of her memory; she talked him through the photographs one by one.

The nurse came after an hour with a glass of water in her hand, placing it on the bedside table, next to the framed newspaper article with a photograph of a younger and trimmer Ross when he was promoted to Detective Chief Inspector. The glass of water was the signal that it was time for him to go. He hugged his mother. The nurse, hovering outside, nodded at Ross, 'She sometimes goes to sleep with that framed newspaper cutting clutched to her chest.'

Ross sat in his car for a while, the nurse's words ringing in his ears. He hadn't told his mother his retirement was imminent. He knew she'd always been proud of his work in the police force. But he hadn't realised how much. He felt he'd let her down in the latter years of his career, had let disillusionment with the politics of the force get the better of him.

He'd brought the disillusionment into his home, wasn't all that surprised when his wife walked out. He could see she was unhappy, but she'd turned away when he wanted to talk about their relationship. It was the deceit he hated. The lies. The going behind his back. He'd had his suspicions, had asked her straight out if she was seeing someone else. She'd denied it. It was after she had left him that he'd started on the sausage rolls.

Ross thought about what Bridges had said about Helen Jackson hankering after him. He wondered if it was true. She was five years younger than him, kept herself trim. He liked her straight talking and considered her the best pathologist he'd worked with. But it had never occurred to Ross that another woman might be attracted to him.

His thoughts turned to Angie Reeves. He'd thought she was going to be a liability, been somewhat brusque with her at the start, saw it as a sink or swim situation. But Bridges was right in his assessment. She'd turned out to be tough. And smart. He had glimpsed his former self in her. She was professional, kept her emotions to herself during the investigation. But he'd seen her tears at their first meeting when she realised who the victim was, heard the fervour in her voice. He knew that for her, finding Walter's killer wasn't just professional – it was personal, too.

It dawned on him he'd been treading a path that could lead to him being lonely and bitter in his retirement. He'd seen it happen to others. He felt a desperate need to extricate himself. He needed to stay on this investigation – his last case – and bring it to a successful conclusion. He knew what he had to do. He would have to swallow his pride when he met with the Deputy tomorrow. Plead with him if he had to. For his mother's sake. For Angie Reeves's sake. For his own sake.

The cold night air had penetrated the inside of the car. Ross shivered. He started the car, put it into gear, turned the heating up as he moved off.

Chapter 20

Thursday morning dawned with grey skies and a gentle breeze, but the autumn sun had found its way through by mid-morning. Leaving her flat in good time for Walter's 11.30 service, Angie parked in a side street, and started on the five-minute walk to the church. It seemed unnaturally quiet; she was surprised there weren't more people making the same walk. Feeling uneasy, she quickened her step. Her growing fear was confirmed as she rounded the corner, and the front of the church came into view. The only person she could see in the churchyard was a man in green wellingtons, crouched down, weeding the bed of roses lining the pathway.

'Excuse me,' Angie said. 'I've come for a funeral service, but I think I'm at the wrong church. Is there another church in Kings Heath?'

'There's a Catholic church. St. Dunstan's.' He stood up. 'Are you in a car?'

She nodded, 'Yes.'

'By rights you ought to be able to drive there in three minutes, but you've got to go along the high street and that's always choc-a-bloc with traffic. And that church has got a parking problem – you'll be lucky to find a space if there's a funeral on. I'd walk if I were you.'

'How long will it take me to walk there?'

He looked at her, saw she was fit. 'You could be there in fifteen minutes.'

He gave her directions. She set off at a brisk pace, quietly cursing to herself. Walter had never mentioned religion; she had assumed it would be Church of England, was surprised he was a Catholic.

The walk took her the full fifteen minutes. She saw the crowd packed along the driveway that ran along the side of the church to the car park behind. Traffic cones across the front of the driveway prevented cars going past; she realised the car park was being used as an overspill area for mourners who had arrived too late to get a seat in the church.

The service had already started; it was being relayed to those standing outside by external speakers. Threading her way through the crowd she found some standing room in the car park. She looked around her, saw the mixture of ages and races, thought she recognised some faces.

She concentrated on following the service. Crackling from the external speakers and the occasional gust of wind didn't make listening easy. The mourners outside recognised the hymn being sung and joined in. Angie sang too. She heard Roxanne reading the W. H. Auden poem, and heard the emotion in her voice, even through the crackling speakers.

They sang another hymn, and then the tributes followed. In faltering words, the captain of the golf club spoke of Walter's character, of his determination, and of his refusal to accept the correlation between age and decline. 'When Walter retired and said he wanted to get to a single digit handicap, we thought he was cuckoo. Only one per cent of golfers achieve that. It took him two years, but he did it. And inspired many of us older ones to look to our game.'

A sudden burst of crackling from the speakers prevented Angie hearing the introduction to the eulogy, but the speaker had a powerful, resonant voice and she heard most of what he said. He spoke knowingly and movingly of his friend Walter, and of Walter's transformation of Longlands. 'Walter went his own way when he became a Head. He decided not to teach but to use the time instead to mentor selected students – two from each year, chosen to give him a true cross-section of the school's population. He met them in pairs for an hour every half-term.'

The speaker paused. Angie looked around, saw the crowd were listening with rapt attention, waiting for him to continue. He painted a vivid picture of Walter's work before concluding, 'Walter Price attracted brilliant teachers – with their help, he took a school that was failing and transformed it into one visited by a Prime Minister. He helped to shape the lives of tens of thousands of students. Many of them, I'm sure, are seated in front of me or are standing outside this church, following this service through the external speakers. To show their respect. To say a simple "Thank you".'

The eulogy had brought tears to many eyes. Angie had come prepared; she took a tissue out and weaved her way through the crowd on the driveway to the front of the church. She made it just as Roxanne emerged from the relative darkness of the church into the autumn sunlight, her face framed by a black lace shawl. She held herself erect, staring straight ahead in her dark glasses.

Walking either side of her was a man and a woman of a similar age; Angie wondered if they were cousins on her mother's side. Four of the pall bearers were older men wearing identical jackets with a crest of crossed golf clubs. The other two were wearing black suits – one was Philip, the other one was a tanned, athletic looking man in his fifties. Angie wondered who he was. She watched until the hearse and the car carrying Roxanne and her cousins moved off on their way to the crematorium.

Walking back to her car, Angie decided against going to the crematorium and the reception. She wanted out. She drove back to the station and climbed the stairs to Ross's office. He was there with Bridges. They both looked surprised to see her. Ross glanced at his watch.

'Shouldn't you be at the reception?'

She shook her head. 'Not for me.'

Bridges gave her an understanding look before responding to her inquiring gaze, 'We were just discussing the investigation. One or two things are puzzling us.'

Ross, who was eating a sausage roll, pointed with his chin at the empty chair. Angie sat down.

'Assuming Walter's murder was to do with the girl and something she told him,' Bridges said, 'how did they know he had befriended her? Surely, if they had seen him in the supermarket car park with her, they would have intervened.'

Ross had stopped eating. 'And how did they know where Walter lived?'

He paused for a moment. Angie remained silent.

'And then there's the break in,' Ross continued. 'All the evidence is that they went straight to the study. Forensics found no sign they'd been in any other room in the house.' He looked directly at Angie. 'You, yourself, know that the study is not in an obvious place. We had enough trouble finding it. So how was it they could go straight to it?'

Angie heard the questions, tried to think of a response, but her brain would not co-operate.

Ross gave her a long look. 'You're grieving,' he said. 'Take the rest of the day off.'

Before she could open her mouth to protest, he added, 'When I see the Deputy at 6 p.m. I'm going to ask him if O'Byrne and Washington are still needed for surveillance. We could do with having them back on this investigation.' He gestured to Angie. 'Go! Try to take your mind off the funeral. Get a good night's sleep. We'll have a briefing in the morning at 9 o'clock and take a fresh look at the case. See what new lines of investigation we can come up with.'

She hesitated. Bridges walked to the door, held it open for her. 'You need the space,' he said. 'And we need you back here tomorrow morning focused with that sharp mind of yours.'

***

Angie went back to her flat and changed out of her funeral suit into jeans, T-shirt and a jumper. Putting on her walking shoes, she drove to the Lickey Hills. The large country park, situated ten miles southwest of the city centre, was one of the most used recreational areas for Birmingham residents, popular with families, courting couples, dog walkers, and people just wanting to escape the din of the city.

Angie had been there many times as a child with her father. Before the accident confined him to a wheelchair. She wandered over the open hills, breathing the fresh air, feeling the warmth of the sun when it escaped from behind the clouds. Remembering Walter.

Unplanned, she stopped at a multiplex cinema on the way back. Walking from the car park to the entrance to the cinema took her past a line of framed posters advertising the films showing. She stopped, closed her eyes for a moment: *'Avoid focusing on images that could remind you of your experience in Iraq. They have the potential to trigger your body's hyperactive alarm system.'* She scanned the posters quickly, moved past the action films, only focused when she came to a romantic comedy.

The screening was about to start but she couldn't risk sitting through the trailers of forthcoming films, so she bought a ticket and a tub of popcorn and sat at a table in the foyer. When she finally went into the auditorium, the film had already started. She followed the story for a while, drifted off when she lost concentration, caught herself, dabbed at her wet cheeks with a tissue and focused on the film for the final twenty minutes. It had a happy ending.

Stopping at a supermarket, she browsed the aisle with bottles of red wine and settled on an Argentinian Merlot. She bought six bottles after the passing attendant told her she would get a 25 per cent discount. She remembered the flickering light on her landing and bought a light bulb.

Back at the flat she ate the last portion of lasagne with some carrots, opened a bottle of Merlot and listened to an Oasis album on her headphones. She was on her third glass of wine when she decided to ring Roxanne. The phone rang and rang; she was about to give up when Roxanne answered.

'Sorry,' Angie said. 'Is this a bad time?'

'Not at all,' Roxanne said. 'I was in the bathroom. Just getting ready for bed.'

'How are you feeling?'

'Tired. Today's been an ordeal. Thank God it's over.'

'I just wanted to apologise. I went to the wrong church, so was late for the service. I heard most of it though, standing in the car park. And I saw you when you came out of the church.'

'Yes, I saw you, too.' Roxanne said. 'But I missed you at the reception. Philip was asking if I'd seen you.'

'I'm sorry. I didn't go to the reception. I didn't feel like mixing socially, just wanted to be on my own.'

'If I'm honest, I felt the same. It's just I didn't have any choice.'

'It was a very moving eulogy,' Angie said. 'Who was the speaker?'

'Oh, that was George Kershaw. I wasn't sure about asking him, but I have to admit it was a good eulogy.'

'He must have known Walter well. Did they work together?'

'In a way,' Roxanne said. 'He came to Birmingham as a young headteacher, knew of Dad's reputation and asked him to mentor him. They spent many an evening in Dad's study discussing school improvement.' She laughed. 'I always think of him as the man who showed me Kosovo.'

'Kosovo?'

'Yes, I heard him mention Kosovo to Dad, and I asked if it was a kind of Greek sweet, like Baklava. They both thought that was funny. Dad had a world map pinned up in his study, so George pointed out Kosovo to me. He said he had several new children at his school whose parents were from Kosovo and Albania. Dad told me later that George thought some of them had criminal connections.'

'Well, he did your dad proud. Did they still see each other after Walter retired?'

'No,' Roxanne said. 'They quarrelled before that when George became a councillor. Dad tried to persuade him not to do it, to stay as a headteacher. But George stood, was elected, and became Chair of the Planning Committee. They didn't talk for years – that's why I wasn't sure about asking him to do the eulogy. But Dad told me they'd been paired together in one of these charity golf days last year. I think they made their peace over the eighteen holes. And Dad approved of George's new role.'

'New role?'

'Yes. George Kershaw. Your George Kershaw!'

'I don't know anyone called George Kershaw.'

'You should,' Roxanne said. 'He's your PCC. Your Police and Crime Commissioner.'

.

Chapter 21

Angie poured herself another glass of wine. So, the Police and Crime Commissioner had known Walter. That must be why he was taking a personal interest, wanting regular updates. Roxanne had been surprised she hadn't recognised the PCC's name, but this was only her second week back in Birmingham. Recalling the athletic-looking pall bearer standing next to Philip, she wondered if that had been George Kershaw. She should've asked Roxanne.

Going into the kitchen for another bottle of Merlot she noticed the light bulb lying on the kitchen table. Staring at it, she couldn't think why she had bought it. Then she remembered the flickering light on her landing. She found the small screwdriver in the kitchen drawer. The bulb had gone past the flickering phase; it was now completely dead. There was just enough moonlight for her to see the heads of the two small screws holding the glass covering in place. She got the screws undone on her third attempt. The hinged glass covering swung down, but even on tiptoes, the bulb was just out of reach. Fetching the stool from the bedroom, she stood on it, reached upwards to unscrew the light bulb and lost her balance as the stool wobbled. Instinctively putting her hands out to break the fall, she felt a sharp pain as she landed on the stone landing. She lay still, waited for the dizziness to go, then staggered back into her flat.

The wrist of her left hand and her left thumb were hurting like hell. Using her right hand to get a bag of frozen peas out of the freezer, she sat on the sofa, with the peas over her wrist and thumb. It was worse after thirty minutes; she couldn't move her thumb. *'I need to go to the hospital.'* She started to search for her car keys, then realised she couldn't drive with one hand. And that she was well over the limit. There was a taxi firm's card in the kitchen drawer, left behind by the previous occupant of her flat. The taxi came inside fifteen minutes; it was a twenty-minute drive to the hospital. She had a two hour wait in casualty before the x-ray was taken, followed by another hour's wait before she was in front of a doctor.

'You've got a scaphoid fracture,' the doctor said. He saw the baffled look on her face. 'Here,' he said, pointing at the X-ray of her wrist. 'This row of bones is the proximal.' He moved his finger slightly upwards. 'This row is the distal. The scaphoid joins them. Yours is fractured.'

Angie nodded. 'How do you treat it?'

'A cast.'

'How long for?'

'Six weeks minimum,' he said. And then seeing her look of consternation, 'How did you do it?'

'Trying to change a light bulb – I was standing on a stool that wobbled.'

The doctor took a step closer, sniffed, and looked at her. 'Never a good idea. Stools tend to wobble. Especially when you've had a drink.'

***

Angie left casualty with a cast all the way from the thumb on her left hand to just below her elbow. It had gone 2.30 a.m. when the taxi dropped her back at the flat. She set her phone alarm for 7.30, climbed into bed, and fell asleep lying on her back. She awoke with a start, lay still for a couple of minutes, going over the events of the previous evening. She reached for her phone and realised she had slept through the alarm. There was a missed call from Ross. She rang him but it went to voicemail. She rang the taxi firm.

'It's going to be around forty-five minutes before a taxi is available,' the man told her.

'Forty-five minutes?!'

'They're all out on the school run. We've got contracts for the special needs kids.'

Waiting in the casualty department had given her time to think. She'd remembered what Ross had said about standing back and taking a fresh look at the investigation, coming up with new ideas. She'd tried to do that, had tried to role play

Walter. Why had he not gone to the police, taken the girl with him? The girl might have been too scared to go on her own, might have thought the police wouldn't believe what she said. Maybe she was in the country illegally. But Walter could have gone with her, could have spoken on her behalf, could have seen that she was taken seriously. For some reason, he had not done that.

Angie felt sure he would not have just left the girl. That was not in his nature. He would have taken her somewhere he thought she would be safe. But where? How would he find such a place? And how would he know how to get there? A thought had been lurking in the back of her mind, but it hadn't materialised. The wine in her blood stream hadn't been conducive to clear thinking.

But clarity had come this morning. When she opened her eyes, and gone over the events of the previous evening, the thought had surfaced almost immediately. Ross had been right: stand back, take a fresh look, and a new idea might come. She would have to wait for the taxi to take her to the station, but after that, Simpson could drive them around in his car. She now knew where she wanted to go.

She phoned Roxanne. 'I was going to ring you today,' Roxanne said. 'I think I've been in a state of shock. Making the funeral arrangements has kept me on the go, but now the funeral is over, I've had time to reflect. There are some things about Dad's murder I don't understand.'

'I'll come over and see you this morning,' Angie said. 'We can go through any questions you have.'

'Thank you. Did you phone me for any special reason?'

'Yes. Is Walter's car back with you yet?'

'Funny you should ask that. It's parked on the drive. I'm staring at it out of the window as we speak. They returned it yesterday while I was at the reception and put the keys through the letterbox with a note.'

'There's something about the car I need to check.'

'You'd better hurry,' Roxanne said. 'I can't stand the stupid car being here, so I'm planning to take it in to the nearest Audi dealer today and sell it. I'll take whatever price they offer.'

'I can understand that, but don't take it in until this afternoon. I'd like to see it when I come to see you later this morning. Are you planning to go out?'

'No, I'll be in.'

She tried Ross again. He answered on the third ring.

'I'm sorry,' she said. 'I'm going to be late for the briefing. I've had a stupid accident and I can't drive. I've ordered a taxi but there's a wait because of the school run.'

'You don't need to come in,' Ross said, sounding flat. 'Take some time off.'

'It's not a problem. Once I'm in, we can use Simpson's car.'

'You don't need to come in because we're going to be off the case,' Ross said. 'The Deputy has instructed me to halt our investigation. I will no longer be the Senior Investigating Officer. Which means my team will be off the case, too.'

Angie's grip on her phone tightened. She took a deep breath, let it out slowly.

'Why would the Deputy do that? Did you tell him the tracker was not on Walter's car when he bought it?'

Ross was back to speaking in his flat monotone, keeping the emotion out of his voice. 'I told him that. And I went through all the steps we've taken to date again, and what we thought had happened.'

'So why?'

'The reason he gave was that this was obviously going to be a long investigation and I am retiring in three weeks. He said it made operational sense to have a handover now. It would ensure continuity of the investigation. He called it operational sustainability.'

Angie closed her eyes. Tried to make sense of what Ross was telling her. She took a deep breath, opened her eyes.

'Who is the new SIO? Who will lead the investigation into Walter's murder?'

'Cunningham,' Ross said. 'Cunningham will be the new Senior Investigating Officer. He's away on a leadership course. He will take over the investigation when he returns to take up his new post as DCI on the first of the month – Tuesday.'

'Do you know him?'

'No. All I know is that he is inexperienced. Recently promoted, so this will be the first time he's leading a murder investigation.'

'What do our team do now?'

'Simpson has been redeployed to join the others carrying out surveillance on this potential terrorist threat. Bridges and I have been told to prepare the handover report for Cunningham. And then we've been told to use our remaining time to go over old cases, get all our files in order.'

'What about me? What do I do?'

She heard Ross clear his throat before answering. 'I know how much this investigation matters to you. I told Henderson your trial period to date has been successful. I recommended that to ensure continuity of the investigation, you be transferred to Cunningham's team with your rank of Detective Inspector.'

Angie waited, still gripping the phone tightly. This time, she heard the anger in Ross's voice.

'I'm sorry. The bastard said he couldn't consider that until the formal assessment of your trial period has taken place.'

Angie swallowed hard. 'That will take weeks. What do I do in the meantime?'

'You've been assigned to desk duties,' Ross said.

Chapter 22

Angie paced up and down, then walked out to the small balcony, and watched the steady flow of traffic on the Hagley Road. She came back into the small lounge cum dining room. The flat felt claustrophobic. The grey exercise ball had rolled into the centre of the room. She lashed out at it with her right foot, sending it sailing across the room. It hit the dining table, the wine glass tottered over and shattered on the wooden floor. She screamed and collapsed onto the sofa. Afterwards she went into the bathroom, filled the sink with cold water and washed the tears away with her one good hand. She needed more space, needed to walk, needed to think. Grabbing her coat, she went down the stairs, and out into the open air. Her phone rang. It was Simpson.

'Has Ross spoken to you?'

'Yes, ten minutes ago.'

'It stinks,' Simpson said. 'This whole investigation stinks. They could have waited until his last week before doing the handover. We might have cracked the case by then.'

'Where are you?' Angie asked.

'In a pokey stockroom on the first floor of a school building. There's a window overlooking the house opposite. I'm supposed to be taking photos with my telephoto lens of the comings and goings, but so far, it's all quiet.'

'Ross said the investigation is being handed over to a new team. The new SIO is going to be Cunningham.'

'Yes, Ross told me. I know him. I've worked with him in the past.'

'What's he like?'

'Hard working. But his early promotion will have surprised many.'

Ending the call with Simpson, Angie walked on with a growing sense of foreboding. She made her way along the side streets, heading in the general direction of a park that she'd driven past. Once in the park, she wandered along the path that wound its way between the flowerbeds, trying to order her thinking.

So, Simpson didn't think the new team would be up to finding Walter's murderer. The man who stabbed him and then cut across his insides, might go free. And what about the girl? Had Walter died in vain? The thought made her angry. There was no justice there.

And what about her own future? She tried to stay calm, to work through her options. She could do what they wanted and go on desk duties. But that was not what *she* wanted. She had returned to work determined to challenge herself, embracing in her mind the psychiatrist's parting words: *'I can't promise a "cure" for your PTSD, but if you are careful you can learn to live with it.'*

She'd had a minor attack in Walter's bedroom at the start, but she had managed ever since. Her confidence in her ability to do the job had grown over the days of the investigation. She was doing more than coping with her PTSD; she had felt the excitement of knowing she was learning to live with it. It would not stop her leading a murder enquiry team. And that was all she had ever wanted since hearing Ross's talk when she was at the Police College.

She realised she couldn't expect Ross to ignore the Deputy's instruction. Particularly if there was bad blood between the Deputy and Ross. To do so would mean he would face a disciplinary hearing on the brink of retirement. There would be consequences.

There was another option – *she* could disobey the Deputy and continue the investigation on her own. To do so would almost certainly put her own career at risk. If she still had a career. She couldn't face the slow death of desk duties. At least she would have a few more days doing the job in the way she loved. And she could pass anything she found out to Ross and Bridges to include in their handover report. It might help Cunningham get closer to finding out the truth about Walter's death.

Ahead of her a couple were walking away from a bench. Angie took their place, sat down and went through her options again. Still deep in thought, she left the bench and walked briskly, out of the park and back to her flat. She made a cup of coffee, buttered two slices of toast and ate them slowly. Finally, when she had made up her mind, she phoned Philip.

'Hello,' he said. 'What a lovely surprise!'

'Are you still suspended from work?'

Surprised by her directness and tone of voice, he paused before answering, 'Yes. Until they finish their investigation and produce a report. Which is likely to take about two weeks. Why are you asking?'

'When we were in the restaurant, you said to let you know if there was anything you could do to help me find Walter's killers.'

'Yes, of course,' Philip said. 'Anything.'

'I've had a stupid accident, broken a little bone in my wrist – it's called a scaphoid fracture.' She didn't hide her frustration. 'My arm is in a cast up to the elbow. I can't drive.'

He didn't hesitate. 'I'm yours for the entire day if you need a chauffeur. Where and when do you want me?'

'Thanks. My flat, as soon as you can make it.' She gave him the address.

'I'm up and ready to leave,' he said. 'It'll take me half an hour.'

'That's great. Text me when you're close.'

She picked up the broken glass as best as she could without using a dustpan and swept the rest into a corner. When Philip arrived, Angie was already waiting outside. She waved when she saw the blue Toyota.

'Where to?' he said, looking at her cast.

'Walter's house. Forensics returned his car yesterday. And I need to have a conversation with Roxanne.' She looked across at him. 'It's better if I do that privately.'

He nodded, asked her about the accident. She told him, went through her visit to casualty. He laughed when she told him what the doctor had said. Then she told him about Ross's meeting with the Deputy. And what she had decided to do. He was quiet, didn't speak until they stopped at a traffic light. Then he turned to look at her, 'It's a big decision you've made, Angie. You're still on trial. This could be the end of your career in the police force.'

'I don't give a shit,' she said. 'Desk duty is not my idea of a career. And I intend to find Walter's killer.'

They moved off as the lights changed. She could see Philip mulling over all that she had told him. Finally, he said, 'What are you hoping to learn from Walter's car?'

'I think, after they left the food bank, Walter took the girl somewhere he thought was safe. I'm hoping the car will tell us where he took her.'

Philip glanced at her, looking puzzled, and mouthed 'How?' But as he was asking, she could see the answer come to him.

***

The police had left Walter's Audi on the left-hand side of the drive; Roxanne's Saab was parked on the right. Philip parked behind the Audi. Angie had just eased herself out of the car when Roxanne came out of the front door and caught sight of Angie's cast. 'Been tangling with a baddie?'

'A bottle of wine, stool, changing light bulb in the dark – in that order,' Angie said, watching Roxanne's look of concern turn into an amused smile.

'That explains the change of car. And your own driver!' Her smile changed to a surprised look as Philip emerged from the car.

'Well, it didn't take you two long to get back together.'

'Philip's off work, and I can't drive.'

'I offered to be her chauffeur,' Philip said. 'But she hasn't mentioned payment, yet.'

They followed Roxanne into the lounge. She disappeared briefly before returning with three mugs of coffee on a tray.

'I know you've got some questions,' Angie said. 'Can we go into the conservatory and talk there?'

Roxanne nodded, led the way. They sat down on the sofa side by side.

'I've been a bit slow on the uptake,' Roxanne said. 'You said in the restaurant that the same men who searched the study had killed Dad. I never asked you how the two were linked.'

'You've not been slow, you've been in shock, and you've been arranging a funeral,' Angie said. 'But yes, the same men who broke into this house were the ones who killed Walter.' She told Roxanne about the DNA match and the tracker.

'But why? I don't see how he could be involved with men like that.'

'We don't know why. That's what we're trying to find out. We do know Walter picked up a girl when he went to the supermarket on the day he was killed. And that she was with him when he went to the food bank.'

'What do you mean "he picked up a girl"?'

'Sorry,' Angie said. 'Wrong use of language. There was a girl in the supermarket car park asking for money. We believe she had run away from someone, and Walter was trying to help her.'

'You think the men who broke into this house and killed Dad were the same men who the girl was running away from?'

'Yes.' Angie explained they thought the girl had given Walter information that he had recorded in his green notebook. And that the men had found the notebook and killed Walter because of what he knew.

Roxanne was silent for a moment. 'Where is the girl now?'

'We don't know who she is, or where she is, but we do know what she looks like. We've been searching for her.'

'Are you close to finding her?'

'No,' Angie said. 'But I'm not giving up.'

Roxanne's head came up. 'You just changed from "We" to "I". Have the rest of your team given up? What about Chief Inspector Ross? Has he given up?' There was an edge to Roxanne's voice.

Angie was quiet for a moment, not wanting to fuel Roxanne's anger, but wanting to be honest with her.

'Ross isn't like that. He's not a quitter. Or Bridges, the Detective Sergeant he works with.' She saw Roxanne take a deep breath, let the anger go.

'It's just that Ross is due to retire in three weeks. Last night, the Deputy Chief Constable took him off the investigation. The reason he gave is that since this investigation is likely to last longer than Ross has got left, it's best to have the handover now to ensure continuity. The new team is led by a man called Cunningham; he'll probably want to come and see you next week.'

Roxanne stood up from the sofa, turned around and gazed through the conservatory windows. Angie followed her gaze, saw she was looking at the arbour at the bottom of the garden.

'He liked to sit there on sunny days, reading.'

She turned back. 'Are you part of this new team?'

'No, I'm not.'

'So, what do you mean when you say you're not giving up?'

'The new Senior Investigating Officer takes over next Tuesday. I intend to carry on until then.'

'Won't that get you into some sort of trouble?'

Angie shrugged, 'Maybe. But I want to do everything I can to find the men who killed Walter. I don't want them to get away unpunished. And I think, if I can find the girl, I'll find the men who killed him.'

Stepping forward to hold Angie's arm Roxanne found herself grasping the cast instead. They both laughed. Roxanne took her right arm this time, squeezed it gently, smiled at Angie through wet eyes.

Philip was reading a newspaper as they came back into the lounge. He picked up a scrap of paper from the side table. 'I hope you don't mind,' he said to Roxanne. 'I saw the car keys with the Audi tab on the table, so I used them to go into Walter's car.' He handed the scrap of paper to Angie.

'What's this?'

'It's the last destination from the satnav in Walter's car. That's what you're after, isn't it?'

'Yes,' Angie said, reading the postcode. 'That's what I wanted.'

She showed Roxanne the postcode. 'Does that mean anything to you?'

Roxanne shook her head, 'No, it's not a postcode I recognise. But I know B44 is on the north side of the city.'

Angie waved the scrap of paper at Philip. 'You're sure this was the last destination?'

'Absolutely. Once the ignition is on, the Audi's satnav takes a few seconds to initialise. Then the screen gives you the option "Go to last destination." This is the postcode that came up as Walter's last destination.'

Looking from one to the other, Roxanne nodded her understanding, 'You're hoping this postcode will show you where Dad took the girl after he left the food bank.'

'Yes,' Angie said. 'And bring us closer to tracking down the men who killed Walter.'

Chapter 23

His companion was getting a magazine for the Friday morning flight to Majorca. Sitting in the departure lounge at Birmingham airport, George Kershaw glanced down at his watch, then looked up at the departures screen again. They should be boarding soon.

The car would be waiting for him at the airport in Palma; it was only a forty-minute drive to his house in Port Andratx, up in the hills, with an unobstructed view of the bay below. The couple who acted as gardener and housekeeper would have made their weekly visit. The house had cost him four million euros; he'd paid cash. Sometimes he pinched himself, marvelling at how far he had come from the council estate in the Shard End area of Birmingham.

It had started when the Albanian children joined his secondary school. After a fight in the playground, he'd excluded both pupils and called their parents in. The Albanian parents were apologetic, co-operative, agreed with him that violence was not the way to handle playground arguments. The father shook his hand, thanked him for how he'd handled the incident.

Three months later, the father told him his daughter was getting married; he would be honoured to have his son's headteacher at the reception being held at a hotel in the Cotswolds. The invitation was for one. George was introduced to a vivacious, young blonde girl when the dancing started. The champagne flowed freely, and the girl's closeness was intoxicating; he didn't protest when she took him by the hand and led him up the stairs.

Two weeks later, the father asked to see him, and right there in his headteacher's office, took out his phone and showed George a video of the vivacious blonde. She was naked in bed. And so was George. The father was apologetic, said the girl had turned out to be under the age of consent. George excused himself, closed the door of his private toilet, and vomited.

'No problem,' the father told him. 'You are an excellent headteacher. We are your friends. This video will go no further, but we thought you ought to know.' They shook hands. It was only afterwards George remembered the use of "we," and wondered what that meant.

He found out three months later when the father came to see him. Over a cup of coffee, he asked George if he had considered standing in the local council elections that were taking place in May. 'You're already the chair of your local party. You have a fine reputation; you're well respected in this area. Your party would be pleased. You would be the favourite to win the council seat.'

George had been flattered but told him he enjoyed being a headteacher – it was what he had always wanted to do. The father smiled and nodded but asked him to think about it.

The next week, the father came back, accompanied by a well-dressed man wearing a mohair overcoat. They asked if he'd reflected on their suggestion that he stand for the council. It was only when the well-dressed man stressed both the importance and the fragility of reputation that George understood it was a suggestion he could not refuse.

He resigned from his post as headteacher, became the councillor for his area, and with his natural ability and their encouragement, was soon Chair of the Planning Committee. Their application for a new casino on the old primary school site, rejected previously in the face of vociferous objections by the local residents, was resubmitted with minor amendments and approved.

George Kershaw knew precisely when he'd had his moment of epiphany. It hadn't been during the fine dining with Albert in London. Or the box at the centre court at Wimbledon. His moment of epiphany came as he stood next to Albert on the yacht in Monaco, a glass of champagne in his hand, and the roar of the engines in his ears as the formula one cars negotiated the chicane. The vision of a new life, a life with riches beyond his boyhood dreams, engulfed him; Albert, bored by racing cars, standing back to observe him closely, smiled to himself.

After dinner, Albert embraced him, told him he needed an intelligent man who would be richly rewarded to work with him. And that he thought George could be that man. George became a willing partner. It was Albert's suggestion that he resign from the council and stand for the vacant Police and Crime Commissioner role. George, already a well-known councillor, stood in the election and won. He was now the Police and Crime Commissioner – the PCC. As a measure of his trust, Albert gave him a special mobile phone so that they could be in direct contact. And shared his plans for the Birmingham area with him.

Having seen the yachts moored on the waterfront in Palma, George wanted one for himself; he thought that with Albert's plan nearing fruition, it wouldn't be long. He resolved to spend part of the weekend taking a closer look at the yachts in Palma harbour.

Looking up again at the departures screen, he saw the "now boarding" sign for his flight flashing. His companion – who had phoned into work sick – appeared, two magazines in her hand.

'I hope we have a good weekend,' she said, standing above him.

The PCC looked up; his eyes were drawn to his new PA's generous cleavage.

'We're going to have a wonderful weekend,' he said.

Chapter 24

Philip keyed in Walter's last destination into his Toyota's satnav. Three consecutive underpasses took them through the city centre, onto the ramp that led to the Aston Expressway, Spaghetti Junction and the motorway to London. They turned right when they came to the Aldridge Road, followed that for a mile before the satnav told them to turn left into their destination street.

The street had seen better times. Large detached Victorian houses lined both sides, most of them now converted to rental flats. Some had front gardens that were grass with the odd flower bed, others had tarmacked the front to provide parking. Philip slowed down when the satnav told them they would reach their destination in two hundred yards. There appeared to be a choice of two houses.

'One of these two?' Philip peered through the windscreen. 'What are we're looking for?'

'I was expecting some kind of charity organisation.'

Getting out of the car, they looked more closely at the fronts of the two houses.

'The one on the right has two CCTV cameras,' Angie said, pointing. 'One on the lamppost to cover the car park, one on the side of the building to cover the approach to the front door. It's got to be that one.'

Philip nodded. 'Do you want me to come in with you?'

'Nice try.' Angie smiled at his eagerness to get involved but shook her head. 'They'll ask for your ID. You stay put in the car.'

She started walking towards the front entrance. Turning into the front, Philip parked so he faced the house and could see Angie approach the front door.

The door was a black, security door with no lock for a key visible; instead, there was a metal keypad attached to the wall, an intercom and a button. Angie pushed the button, heard the buzz on the other side of the door. A woman's voice said, 'Yes?'

'Police. Detective Inspector Reeves,' Angie said. 'I'd like to have a word.'

'How can I help you?' the woman said.

'I'd prefer to discuss it inside. Open the door please.'

Angie waited. There was a momentary pause before the door release buzzed. The heavy door opened inwards. She found herself in an enclosed foyer. Ahead of her, a set of double doors guarded a corridor, again with a keypad at the side. On the right, she saw an office-cum-reception with a glass front and sliding windows. The woman had left her desk, stood unsmiling behind the sliding windows, watching Angie. She was in her forties, a little overweight, with black hair piled high on her head, lots of dangling jewellery and oversized glasses with red frames. A low-cut top exposed the top half of her generous breasts. She looked like she had lost track of time on the suntan bed. She was chewing gum.

Sliding the window open, she took in Angie's cast with a smirk. 'What can I do for you?'

Angie showed the woman her warrant card. 'Could you tell me what this place is?'

'This is The Women's Refuge for abused women. Single or married with no children. We don't take children. Just abused women.'

A memory flashed through Angie's mind. A memory of being woken up and abused by her drunken boyfriend. The physical damage had faded but the emotional scars lingered. She hadn't been in a serious relationship since then.

She pushed the memory out of her mind. 'I need to ask you some questions.'

The woman slipped another piece of gum into her mouth, 'Ask away.'

Angie stared at the woman. Her general unhelpful demeanour, the rhythmic movement of her jaw and her smirk on seeing the cast were getting on Angie's nerves, triggering the release of her pent-up feelings since Ross's phone call. She let it out, knowing she was being unnecessarily aggressive.

'We can do this in one of two ways. Either we sit down in your office, and you answer my questions, or I take you back to the police station and you answer them there.'

The woman stopped chewing. 'There's no need for that.' She beckoned for Angie to move around to the office door at the side, let her in, and moved a plastic chair from the corner to the other side of her desk. Picking up the chair with her good hand, Angie took it to around to where the woman was sitting and placed it about two feet from her.

She took out her notebook. 'What's your name? And what is your role here?'

The woman had resumed her chewing. 'My name is Marion Hayes. I'm the manager here. Which means I'm also the receptionist when I'm on duty.'

'How many others are on duty during the week?'

'There are three of us. We share the eight-hour shifts – either 6 a.m. to 2 p.m., or 2 p.m. to 10 p.m.'

'What happens if there is a problem between 10 p.m. and 6 a.m.?'

'We have a small accommodation block at the back. One of the assistant managers has a room. She's on call during the night if there's an emergency.'

'Who was on the late shift a week last Wednesday?'

Marion Hayes didn't hesitate. 'I was. I always do the late shift on Wednesdays.'

Angie had a large handbag with her. She took out the photograph of Walter, put it face up on the desk.

'Do you remember this man coming here a week last Wednesday afternoon?'

Marion Hayes didn't bother to look at the photograph. 'We don't allow men in here.'

Angie took out a rolled sheet of A3. She put Margaret's pencil portrait of the girl – the one without the shawl – on the desk, using a paperweight at one end and her cast at the other end to keep it flat.

'What about this girl? Did she show up here last Wednesday? Either by herself or with this man?'

Marion Hayes took her time, looked at the portrait of the girl. 'Pretty girl. But she's not been here. I've never seen her. Sorry.'

Angie sat back in her chair. Shit! Maybe Walter had driven the girl to the refuge, left her to go in by herself, knowing that men were not allowed in. And maybe the girl had got scared, run off instead of ringing the bell. Run off to hide again from whoever she had escaped from.

But if the girl had even stepped into the car park, or approached the front door before running off, she should be on the CCTV.

'Just one more thing. I'd like to look at your CCTV for that day. Where are the recordings?'

'Our CCTV doesn't work,' Marion Hayes said. 'It's just for show. Puts people off. You know – like those dummy speed cameras you people use.'

'I'll leave this portrait of the girl with you,' Angie said. She stood up and handed Marion Hayes her card. 'This is my mobile number. Perhaps you could talk to the two assistant managers, show them the portrait. Ask them if they've seen the girl loitering in any of the side streets when they've been coming in to work.'

'I'll do that,' Marion Hayes said. 'I'll talk to them and show them the portrait. And I'll be sure to give you a ring if they've spotted that pretty, blonde girl.'

Angie stood still for a moment, looked pointedly at Margaret's pencil portrait and then, with a fixed stare, at Marion Hayes. The woman's hand had flown up to her mouth; tell-tale pink blotches appeared above her low-cut top, and on her neck. Angie sat back down and beckoned for Marion Hayes to do the same.

'This is a murder investigation,' she said. 'Tell me one more lie, and I *will* take you in to the station.'

***

There was a hold up on the Aldridge Road on their way back; a container lorry had broken down on the inside lane. They crawled along on the outside lane. 'So, after you'd shown her Margaret's pencil portrait of the girl, she told you she'd let you know if anyone had seen the pretty blonde girl?' Philip laughed. 'What happened then?'

'I asked her how she knew the girl was blonde. She blustered, said it was just a guess, but even through the fake tan, I could see the nervous pink blotches appear on her chest and her neck. She fell apart when I asked her if she wanted to be charged with being an accomplice to murder.'

'And when she showed you the CCTV, you saw Walter with the girl?'

'Yes, the camera covering the car park was broken. But there was nothing wrong with the camera covering the approach to the front door.'

'Tell me the story again. It might help you get it straight in your mind if you talk it through.'

'The Chair of Trustees of the refuge rang Marion Hayes to check if the emergency room was vacant. Then she rang her back to say a man – she gave her Walter's name – would arrive with a girl. She was to give the girl the emergency room, and she was to allow the man to enter the refuge with the girl. Walter turned up about forty minutes later with the girl.'

'But she couldn't keep her nose out of it.'

'No. She said she went into the room without knocking, because the man had been in there alone with the girl for over half an hour, and she was concerned for the girl. But I think she's just the nosey type. When she went in, Walter was making notes in his green notebook, taking down what the

210

girl was saying. He shooed her out of the room, but she had seen what he was doing. She said Walter left after another half hour, telling her he would be back for the girl the next day. And then the men turned up, the ones we think killed Walter.'

'How did they know the girl was there?'

'I don't know where they got their information from,' Angie said. 'But they knew where Walter had taken the girl. Just like they knew the notebook was in his study.'

'The CCTV shows Walter at the front door with the girl at 14.50.' Angie glanced across at Philip. 'It was hard seeing Walter. Knowing what happened afterwards.' Angie was silent for a moment before continuing. 'Then Walter leaves on his own at 15.55. The men turned up two hours later. Marion Hayes said she only saw one man. He rang the bell at 17.54, told her the blonde girl was his sister, and that she had run away without her medication. He said she would go into a coma without it. He offered Marion Hayes two hundred pounds if he could give his sister her medication and take her back home.'

'So she took the money and then he asked her what Walter had done while he was there with the girl?'

'Yes, that's when she told him about seeing Walter making notes in his green notebook. The money was to buy her silence. She said the girl was already unwell by the time the man left with her –

he had to carry her. The CCTV showed him leaving with the girl at 18.08.'

Philip looked across at Angie. 'You think he drugged her?'

'I'm sure he did. I don't think the girl would have gone quietly otherwise.'

'Did Marion Hayes see the van?'

'Not on CCTV because of the broken camera. But she said she looked through the window and saw them put the girl in the back of a white van.'

'Them?'

'There were two of them. A man got out of the driver's side and helped to put the girl in the back of the van. She didn't see his face.'

'But you've got the other one on CCTV – the one who rang the bell and drugged the girl?'

'Yes. We've got crystal clear images,' Angie said. 'Front and back.'

She looked across at Philip. 'He's got a ponytail.'

Chapter 25

Angie had the name and phone number of the Chair of Trustees of the refuge. She dialled the number when they were stationary at a traffic light. The voice that answered sounded crisp, authoritative.

'Theresa Vines.'

'Mrs Vines, I'm Detective Inspector Reeves from West Midlands Police. I'm involved in investigating the death of Walter Price. I understand you knew him.'

Her voice was softer. 'Yes, I knew Walter. He and my husband are… were… members of the same golf club. We were at his funeral earlier this week. John was a pallbearer.'

'I see.' Angie paused for a moment to allow for a change of topic. 'I wanted to talk to you about your role as Chair of Trustees of the The Women's Refuge in Great Barr.'

The pause came from Theresa Vines this time. Angie noted the more cautious tone.

'How can I help you, Inspector?'

'I believe Walter phoned you a week ago last Wednesday,' Angie said, making an educated guess from what Marion Hayes had told her. 'It would have been in the afternoon, probably just after 2 p.m.?'

'Yes?'

'I need you to tell me about this conversation. Why did Walter Price phone you?'

Theresa's voice was back to being crisp and authoritative. 'Why? Is this relevant to your investigation?'

'It might be,' Angie said. 'We're following up all the interactions he had earlier on the day he died.'

There was a lengthy pause. Angie waited with the phone held against her ear while Theresa Vines came to a decision. 'I'm willing to co-operate with the police in any way I can, Inspector. But I'm not comfortable talking on the phone about a private conversation I had with Walter. If you really think this is relevant, then I suggest we meet in person.'

'I'm happy to do that,' Angie said. 'When would be a convenient time?'

'Is this urgent, Inspector?'

'Yes, it is.'

'Very well. It's two thirty now. I have to go out at four thirty. How far away are you? My address is 34 Railton Road, Edgbaston.'

Philip mouthed at Angie. 'We could be there in twenty minutes,' she said.

'That would be fine,' Theresa Vines said. 'You can park on the drive.'

Philip knew the Edgbaston area. Angie left him to drive, sat back and wondered about Theresa

Vines. Wondered how she'd got involved in the world of domestic abuse. She was probably retired now, doing voluntary work after a professional career. Lawyer, social worker, teacher, magistrate – they could all draw you into the sordid world of domestic abuse. Angie had seen the statistics for England and Wales: two women killed and three committing suicide every week.

She thought about her own experience with Rob. They'd been together for just over a year and she was beginning to think they might have a future together when it had happened. Her father had warned her about the power of alcohol to change a man's behaviour, to bring to the surface what he called the latent forces in an individual's character. Rob had told her he got blotto when he was away watching the Six Nations rugby games with his friends – part of the experience he had said. But she had never seen him really drunk until that night.

It had been at his friend's wedding in Newcastle. She'd excused herself at midnight and gone to bed, exhausted after having driven them from Birmingham. Rob came up much later, pulled her out of bed, accused her of making him a laughingstock in front of his friends. She hadn't seen the first punch to her stomach coming. Or the second one to her face. She left him after that, refused to see him again. She hadn't been in a relationship since then.

Two weeks later, when the swelling in her jaw had gone down and her fading black eye was masked by makeup, Angie took her dad out for dinner and insisted on picking up the bill.

'Alright, what's going on?' he said, with a broad smile from his wheelchair.

Angie hugged him, kissed him on the cheek, and smiled back at him. 'More than you need to know. This is just to thank you for being such a wise father.'

***

Number 34 Railton Road was halfway down on the left, a large white detached house with an impressive wooden front door. There was plenty of parking space on the drive. Angie had agreed Philip could sit in with her, provided he kept quiet, and asked no questions. 'And if Theresa Vines doesn't ask to see your ID.'

She must have been looking out for them because the front door opened as they got out of the car. Theresa Vines held out her hand, then caught sight of Angie's cast.

'Oh dear, what happened to you? In the line of duty, I expect?'

Angie took out her ID and shook her head, 'Just a silly domestic accident.' She turned her head to indicate Philip. 'Philip Maddox. He's stuck with all the driving.'

Theresa Vines nodded at Philip and led the way into the house, past the open door of the lounge. 'I thought the kitchen table might be the best place in case you want to write anything down.'

They sat around the kitchen table with its cream granite top, accepted the refreshment Theresa offered. She poured the tea. 'I assume, since you are here, you already know that Walter took a girl to the refuge.'

Angie nodded, 'Yes. We're hoping you can tell us why he did that. And who the girl was. So perhaps you could go over the telephone conversation you had with Walter on the Wednesday?'

'There were three telephone conversations with Walter on that Wednesday,' Theresa Vines said. 'Is there a specific one you are interested in, or would you like me to go through all three in chronological order?'

Angie put down her cup of tea, caught the glance Philip shot her, 'Chronological order, please.'

'The first one was around 9.30 on Wednesday morning. Walter sounded happy, even excited. He said he had some good news for me – he'd received an unexpected windfall that he wanted to donate to the refuge. He suggested we use it for the refurbishment we needed.'

'How much was the windfall? And did he say where it came from?'

'Three and a half thousand pounds. He said he saw it as a long-term investment that had borne fruit.'

Philip was having a coughing fit. Theresa Vines fetched him a glass of water and handed him a tissue. Angie waited before resuming her questioning.

'You said Walter sounded excited. Was that because of the windfall?'

'No, he was matter of fact about the windfall. He was more excited about the dinner he had been invited to on the Thursday night.'

'Do you know who he was meeting?'

'No, I don't,' Theresa Vines said. 'Many women found Walter attractive, but he was rather evasive when I asked him if he'd been snared by a bold, new woman. He laughed and made a cryptic comment about it being more like the return of the prodigal son.'

'Do you know which restaurant?'

'Yes. The fine dining one in Moseley.'

'When was your second conversation with Walter?'

'I suspect that's the one you're really interested in,' Theresa Vines said. 'It was just after 2 p.m. I was sitting at this very kitchen table when he phoned.' She paused as if to gather her thoughts. 'He was quite serious. There was no small talk. He just came right out and said he needed a favour from me.'

'A favour?'

'Yes, he told me there was a young woman with him who desperately needed a room for the night. He said he knew we didn't work that way, that it wasn't normal procedure, but was the emergency room vacant that night?'

'And what did you say?'

'I asked him if he had tried the homeless shelters first. He said he couldn't. She wouldn't go to a homeless shelter because the people who were after her would look there first.'

'What did you say to that?'

'I asked him why he didn't take her to the police if she was in trouble.'

'That seems a fair question,' Angie said.

'He became impatient,' Theresa Vines said. 'I could hear it in his voice. Which was not like Walter. He said it was a complex situation because she was an Albanian from Kosovo; she wouldn't go to the police, and she was in fear of her life. He couldn't say more on the phone, so it was a question of me trusting his judgement. Could she have the emergency room if it was free?'

Angie heard the catch in her voice. Theresa Vines took a sip of tea.

'I rang Marion Hayes, the duty manager at the refuge. She confirmed the emergency room was free. I gave her Walter's name and told her that once she had seen Walter's ID, she was authorised by me as Chair, to let him enter the premises with the girl. I told her to put the girl up in the emergency room overnight. I also said I would be immediately confirming this instruction to her by email. Theresa paused, 'I intended to report it at the next Board meeting.'

'And then you rang Walter.'

'Yes, I rang him back straight away. He thanked me, sounded very relieved, and said it would be for a maximum of two nights. He asked me for the address and postcode of the refuge. That was the last time I spoke to him.'

Angie asked Theresa Vines how she knew Walter. She said her husband, John, and Walter, were members of the same golf club. They started going out to restaurants together, Walter bringing his latest date. 'Walter had a bank of amusing anecdotes, usually at his own expense, from his years as a headteacher. He was fun to be with.'

She paused. 'I can't believe he's dead. This is such a tragedy.'

'Did Walter have much to do with The Women's Refuge?'

'I used to be a social worker,' Theresa Vines said. 'I was Deputy Director of Community Care before I retired. Then I took on the voluntary role of Chair of Trustees of the refuge. Walter and I had plenty to talk about – his career had involved working with deprived communities, and he had experience of the effects of domestic violence. We don't have men as Trustees, but unknown to my board I used Walter as a de facto Trustee. I found it very helpful to sound him out when there was a problem.'

'Had Walter ever visited the refuge?'

'Oh no. Men are not normally allowed inside the refuge.'

***

'Where to?' Philip said when they were back in the car.

'To the station. I've got to let Ross and Bridges know what we've found out.'

Philip didn't speak during the drive to the station. Angie glanced across once, saw the intense look on his face. When they reached the station, Angie eased herself out of the car and walked around to the driver's side. Philip lowered his window.

'Thank you for driving me,' Angie said. 'I couldn't have found all that out without your help.' She straightened up, 'You've done enough. I'll get a taxi home.'

'Text me when you're ready,' Philip said. 'I'll pick you up. Why don't we go out for dinner tonight?'

'I'm too tired to go out. Don't forget I spent almost four hours in casualty.'

'We could get a take-away, something you can eat easily with your one hand. Pizzas?' Before she could shake her head, he said, 'Please. There's something I need to tell you. It's important to me.'

She saw the pleading in his eyes. 'Okay, I'll text you.'

Philip's phone rang as he started to move off. He looked at the screen, saw who it was. Anna didn't bother with any small talk. 'I need to see you,' she said. 'As soon as possible.'

**

The two of them were in Ross's office: Bridges sitting in front of a computer at the table, typing away on the keyboard, Ross opening a file from a stack on his left. There was a shorter pile on his right. Old case files. She saw the small white paper bag with the sausage roll.

Angie knocked and pushed the door open. They both looked up, surprise written large on their faces.

'You shouldn't have come in,' Ross said. 'I told you there was no need. I've told them you've had an accident and will be off for several days. I didn't think you would be in a hurry to take up desk duties.'

'I'm not,' Angie said.

'It'll be Lloyd House when you're ready to come back,' Ross said. 'Police Headquarters in the city centre. That's where you'll be based.'

'But now you're here,' Bridges said, eyeing her cast, and pointing to the empty chair. 'Do tell us how you did it.'

She told them about the accident. And then, when they'd stopped smiling, she began to tell them about her day.

Bridges made her start again so he could make notes. Angie told them about following Walter's last satnav destination, about Walter and the girl, and what Marion Hayes observed when she entered the room. She showed them the CCTV pictures of Walter and the girl approaching the front door. They saw Walter leaving. Then the face of the man at the front door. And fourteen minutes later his back, the ponytail clearly visible, as he carried the girl out of the refuge. They listened intently as she recounted what Theresa Vines had told her.

They sat back in silence when she finished. She looked from one to the other, but both were staring straight ahead. Then they looked at each other and communicated their decision with a nod before turning to her. She saw the steely determination in their eyes, felt the renewed energy in the room. Ross came from behind his desk and shook her hand. 'You've done well,' he said. Angie felt herself glowing. Bridges, watching them, gave her a moment before speaking.

'Theresa Vines was certain Walter told him the girl was from Kosovo?'

'Yes.'

'Then the chances are that our pony-tailed friend is from Albania,' Bridges said, 'which makes it a whole new ball game. Walter had no idea what he was getting into.'

Angie looked questioningly at Bridges, but it was Ross who answered. 'The National Crime

Agency briefed us six months ago. Albanians are heavily involved in organised crime, and they've been increasingly active in Birmingham and the surrounding areas.'

'I'll circulate ponytail's image,' Bridges said. 'To Interpol too. He might be known to them.'

'Let's do that straight away,' Ross said. 'We might get a result overnight.'

He turned to Angie. 'You go home now. You'll need some sleep after your experience in casualty. We'll meet here tomorrow morning at 8 o'clock.'

Angie's heart soared as she realised the implication of what he had just said. *They were going to carry on with the investigation.*

'What about the Deputy?' she said. 'Shouldn't we update him? He might change his mind about you leading the investigation.'

Ross stiffened, looked at her with flashing eyes. 'Fuck the Deputy!' he spat it out, reaching for his sausage roll. 'We tell him nothing.'

Chapter 26

The Starbucks was at the town hall end of Colmore Row, in what used to be a Lloyd's bank building. Sitting down with a latte, Philip waited for Anna to arrive. He realised they weren't meeting in her office because he wasn't allowed on the premises during his suspension. He wondered why she wanted to see him; he was still waiting for his interview with the audit team investigating what they were calling fraud.

Anna came in, glanced in his direction. She got her coffee and joined him.

'Thanks for coming in at such short notice.'

'No problem. I assume this is to do with the audit investigation.' There was a long moment's pause before she answered. 'Philip, I'm not sure I should be meeting you in the middle of an investigation, so let's treat this as an informal conversation. The auditors are interviewing Becky, your PA, today. They're going to call you for an interview, probably early next week, once they've got their ducks in line. Given your current position at the college, and our hopes for your continued employment at the college, I thought it only fair to give you a heads-up.'

Philip scratched his head. 'I'm sorry, I don't understand. What are you giving me a heads-up about?'

She was watching him intently. 'Do you know of a company called Progress?'

'No, I've never heard of them.'

'They used to be one of our sub-contractors. We used them to deliver courses for us on their premises: basic maths courses and literacy courses to our refugee students and returning adults. We claim the funding and use some of it to pay for the sub-contracting, which makes us the ones accountable for the funding.' She looked at Philip, waited for him to nod his understanding before continuing.

'We stopped using Progress three years ago. Before you joined us. We had many complaints from students about the quality of their teaching. After an investigation, we decided it was unacceptably poor. We've had no contract with them for the last three years.'

'I'm obviously missing something here. If we don't have a contract with them, why are they part of the audit investigation?'

Anna leant forward, her hands resting on the table with fingers interlocked. 'Because the auditors have discovered we paid Progress over £170,000 in fees during the last financial year.'

'Right. I see now. That would certainly be fraud. But how could that happen if our contract with them ceased three years ago?'

'The thing is the payments made to Progress have been authorised by you.'

Philip started to laugh, then stopped when he saw her expression. 'You're being serious, aren't you?'

'The authorised payments have your signature on them. The finance department wouldn't have made the payments otherwise.'

Philip made himself take two deep breaths, let them out slowly, kept his calm.

'Do you think I've done this?'

'No, Philip, I don't. But I'm not the auditors, I'm not the barrister in court that will prosecute you, and I'm not the judge that will sentence you if you're found guilty. All I can do is give you a heads-up. So go home, think long and hard, and come back with an explanation as to how this could have happened.'

She stood up, leaving her unfinished cup of coffee. 'I'm sorry but I've got to go. Another appointment.' She gave him one last look. 'I just thought you ought to know what you'll be walking into.'

Philip remained seated, nursing his coffee for a while after Anna left. He'd parked at Snow Hill Station, at the other end of Colmore Row from Starbucks. Walking back to the car park, his thinking focused on what Anna had said about the impact of the evidence the auditors had found. She was right; he would be damned in a court. He was the only one authorised to make those payments.

What defence would he be able to offer if his signature was on the claim forms?

He knew now that this was fraud, that someone had forged his signature. But who? Only his PA, Becky, could access his electronic signature. He trusted Becky; she gave him no reason to doubt her honesty. She was competent at her job. He would have described their relationship as one of mutual trust and respect. He kept it professional, resisted the temptation to probe into her personal life. She too was suspended while the auditors carried out their investigation. When they interviewed her, the questions would be about him. '*Come back with an explanation,*' Anna had told him. Philip sat in his car, trying to make sense of what was happening to him. His phone pinged. It was a text from Angie, telling him she was ready to be picked up.

***

It was on the eighth evening when Bujare brought the food that the girl at last spoke. This time, getting up straight away, she picked the tray up from the hatch and carried to the fold down shelf against the back wall of the cell. Sitting on the white plastic chair, she ate without speaking, her back to Bujare. When she'd finished eating, she sat on the bed, her head down. Bujare waited. The girl finally made up her mind; she raised her head and looked at Bujare.

'Good food.'

It was not what Bujare had expected her to say. But she'd made a special effort for the girl. 'Thank you. My name is Bujare,' she said. 'What is your name?'

The girl hesitated before she answered. 'My name is Elira.'

'Why are you here? Why did they bring you here?'

'I ran away from them, then I trusted a man who promised to help me. He took me to what he said was a safe house, but then I think he betrayed me, and told them where I was hiding. They came for me and then brought me here.'

'We had another girl here who had tried to run away from them, but you are not like her. She was from the streets.'

Elira held her head slightly to one side, stared at Bujare for a long moment. Bujare noticed she had green eyes.

'I am a second-year student at the University of Medicine in Tirana. I wanted to come to England for the last few weeks before my university started back. I met a man in the students' union who promised I could be the Assistant Manager in a restaurant in London. He said they would pay my ticket from Tirana to Gatwick. But there was no restaurant in London. They took me in a van to Birmingham and wanted me to work as a prostitute for their important friends.'

Elira stopped talking. Bujare could see the anger had returned to her eyes. The girl, still with her head to one side, continued to stare at Bujare.

'Why are you doing this?' she asked. 'Why do you work with these people?'

Bujare didn't know what to say. She could have said, 'I'm here because my husband, Pavel, is here, and I love him.' But instead, she said, 'I have to go. Pass me your tray.'

Elira brought the tray over, put it down on the shelf inside the hatch; as she did so, her fingers splayed and Bujare saw the little finger of her left hand was a stump, cut off at the first knuckle. Taking the tray, Bujare closed the hatch and bolted it. She turned away, her heart beating wildly.

Chapter 27

They got the pizzas from Domino's in Selly Oak – two, 12-inch Margaritas. Angie had greeted him cheerfully, tired but still excited that the investigation was back on. But Philip was unnaturally pensive. Seeing the tension in his face, Angie wondered what he was going to tell her. He only spoke to suggest they stop for a bottle of wine, but she told him she had plenty. They took the pizzas back to Angie's flat. Angie fetched a knife from the kitchen. Philip cut the pizzas into 4 slices, opened a bottle of Angie's Argentinian Merlot, and poured two glasses. From where they sat at the dining table in the lounge with the curtains open, they could see the balcony in the fading sunlight.

Angie ate two slices of pizza, picked up her glass of wine. 'You said there was something important you wanted to tell me.'

'There's quite a lot I want to tell you, but something else has just happened,' Philip said. He told Angie about his meeting with Anna, the heads-up she had given him about how the investigation at the College was progressing.

Angie gazed at him intently. 'What are you going to do?'

'I've decided to wait until I'm called for interview by the investigative team. Anna thinks that will be early next week. After that I'll have a better idea as to whether I'm going to need legal representation. I really need to see the evidence they would use against me. They'll have to show me the claim forms with what they're saying is my signature. I'm not sure what else I can do before then.'

He paused, put down his glass of wine and looked directly at her. 'But that's not what I wanted to talk to you about.' Angie held his gaze and saw he was trying to keep his emotions under control.

'First of all, I owe you an apology. I realise I trust you more than anyone else in my life. Surprises me that, as I haven't seen you for the last fifteen years. But I guess it's down to those seven years we had together. I think I talked to you then more than I've talked to anyone since.'

Angie didn't reply, but her mind went back to the conversations they had had, the confidences they had shared during their years together at Walter's school.

Taking a sip of wine, she smiled while she kept her eyes on his face. Waited.

'When my mother was diagnosed with cancer, we thought it was treatable. When it turned out to be aggressive and she died two months later, it was the biggest shock of my life. I couldn't cope. Walter wouldn't let Social Services take me into care. He persuaded them to let me live with him. I had the room their au pair used to have. I withdrew completely into myself. I realise I cut myself off from you, from our friendship. And then later, when I wanted to explain, you'd started going out with Ian Gill.' Philip paused, then looked up and met her eyes. 'I behaved badly. It's taken far too long, but I'm saying sorry now.'

The old hurt surfaced. Angie felt the tightening in her stomach but managed to mouth 'Thank you.' She remembered how she'd been, the nights she had lain on her bed wondering what she'd done wrong.

Philip stood up abruptly, insisting he was going to change the bulb that had caused her accident. 'But I'd better do it now before I have any more wine. Wouldn't do to end up with both of us having a fractured wrist.'

Angie had composed herself by the time he came back in. She poured a glass of the Merlot and handed it to him. 'What brought you back to Birmingham?'

'Give me a minute.' Philip took his glass of wine out on to the narrow balcony, stood gazing out at the traffic flowing by. She realised he was gathering his thoughts, deciding how much he wanted to tell her. He came back in from the balcony, sat down opposite her, and took a deep sip of wine.

'I did a bad thing to Walter. And it's been on my conscience for fifteen years. I've suffered from depression, been unable to sustain a long-term relationship. I didn't realise the two were linked. I finally saw a therapist when I was on the verge of a nervous breakdown. She advised me to return to Birmingham and to talk to Walter.'

'Did you see him?'

'I couldn't bring myself to see him face to face. And then the week before he was murdered, I saw him at the Apple store in Touchwood. I watched him for a while, talking to one of the staff about his mobile phone but I didn't have the courage to approach him. Instead, I went home, wrote him a brief note and posted it before I could change my mind.'

'What did you say in your note?'

'I invited him out for dinner at the fine dining restaurant in Moseley that Theresa Vines mentioned. We were supposed to meet at 8.30. I sat and waited in the restaurant until 9.15. When he didn't show, I thought it meant he didn't want to meet me. And then when I got home, I saw on the local news that he'd been killed the previous evening.' Philip finished his glass of wine. 'I still don't know if he would have met me for dinner. And if he had forgiven me.' Philip's voice tailed off. He stared intently at the glass of wine in his hand. A tear made its way down his right cheek.

Angie reached out and held his hand. 'You heard what Theresa Vines said. Walter was excited to be meeting you, likened it to the return of the prodigal son. That sounds very much like he'd forgiven you for whatever you did.'

He held on to her hand without speaking, without looking at her.

Then he said, 'You haven't asked me what the bad thing was I did.'

Angie raised her head and met his eyes.

'I'd like to tell you,' Philip said. 'But can we go for a walk? I'd find it easier that way.'

***

It had gone dark, there was a chill in the air. They walked side by side, along the side streets. He told her that during the summer holidays of that year, in the three months between taking his exams and going up to Cardiff University, he'd taken a job selling hot dogs at nights from a cart in the city centre.

'My pitch was on Stephenson Place, at the bottom of the ramp leading to the train station. I saw you with Ian once. I think you must have been coming from a film or a concert at the Odeon in New Street.'

He told her one of the other hot dog men had taken him to a betting shop. 'There was one in Needless Alley, just off New Street. George took me there, showed me how to write out a betting slip. We bet on the evening flat racing. My first bet was on a horse called Wild Nettle – it won. I won twice as much money as I earned selling hot dogs for six hours that evening.'

He told her he had taken the betting on horses seriously, started buying the racing paper, studying the form.

'The winners kept coming. I thought I'd worked out a successful system.'

Then he had a long run of losers. George told him he could get him credit from a friend, could place his bets for him until his winning streak returned. So, he had kept gambling, increasing the size of his bets. Then, in mid-September, three weeks before he was due to go to Cardiff, George told him he owed £1500.

'I was earning £12 a night. I told him I didn't have that sort of money, but I could pay in instalments out of my student grant.' George told him his friend wanted immediate payment, but there was another option if Philip couldn't repay what he owed.

'It turned out that his friend also ran a prostitution racket. The option he gave me was to be one of his rent boys until I paid back the £1500. So it was find the money or become a rent boy. Otherwise, the men who worked for his friend would break both my legs. And he said not to try running away. I'd told them I was going to Cardiff University. They would find me.'

Angie, who had been silent to this point, gasped involuntarily. Philip seemed not to notice.

'I was terrified. I didn't know what to do. I panicked.'

Walter had gone away for the weekend with one of his girlfriends to see a show in the West End. Philip said he had the run of the house. He'd gone into Walter's bedroom, to the drawer in the dresser where he knew the jewellery belonging to Roxanne's dead mother still lay. He took a diamond and emerald necklace to a pawn shop in Corporation Street, was given £1800 for it.

'I paid them their £1500, left Walter a note saying I felt strong enough to be independent and was going to my aunt in London for two weeks before going to Cardiff. Walter tried to contact me several times during my first term in Cardiff, but I didn't reply. He never mentioned the theft and I don't know if he realised the necklace was missing. But I knew and I've never been able to forgive myself for what I did.'

Angie remembered Philip's coughing fit when they were seated in Theresa Vine's kitchen. 'The windfall Walter told Theresa Vines about was from you, wasn't it?'

'Yes, it's today's equivalent of the monetary value of the necklace. I thought he would understand why I had sent it.'

They walked in silence for a little while, then Philip stopped as they came to a lamp post and turned to face Angie. 'I know the money doesn't make things right. It was the betrayal of Walter's trust, when he had done so much to help me. That's why I despised myself. That's why I lost my self-respect.' His voice broke. 'That's why I wanted his forgiveness.'

Angie held his hand without speaking. In the light from the lamppost, she saw the tears glistening on his cheeks.

'You're the first person I've ever told.'

'You were eighteen. Walter would have understood.'

When they got back to the flat, Angie opened another bottle of the Argentinian Merlot. Sitting at the dining table, they reminisced about their school days, about their mentoring sessions with Walter. Then Philip said, 'There's something else I want you to know.'

Angie took a long sip of her wine.

'Remember how we'd all talked in the sixth form about ways in which we could celebrate after our last exam?'

Angie nodded, smiled at the memory.

'Well, I'd talked it through with my mother the week before she was diagnosed. She knew how hard I'd been working for the exams; she asked me how I wanted to celebrate when the results came out. I told her I wanted to go away, maybe back to Devon for a week's holiday. So, we'd looked together and made a provisional booking for a cottage in Dawlish, overlooking the beach.'

'For you and your mother?'

'No,' Philip said slowly, looking directly at Angie. 'For me and you. I was going to ask you to come away with me for the week.'

Angie felt herself tingling. It started at her shoulders and ran all the way down through her body. She tried to keep still, to keep quiet. But the words escaped.

'That would have been nice. I would have liked that.'

Breaking eye contact, Philip looked down at his glass. It was Angie who broke the awkward silence. 'You sit on the sofa,' she said brightly, springing up from her chair. 'I'll make us some coffee. I've been dying to try out this new percolator I bought.'

Using her one good hand, the percolator took a while to unpack and master. She thought about Philip's vulnerability while she waited for the coffee to percolate, recognised how hard it had been for him to tell her what he had done. She felt a tenderness towards him, wanted to share with him her experience in Iraq and her battle to recover from PTSD.

But when she emerged triumphantly from the kitchen, two cups of coffee balanced on a tray held in her right hand, Philip was stretched out on the sofa, fast asleep. She put the tray on the table, sat down on the wooden floor so her face was level with his, thought about what he had just told her. *He had wanted the two of them to go away together for a week in Dawlish.* She knew Dawlish was the seaside resort town in Devon where he had been born and lived before coming to Birmingham. She gazed at him for a long moment, then caught herself – that was fifteen years ago when they had both just turned eighteen. She shook her head, stood up, fetched a duvet from the cupboard in the spare bedroom, and lay it gently over him.

Chapter 28

Waking up on the sofa just after 5 a.m., Philip took a moment to realise where he was. And then he remembered the previous evening. He folded the duvet, ignored the percolator in the kitchen, opted instead for a cup of instant, black coffee. Angie had told him she was meeting Ross and Bridges at 8 – he left her a note saying he would be back for her at 7.15.

The streets were quiet on the drive back to his flat. He took his time, driving with the radio off, his driver's window open to let the fresh morning air in. He felt different. Less tense. And only now did he fully realise the price he'd paid over the last fifteen years. It was like when he wore glasses for the first time – until then, he hadn't realised what normal was. He felt normal now.

His conversation with Anna resurfaced. He tried to put it to the back of his mind for now, not wanting to dampen his mood.

Back at his flat, he showered, put on some fresh clothes, and had two fried eggs for breakfast. The traffic was heavier on his way back. The lights were against him, but he didn't mind; he used the waiting time to think. He wondered how Angie felt about him this morning. His memory was that she'd been supportive. But that was last night. What about this morning after a night's sleep and time to reflect on what he'd done? Would she understand his need to play a part – even a small part – in finding Walter's killer? Or would she despise him, want to end their friendship? Was there any chance she would want to be more than a friend?

The parking space he had vacated was still there. Angie came out of the building as he pulled in. He opened his car door and got out to greet her. Noticing the shirt cut away to fit over her cast, he wondered how much longer it took her to get dressed using one hand. She looked him up and down.

'Shower and a change of clothes?'

He nodded. 'I slept well on your sofa.' He pulled an apologetic face. 'Sorry about falling asleep while you were making coffee. How was the percolator?'

'No problem with you dropping off,' Angie said. 'But you missed a great cup of coffee.'

He took a step forward, held her good right hand in both of his. 'Thank you for listening to me last night. Like I said, you're the only one I've ever told. And I feel so much better for it.'

She left her hand between his two, leant forward, and kissed him on the cheek.

He dropped her outside the station at ten to eight, watched the back of her as she headed for the building. Just before she disappeared through the entrance, she turned around and waved.

***

Ross and Bridges were already in the office. Ross was at his desk engrossed in reading a file; Bridges was sitting at the table, concentrating on the computer screen in front of him. They looked up, smiles on their faces as Angie entered the room. Noticing four plastic cups in the bin, she looked at them suspiciously.

'Drinking coffee from the machine! What's going on? How long have you two been in?'

'We circulated the CCTV image you got from the refuge before we left last night,' Ross said. 'Our chain smoker with the ponytail. I told the Duty Sergeant to ring me at home if anything came through.' Ross paused. Angie held her breath, waited. 'He took me at my word,' Ross said, 'woke me up at 4.30 to tell me something had come through from Interpol. I rang Bridges, and we came in.'

And with that, they both ignored her. Ross went back to reading his file. Angie turned to Bridges, but he was focused on his screen. Confused by the long silence that followed, she stared from one to the other. Bridges broke first. He looked up and grinned. Ross followed suit. Angie looked at the two older men, saw the excitement in their faces.

She realised with a start that they were teasing her. She had never seen them like this.

'Interpol came up trumps,' Ross said. 'Ponytail was on their data base. And it's looking likely we're dealing with an Albanian Organised Crime group. His name is Rumesh Zeka, aged thirty-four, from Kosovo. He had a string of minor offences to his name before graduating to more serious crimes. He was heavily involved in a gang stealing upmarket cars to order for Italian customers. They also think he was involved in the murder of a rival dealer but couldn't prove it. He did a five-year stretch for armed robbery, then disappeared after he was released from Dubrava prison in Kosovo four years ago. They didn't know he was in England. They're going to forward all the information they have on him, including known associates.'

'We'll get him,' Bridges said. 'He didn't have a ponytail when he was released from prison – he must have grown one since. He might cut it off, so we've circulated both images - with and without ponytail – to the ports and the airports in case he tries to leave the country.'

'What about Eurostar? He might try to get to France by train.'

'We've got that covered too,' Bridges said. 'We'll get him. Then we'll find out who killed your headteacher.'

'And why? Why did they kill him? What did Walter know?'

'Rumesh Zeka can probably answer those questions,' Ross said. 'We need to brief you on Albanian Organised Crime groups.' He nodded at Bridges.

Angie looked at the screen on Bridges's laptop as he turned around, noticed he'd been reading the latest National Crime Agency report on Organised Crime Groups.

'Albanians make up just under one per cent of organised criminals in the UK,' Bridges said, reading from the report. 'British nationals are sixty-two per cent, the rest is a mixture of nationalities, including some unknown. Albanians are a group that is small but big in impact. Human trafficking of both men and women used to be their mainstay: the men used as cheap labour on their building projects, the women for prostitution. But in recent years they've used their proceeds from human trafficking to buy into the drugs market. They now dominate the cocaine trade in London. And in the last eighteen months, they've been expanding, muscling in on the supply of cocaine in the West Midlands. And in Scotland, too.'

Ross leant forward, closed the file in front of him, 'The National Crime Agency briefing was an eye-opener. They said the rise of the Albanian Organised Crime groups is unprecedented compared with other recent developments, due partly to their readiness to use extreme violence.' He paused, then looked directly at Angie, 'That's the world your headteacher might have stumbled into.'

Angie thought of Walter, dying on the tarmac in the car park. A knife plunged into his chest and then drawn across. A victim of extreme violence.

'The advantage we've got,' Ross said, 'is they don't know we've identified Ponytail, circulated his photograph on our intranet, and have the border points covered if he tries to leave the country.'

'We know that Rumesh Zeka is a chain smoker,' Bridges said. 'Buying a single packet of cigarettes on the night of Walter's murder was probably a one-off because they were in a hurry. I bet he normally buys cartons of 200 cigarettes from the supermarket.'

Ross saw where he was going. 'You're suggesting we show his photograph to supermarket staff.'

'The big supermarkets. The ones where he can feel more anonymous, even though cigarettes are usually sold at a separate counter. We might get lucky if we show his photograph to staff behind the tobacco counter.'

'Worth a try while we're waiting for him to be spotted,' Ross said, picking up his car keys.

'What do you want me to do?' Angie asked.

Ross eyed her arm with the cast. 'You wait here in case anything else comes through from Interpol. Phone us immediately if it does.'

He handed her the report they'd been working on. 'This is everything we have on the case since the investigation started. Read though these notes again; it might spark some fresh thinking.'

'And we've been pondering the fact that the van was stolen in Aberystwyth,' Bridges said. 'It makes us wonder why they would go so far to steal a van. Unless they already had reason to be in that area. They might have a base there.'

'You're thinking that's where they might have taken the girl.'

'Maybe. And if so, the route to that part of Wales would take them along the M54. We were going to go back over the ANPR cameras on the M54, try to spot the van.'

'I'll do that,' Angie said. 'They would have wanted to move the girl quickly. I'll start looking at M54 ANPR footage for the night of the murder and the following morning.'

'Don't forget to take a fresh look at those case notes,' Ross said as he followed Bridges out. 'I've got a nagging feeling we're missing something, but I can't put my finger on it. You might have better luck.'

Chapter 29

The red SUV had come down the farm track the night before, Rumesh and Erag bringing a man they put in the cell farthest away from the girl. After they left, Pavel told Bujare the man was a recent arrival who had tried to run away. He said the man wouldn't find it easy to eat; his face was a mess after Erag had his fun.

'What do these men, like the one they just brought, do for them?'

'You don't want to know,' Pavel said. 'It's best if you don't ask questions. That way, if there is any trouble, you won't be so involved.'

'Tell me,' she said. 'Please. I am not stupid. I know that the men who bring them here are not good men. We can't pretend I am not part of this.'

Pavel had sighed, took his time drying the plates before he sat on the sofa next to her.

'The men they bring are mostly skilled workers: carpenters, bricklayers, electricians or plumbers. They keep them living together, make them work for them on the run-down houses they buy at auctions. Sometimes they resell the houses, but most of the time they convert them into rented flats for the students at the universities in Birmingham

– there is a great shortage of student accommodation so there is no problem renting them.'

'Do they pay the men?'

He shook his head, 'No. They feed them, but they don't pay them. Maybe sometimes they give them a little allowance.'

'Why do the men do it?'

'There is a man in London who is the big boss,' Pavel said. 'He is the one who owns this farm. He has contacts in the prisons in Albania and in Dubrava prison outside Kosovo who tell him which ones are craftsmen, and on which day they are going to be released. These men are all ex-prisoners. His people are waiting when they step outside the prison gates without a job. They promise them work in England using their skill to earn good money. Then once they are over here, they force them to work on their houses. If any of them have passports, they confiscate them. If they cause trouble, they bring them here to the punishment block. It is a warning to the others.'

'What about Erag – the young one with the pockmarked face and the mad eyes? The one with the knife strapped to his back. He is not a craftsman. What does he do?'

Pavel didn't answer. He pressed the remote control on the TV and started to flick through the channels. Bujare knew not to ask him any more questions. She didn't need to ask him about the girls; she already knew what they were made to do.

After seeing the girl, Elira, the previous evening, Bujare had returned with her head spinning. She had a sleepless night, tossing and turning, while next to her, Pavel slept soundly. At 5:30 in the morning, Bujare felt herself shivering. Getting out of bed, she dressed in the dark, and went into the kitchen. She gathered the ingredients she needed together. She enjoyed making spaghetti bolognese; it had been a treat on special occasions when she was a child. Her mother used to let her and her sister, Altina, take turns grating the parmesan cheese to be spooned over the pasta.

The sisters had been close to each other, but they quarrelled over what was left after their mother died. Bitter words had been said by both. Altina had moved away to Tirana; the sisters had not seen or spoken to each other for over twenty years. But before the quarrel Altina had had a baby girl. Holding the baby in her arms at the christening, Bujare had smiled as the baby gurgled, had kissed the stump of the little finger that the baby had been born with. Their grandmother chose her name. They'd called her Elira.

Bujare turned the heat down and left the sauce to simmer. She looked in the bedroom. Pavel was still asleep. Going back into the kitchen, she ate a bowl of cereal, and had a cup of coffee. When the sauce was finished, she set it aside for the evening meal. Raising the kitchen blind, she looked out across the farm fields. In the first glimmer of daylight, she could see it had rained during the night; the fields would be muddy. Putting on her green wellingtons she kept by the farmhouse door, she went for a walk. Past the punishment block and across the fields. The air smelt wet and fresh; she could hear the birds chattering as she breathed deeply.

Ahead of her, a young fox in the field pawed at what she thought must be a hole in the ground, trying to push his nose down it. The fox sensed her when she got to within thirty yards and looked up, his head perfectly still as he watched her. Bujare stopped, stood up to her full height, and stared back at him. She thought he had a handsome head, was admiring the way he held it, when he suddenly turned and ran off through the far hedge, into the next field.

She felt better after her morning walk. Pavel was still asleep. Bujare poured some cornflakes into a bowl, added milk, put the bowl and a spoon on a small tray, and walked over to the punishment block.

When she pulled the hatch back, the sound woke the girl. She sat up on the bed.

'I've brought you some cereal,' Bujare said. She put the tray on the shelf.

The girl stood up and stretched, then took the bowl and spoon off the tray without speaking. She sat on the bed eating the cornflakes. When she finished, she put the empty bowl and spoon back on the tray.

'Thank you.'

Bujare nodded. Then she said, 'Elira is such a pretty name. How did your mother choose it?'

'She didn't choose it. My great-grandmother chose my name. She was good at choosing names.'

'So which name did she choose for your mother?'

The girl gave her a curious look, stared at her before answering, 'Altina. My mother's name is Altina. Why do you ask?'

Bujare shook her head slowly, smiled at Elira, and picked up the tray with one hand. She took slow steps walking back to the farmhouse because her heart was racing, and she felt a little dizzy. Halfway between the punishment block and the farmhouse, she sat down on the wet grass and cried. Big sobs wracked her body. She didn't see the young fox standing still, his head up, watching her.

Pavel was still asleep but beginning to stir. Locking the bathroom door, Bujare turned the bath taps on so he could hear running water. She sat on the side of the bath and tried to think.

She would have to free Elira. They could say she had escaped. They would get into trouble but maybe not too much trouble. She was only one girl. And they had lots of other girls. But she needed to talk it over with Pavel – he would know what they should do.

Pavel was already dressed when Bujare came out of the bathroom.

'Where are you going?' she asked him.

'It's Saturday,' he said. 'I'm going to Machynlleth for the street food.'

'I need to talk to you. It's important.'

'Not now,' Pavel said. 'You know I have to get there early to be sure of getting some street food. We can talk when I get back.'

She walked with him to the shed, waited next to the white van with the dust cover over it. He felt in his pockets for the keys to the old green SUV.

'When are you getting the clutch fixed?' Bujare didn't want to nag him again, but she had seen the car stall, and felt anxious about him driving it. He told her it was booked to go into the garage the next week; they would need it for the entire day.

'How are you going to get back to the farm?'

'A courtesy car,' he said. She didn't understand. 'They will give me one of their cars for the day while they replace the clutch.'

He backed the SUV out of the shed; she heard a crunching noise from the gearbox as the car stalled. Then he found the gear, and she waved to him as he drove off down the track.

Bujare loved Pavel. Loved that he tried to please her. Not like her first husband who used to beat her when he had too much to drink. Pavel was different. He was gentle with her. His first wife had died in a car crash on the road from Kosovo to Pristina; he'd told Bujare they'd been childhood sweethearts from the same village. He said he'd gone crazy after her death, spent the next year mixing with the wild ones and ended up in Dubrava prison. When he was released after two years, the man waiting outside had told him he needed a carpenter. But the work was in England.

Bujare walked back to the farmhouse and sat in the kitchen with a cup of tea. Pavel would be back in two hours. She would sit him down and tell him Elira was her niece. Then they could plan how to make it look like the girl had escaped.

Chapter 30

For seven years, ever since they were waiting for him outside Dubrava prison on the day he was released, Pavel had worked on the houses in Birmingham. They had kept his passport. They gave him a pittance but said they were taking care of his elderly mother in the village outside Tirana. He enjoyed his work as a carpenter, so he just kept his head down and let each day come and go.

But after the fall from the scaffolding, he'd had to wear a back brace and couldn't work at the pace they wanted. They were sympathetic, allowed him a little more freedom, let him stay behind if he was having a bad day. He'd hoped they'd give him his passport back and let him return to Tirana.

And then he'd met Bujare by chance, in the fish and chip shop. She had dropped her packet of chips; he winced as he stooped to help her. But their eyes met. He started to meet her secretly.

Three months after he had met Bujare, Pavel was taken to a hotel in the city centre. The man who greeted him warmly and bought him lunch, wore an expensive suit and a green silk tie. Afterwards, while they were having coffee, he said, 'I have a proposal for you. I have a farmhouse in Wales. A couple – a man and his wife – have been looking after it for me, but the man has died suddenly.' And then he had leant forward and put his hand over Pavel's. 'I know you've been struggling on the building sites since your accident. I thought maybe you would like to go to the farm and be my new housekeeper.'

Pavel had been taken aback. 'But you said there was a couple there. I don't have a wife.'

Albert had smiled, 'I thought you might persuade the woman you've been meeting secretly to go with you. You two make a fine couple.' He leant forward and spoke quietly, his eyes watching Pavel closely. 'I still have your passport in safekeeping. After three years as my housekeeper, I'll give it back to you. And I'll set the two of you up with a small bar or café in Tirana. Whichever you prefer.'

Pavel and Bujare were married at the registry office in Birmingham. She had come with him to the farm just over a year ago. He tried his best to make her happy.

***

The road from Pennal to Machynlleth ran alongside the river. Pavel drove steadily, deep in thought. He was worried about Bujare. She wasn't herself, asking lots of questions, then lapsing into long silences. And he had noticed her empty side of the bed when she'd gone for an early morning

256

walk. He knew she only stayed at the farm because of her love for him. And the promise of the little bar in Tirana they would run together.

Bujare would be looking forward to the Indian street food. The woman who cooked it had a stall on Saturdays; she had told him she was from Kerala, a state in the south of India. He and Bujare both liked the flavour of her food; he took some back to the farm every Saturday. He decided he would open two bottles of wine that evening – Bujare needed cheering up. And maybe it would mean less time in front of the TV and more time in the bedroom.

Pavel was still smiling at the thought as he waited to take the sharp right-hand turn that would take him over the bridge, into the town centre. He moved off in first gear when there was a break in the oncoming traffic, heard the grating noise from the gearbox as he tried to find second gear. The SUV stalled before he reached the safety of the bridge. He saw the oncoming container lorry, tried frantically to find the gear as the lorry loomed ever closer. The collision was broadside, toppling the SUV over. The heavy container lorry pushed the car along the road; sparks flew off the tarmac before it came to a juddering halt.

***

Bujare vacuumed the carpets in the lounge and their bedroom and cleaned the work surfaces in the kitchen. She enjoyed this housework – it reminded her of her old cleaning job. Sitting down with a cup of tea she heard a car coming up the track and smiled to herself at the thought of the street food. Then looking out of the window, she saw a police car come to a halt by the shed where the van was parked.

The van had the dustcover over it. She thought of the punishment block, felt a knot in her stomach. She threw the tea away, drank a glass of water, and opened the door as the police officers reached it. There were two of them in uniform: a middle-aged man with a serious looking face and a younger, slimmer female officer. They waited until they were all seated around the kitchen table and then the male officer told her about the accident, told her the firefighters had cut Pavel free, and the paramedics had taken him in the ambulance to the hospital in Aberystwyth. Bujare thought she was going to faint and held on to the tabletop. She managed to ask how seriously Pavel was hurt. They didn't know.

'But it's an excellent hospital,' the officer told her. 'Your husband will be in expert hands.'

The officers offered to make her a cup of tea, but fearful of the punishment block, she declined, desperately wanting them to leave. They asked her if she had any family close by – she said no, but she would call a friend. They wrote down the phone number of the hospital, tore the page from the notebook and handed it to her. She held it in her hand as she leaned in the doorway and watched them drive away.

Sitting down with another glass of water, taking little sips, Bujare waited for her pounding heart to slow down. With trembling hands, she unfolded the piece of paper with the number and rang the hospital. She gave Pavel's name, told them she was his wife, asked if she could speak to him.

They put her through to a senior nurse with kind voice. 'Your husband was taken straight to the operating theatre. He has serious injuries, but they are not life-threatening.'

Bujare struggled to breathe. 'Do you mean he might die?'

There was a pause before the nurse answered, speaking slowly. 'No, I don't mean that. His life is not in danger. But your husband was seriously injured in the accident. The doctors needed to operate straight away.'

Bujare had to take another sip of water. 'How long will he have to stay in the hospital?'

'I'm sorry,' the nurse said. 'You'll need to speak to the doctors. After the operation, they will be able to give you more information about his injuries, and an indication as to how long it will take him to recover.'

'When can I see him?'

The nurse told her there was no point in her coming to the hospital before 7 p.m. as Pavel would be in the operating theatre for around three hours. He would be unconscious afterwards and it would take time for the effect of the anaesthetic to wear off.

Bujare put the phone down and sat with her head in her hands. Then she went into the bedroom, searched in the bottom of the wardrobe where she kept her shoes, found the hidden packet of cigarettes and the lighter. Pavel didn't like her smoking. Taking a cigarette out of the packet, she lit up, sat at the kitchen table and tried to work out what she should do.

***

Albert was a habitual early riser, even on the weekend. He had just cracked two eggs when his phone rang. It was one of the Aberdeen phones – the number 2 with the one blue dot. The woman on the other end was the widow of Albert's rival, the man who Erag had killed in the park. She propped up the pillows, stretched out her long, slender legs.

'Good morning! I knew you would be up, even if it's seven o'clock on a Saturday morning. I woke up thinking about you and that video we watched together. I had a wonderful time.'

'Me too. You're a quick learner,' Albert said, smiling at the memory. He'd shown her the video of the Deputy with the tall brunette in Monaco. 'How was your flight back from London?'

'No problem. It's easy when you've only got hand luggage. When can I come down again?'

'When our current situation has been resolved. Is everything still going smoothly?'

'Yes,' she said. 'All the arrangements are in place. I don't see any problems.'

'Good. I'll be in touch.' Albert ended the call, returned to making his breakfast.

The second phone call came just as he finished his Eggs Florentine. It was from a senior officer at Interpol, the one Albert paid well to keep him informed of developments. Albert listened without interrupting, asked two questions before ending the call. He had two slices of toast and thick marmalade, ate slowly while he considered how to respond to the new information. Having made his decision, he used his number 3 phone with the red dot to make the call. He let it ring three times, waited a full minute, then rang again. It was answered straight away.

'Are you by yourself?'

'Yes.'

'Listen carefully,' Albert said, 'this is what I need you to do.' He gave his instructions, then made the person he was speaking to repeat them back to him. When he was satisfied, he said, 'You'll need to act quickly. Phone me when it is done.'

Chapter 31

Philip had made his decision after he confided in Angie. He would talk to Walter. And then he would talk to Roxanne. He drove through the black wrought-iron gates of the Lodge Hill Cemetery and Crematorium. The main building of the sixty-one-acre site in Selly Oak was a half-mile further on, with a car park on the right. It was a map of the large site that he was after; he soon found the section listed in Walter's Order of Service.

He walked back along the road towards the entrance, until he came to the short flight of stone steps, flanked by wooden railings, that led to a path. On the right side of the path, old, faded, concrete gravestones, some of them cracked, stretched into the distance; the left side provided a striking contrast of raised, black marble plaques. Fifty yards ahead, on the left, he saw Roxanne.

As Philip came to a halt, unsure whether to go on, she raised her head and saw him. She stood up as he walked forward.

'I just wanted some time with him on my own,' she said. 'But I was just leaving. Please stay if you want to.'

He nodded. 'I'd like to stay for a few minutes. There are some things I want to tell him.'

Roxanne looked him in the eye. He thought she was about to say something, but she just nodded and turned to go. She'd taken a few steps before Philip caught up with her.

'I won't be long,' he said. 'There's a café at the first roundabout, if you turn right out of the exit. Do you fancy a coffee?'

He saw her beginning to shake her head. 'Please, Roxanne. There's something I need to tell you.'

She looked at him speculatively, without smiling. 'Okay,' she said quietly. 'I'll wait in the café.'

A young mother pushing a buggy, a young boy holding on to her other hand, was walking slowly up the path. Philip waited until they had gone past. Then he crouched down by Walter's graveside, spoke to him haltingly, forcing himself to continue until he had said everything he'd longed to tell him.

***

Roxanne was the only customer in the café. A round faced middle-aged woman with a friendly smile brought two mugs of tea to the table as Philip sat down opposite her. They both shook their heads when she asked about cakes.

Philip's tea was too hot to drink. Roxanne was sipping hers. He blew on his and they sat in silence for a moment before Roxanne spoke.

'You said you wanted to tell me something?'

Philip took a breath. 'Walter must have wondered why I disappeared and never contacted him again. Given how much he did for me.' He paused. 'He must have mentioned it to you?'

Roxanne nodded but remained silent.

After a moment, Philip continued. 'I disappeared – or more accurately I ran away – because I did something terrible. Something I am deeply ashamed of.'

Roxanne raised her cup to her lips, cradling it with both hands while she sipped, her eyes focused on Phillip's face.

'I stole your mother's emerald and diamond necklace,' Philip said, forcing himself to maintain eye contact. 'I stole it from the dressing table in your dad's bedroom and I pawned it. It's the single worst thing I've done in my life.' He put his mug down, his hands under the table rested on his thighs, squeezing them.

Her eyes were still on his face. His throat was dry. He found the long silence before she spoke unbearable.

'Dad knew you took the necklace. He didn't go into my mother's jewellery drawer until Christmas – he gave me a piece of her jewellery every Christmas – so he didn't realise it was missing until then. He thought it was you, said it was the only thing to explain why you ran away.'

'And he told you?'

'Only much later, when we took a walking holiday together in Majorca. He told me then.'

'Why didn't he report me to the police?'

'I asked him that. He said you must have been desperate, and he didn't want you to have a criminal record. And that in any case you would punish yourself more, that your conscience would eat away at you. He also said one day you would return of your own volition.'

Roxanne paused, cocked her head slightly to one side, kept the eye contact. 'He was right about that. Shame you left it too late.'

'I wrote to him. We were going to meet up for dinner the day after he was killed.' Philip looked down, noticed he hadn't drunk his tea. 'I missed the chance to say sorry to him, face to face. So, I wanted to say sorry to you.'

Roxanne still held his gaze. 'Why did you do it?'

'I had a gambling debt. The people I owed gave me the option of paying up or working for them as a rent boy. Or they would break both my legs.' Philip, with his head now lowered, didn't notice Roxanne's hand fly to her mouth, didn't see her widening eyes.

'I pawned the necklace to pay them off.' He drank his tea, not knowing what else to say, then without meaning to, added, 'I've told Angie. I didn't want to keep any secrets from her.'

Roxanne played with her empty cup, moved her finger around the rim, waited until he looked up. She let her eyes wander over his face before she spoke.

'My father knew your mother.'

Her statement surprised him. 'Yes, of course. They met at parents' evenings. And he came around to our house when she had a car accident. And after she was diagnosed with cancer.'

'I didn't mean that. They knew each other before you were born.'

Philip sat up, gave her a baffled look. 'What do you mean? How could they have known each other?'

'Dad told me when we were walking in Majorca. You used to live in Devon, didn't you?'

He nodded slowly, 'Yes, we lived in Dawlish.'

'Dad was Head of the English Department at a school in Dawlish. Your mum was placed in his department during her training year. She trained as an English teacher, didn't she?'

Philip nodded again.

'They had a relationship,' Roxanne said. 'It lasted six months. Then he met my mother.'

Philip's head was spinning. He realised Roxanne was talking again.

'He moved to a London school as Deputy Head. Then, when I was six, he got the Head's job at Longlands.'

Philip's mother had never fully explained to him why they moved from Devon to Birmingham. He realised now it was not a coincidence that had brought him to Walter's school.

'Was that why he chose to mentor me? And why he took me in when Social Services were going to take me into care?'

She shrugged, 'Maybe. But that was his way. You weren't the only one he mentored. He helped lots of others too.'

'Anything else for you?' The round-faced woman was back at their table, still smiling. Roxanne shook her head, paid the bill. They stood up to go.

'One other thing,' Roxanne said. 'My mother had a miscarriage just before we left Devon. It would have been a boy – my younger brother. She couldn't have any more children after that.'

Philip wondered what she was going to say next.

'He didn't say so,' Roxanne said. 'But I think Dad might have regarded you as the closest thing to the son he never had.'

Chapter 32

Erag had just parked the red SUV when his phone rang. He twisted to one side to slip the phone out of his jeans pocket. It was an angry Rumesh.

'You're late! I've been standing here waiting. The racing will have started by the time I get back.'

'I was about to phone you,' Erag told him. 'You don't need to come out today.'

'What are you talking about?'

'I woke up early. I've done the shopping and taken the food to the men. You don't have to do anything.'

'Okay. That's good. But I don't like to be kept waiting on the street. You should have phoned me earlier,' Rumesh said. Then he added, 'You need to pick me up this evening. Albert phoned me earlier. There is a parcel he wants us to pick up. Bring the bolt cutter when you come.'

'What's in the parcel? Why do we need the bolt cutter?'

'Don't ask so many questions. He gave me an address with the directions. You just have to drive. Pick me up at half-past seven.' Rumesh rang off.

Slipping his phone back in his pocket, Erag smiled grimly. He hated that Rumesh took all the credit for the work they did. It was Erag who'd found the green notebook in the man's study, hidden in the lining of the sofa cushion. But Rumesh had taken it from him, phoned Albert. 'I have the notebook.' Erag had been seething. And Rumesh showed him no respect, sneered at his regular workouts at the gym or the gymnastics centre. Rumesh didn't do any exercise, said he didn't need to with the small gun in the holster at the back of his waist.

Erag had been to the wholesale supermarket earlier, filled a trolley with bags of rice, pasta, big tins of frankfurters, meatballs and tuna. He also bought twelve protein bars and twelve 1.5 kg bags of flour. At the checkout, the food went into eight large plastic bags; he asked them for a cardboard box he could put the bags of flour in. Before leaving the supermarket, he pushed the trolley to the separate pharmacy counter and asked for an elastic bandage.

On the way back he'd stopped at a hardware store and bought two heavy duty padlocks. Then he took the bags of food to the house where the men stayed but left the flour in the SUV. The men were quiet; he knew they were wondering what had happened to the one who'd tried to run away.

Afterwards he'd driven to an area of Birmingham that he didn't know and done what he had to do. Back in the SUV he unwrapped a protein bar and decided he would go to the gymnastics centre later that afternoon for another workout on the new mat, the special one that told you how high you jumped from a standing start. Watching a YouTube video, he'd seen a young, black gymnast from California jump his own height – 5 foot 9 inches – from a standing start. Erag thought that was incredible. It was a feat beyond him, but he liked the challenge of finding out how high he could go.

He'd found he went higher when he jumped backwards from a standing start, somersaulting through the air before landing on his feet. He enjoyed experimenting, seeing how much higher he could go if he took three or four steps backwards, before launching himself into the air. He would practise that for an hour and afterwards workout with the free-standing weights. There was plenty of time before he picked Rumesh up at seven thirty.

***

Ross and Bridges had no luck taking the photograph of Rumesh Zeka around the supermarkets. And nothing more came through from Interpol. 'We could release his photograph to the media,' Bridges said. 'Newspapers, television and social media. Enlist the support of the public. But that would alert him to the fact that we were after him. He would go underground.'

Ross agreed. 'Let's give it a couple of days. Rumesh Zeka doesn't know we're after him. He might well venture out. And if he does, there's a chance we might nab him. All our officers are on the lookout for him. They've been told he is highly dangerous, that they should follow but not attempt to arrest him.'

They went through to the incident room where Angie sat watching CCTV. She was rubbing her eyes.

'ANPR fatigue?'

She looked up. 'Yes. It's tiring looking at the CCTV footage all day. But I've found something.' She stood up and stretched. 'I picked up the white van on the M6 heading north. Early on the Thursday morning, the day after Walter was killed, I picked it up twice just after junction 7 and then again after junction 9. But I lost it after that.'

'The M54 is at junction 10,' Bridges said. 'That's where they would turn off if they were heading for the Aberystwyth area.'

'I couldn't find anything on the M54 footage or anything further on the M6.'

'They'll have hidden the van,' Ross said. 'It might eventually return with a respray and different license plates. But in the meantime, they'll be driving a new vehicle. And we have no way of knowing what that's like.'

'What about the case notes?' Bridges asked her. 'Did they spark any fresh thinking?'

'I was just about to start on them.'

'No, you won't,' Ross said, taking the folder from her. 'You won't get any fresh thinking with those glazed eyes. I'll go through these again. Why don't you go outside and get some fresh air? Take a walk around the boating pool and clear your head.'

Angie breathed the fresh air as she stepped out of the building. Crossing the road to the wide boating pool she saw the ducks had congregated at one end, watching two remote controlled model boats following each other around the water. She thought it was a father and son, the father controlling the leading boat, making unexpected turns; the son doggedly keeping in his wake.

She walked around the pool twice, then sat on a bench. The father and son had exchanged roles; now the son's boat was leading, zigzagging its way across the pond. The father made a wrong turn, the gap between the two boats grew, and then father and son were both laughing.

Walking in the fresh air had cleared the fuzziness from her brain. She was ready for the case notes Ross had asked her to read. He'd said he thought they were missing something.

Back in the incident room she found them waiting for her, Ross with the notes of the investigation in his hand.

'Got it!' he said. 'Something that doesn't add up. It's Walter's phone calls.'

He beckoned for her to sit down. 'According to our notes, Theresa Vines, the Chair of the refuge, told you she had three telephone conversations with Walter on the day he died. He phoned her at 9.30 in the morning to tell her about his unexpected windfall, then again around 2 p.m. to ask for a place in the refuge for the girl, and she phoned him back a few minutes later.'

'That's right. That's what Theresa told me.'

'But you told me the daughter said Walter didn't have a phone. That he had ordered a reconditioned one.'

'Yes, that's what Roxanne said.'

'So how is it that Walter could have three phone conversations? Whose phone was he using?' Ross was looking at her intently, waiting for her response.

'That's the nagging doubt you couldn't put your finger on, isn't it?'

'Yes!'

'I don't mean to pour cold water, but maybe he was at the food bank when he rang Theresa Vines,' Bridges said. 'And got her to ring him back there.'

'We can check that out,' Ross said, 'but it wouldn't explain the first phone call he made to her at 9.30 when she said he was at home. According to our notes, there is no landline in the house.'

'Maybe he did have another mobile phone,' Angie said.

Ross said, 'Forensics state categorically that the glove box in his Audi was locked, and that it had not been touched. So, did Walter run with a mobile phone in his tracksuit pocket? If he did, what happened to it?'

'I didn't meet the two students who discovered his body,' Angie said. 'But they were alone with him for a few minutes. Do you think they might have been tempted to take his mobile phone?'

'They just seemed normal, decent girls,' Bridges said. 'But one thing you learn in this job is never to make assumptions about anyone. We'll have to interview them again.'

'I'll try to get hold of Theresa Vines,' Angie said.

***

Theresa Vines seemed pleased to hear from her. 'I've been wondering how the investigation is going. Are you any closer to finding out who killed Walter?'

'We're still in the middle of our investigation. I just wanted a quick follow up on our conversation from yesterday.'

Theresa Vines told her she didn't know where Walter was when he phoned her in the afternoon. He had given her a number to phone him back on and he had answered on the first ring. She'd written it down on the back of a shopping receipt, but that had gone in the bin and the bins had since been emptied.

'What about the first phone call? The one in the morning when he phoned to tell you about his windfall. Do you know where he was when he made that phone call?'

'Oh, yes, he was at home,' Theresa Vines said. 'He told me he had been for an early morning walk and was just about to make his breakfast. I remember him saying he felt like scrambled eggs and bacon.'

Angie rang the food bank. Margaret wasn't there, but Angie explained who she was, and they gave her Margaret's home phone number. She answered straight away. They exchanged pleasantries and then Angie said, 'Margaret, that day when Walter was at the food bank, and you saw the blonde girl with him. Can you recall whether you saw him make any phone calls?'

Margaret didn't hesitate. 'Yes, dear. He did make a phone call.'

'Are you sure?'

'Quite sure. I remember closing the office door to give him some privacy. He said he had to make an important call.'

'He made the call from your office, not from his car?'

'Yes, dear. He said he didn't have his mobile phone with him. That's why he asked if he could use the phone in our office.'

'Was he in your office long?'

'A little while,' Margaret said. 'He had to wait for someone to phone him back.'

Angie told Ross and Bridges what Theresa Vines and Margaret had said.

'So,' Bridges said, 'Walter didn't have a mobile phone when he was at the food bank with the girl.

But we don't know if he had one earlier in the day when he rang Theresa Vines from home at 9.30 in the morning.'

Ross turned to Angie. 'Talk to Walter's daughter again. See if she knows how Walter could have made that first phone call.'

Chapter 33

The nurse had told Bujare that Pavel should be conscious and back on the ward by 7 p.m. Bujare phoned the taxi company, asked them to send a car for 6 p.m.; although the journey wouldn't take much over thirty minutes, she wanted to be sure to be on time. The taxi company was a small one; they told her there wasn't a car available then, the earliest they could send one would be half past six.

Keeping herself busy in the kitchen, doing what she called tidying up, she emptied the cupboards that were filled with crockery, putting the dishes back in different places, the plates at the back this time and the bowls in the front. Then she rearranged the cups they kept in the narrow cupboard so those with the same design were next to each other. After that, she took a break, sitting at the kitchen table with a cup of tea and a cigarette, before going back to work.

Starting on the lower cupboards, she knelt on the tiled floor to see all the way to the back; the tiles were hard on her knees, so she used two double folded kitchen towels to cushion them. They both liked wine – the bottom cupboard was full of bottles of red wine and white wine. But when she opened the cupboard, the first thing that caught her eye was the bottle of champagne. It was a fat bottle, making it difficult for her to reach past it to get at the slimmer bottles of wine behind.

She had been cross with Pavel when he came back from Machynlleth with what she called the fat bottle. He'd laughed at her. 'It's called a magnum, twice the size of a normal bottle of champagne. There was a special offer on. I got the last one at half-price.' She read the label, "Veuve Clicquot Yellow Label Non-Vintage Champagne", asked him what 'Non-Vintage' meant; he explained it just meant the grapes were from more than one year. Bujare relented when Pavel told her he had bought the magnum of champagne to celebrate their coming wedding anniversary.

But that was before his accident. She wasn't sure if he would be allowed to have alcohol when he came home from the hospital, but she liked the idea of celebrating his return to her with champagne. The thought made her smile. She emptied the cupboard, then put the bottles back in, the red wine in two rows on the left, the white wine on the right. And in front of them she put the magnum of champagne.

At six o'clock she took the reheated pasta out to Elira and the man in the punishment block. She couldn't risk speaking to Elira, didn't trust herself not to breakdown. She opened the hatch, put the food down quickly and walked away. Then she sat in the kitchen and had a smoke.

The taxi came promptly at half past six, but by the time she'd waited at the hospital for the lift to the sixth floor, then found her way along what seemed like endless corridors, it was almost an hour later. She pushed the double doors to the ward open. Two nurses were seated at the central desk. They looked up as she approached, waited until she was beside them.

'Who have you come to visit?' one of them asked. Bujare thought she spoke kindly.

'My husband, Pavel. He was having an operation but when I phoned, the nurse said I could see him after 7 p.m.' Then she added, 'My name is Bujare.'

'Hello Bujare,' the other nurse said. 'I'm the one you spoke to when you phoned. Pavel is not back yet.' She saw the concern growing on Bujare's face.

'There's nothing to worry about. The operation has gone well, they should bring Pavel back to the ward anytime now. Let me take you to where they're going to bring him.' Bujare followed her to the end of the corridor. There were spaces for eight beds in the room on the right, but the bed that should have been closest to the door was missing. The nurse pointed to the vacant space.

'That's where Pavel's bed was. They will bring him back here.' She pointed to the plastic chair just outside the room, with its back against the end wall of the corridor.

'Why don't you sit here and wait for him? Would you like a cup of tea?'

Bujare nodded, feeling an immense sense of relief. These nurses were so kind. They would be kind to Pavel, too.

They wheeled Pavel out of the lift before she finished her cup of tea. Her face lit up when she saw him. She gave him a wide smile and waited patiently outside until the orderlies had manoeuvred his bed back into its place. He had a drip attached to his arm. She asked the nurse what it was for and was told it was morphine to help him with the pain. The nurse called it a controlled drip, showed her the tube that ran from the morphine had a clicker at the end that lay on Pavel's bed; she said he could control how much morphine entered his body by pressing the clicker.

Sitting on the plastic chair at the head of Pavel's bed, she held his hand. He was conscious but drowsy and kept dozing off. Once, he smiled at her weakly and squeezed her hand. Sometimes she talked to him quietly – not about Elira or her fear of being alone when Rumesh and Erag came, because she didn't want to worry him. When she talked, it was about the little café bar in Tirana they were going to run together. And she told him she had rearranged the wine cupboard and put his magnum of champagne at the front ready to celebrate him coming home.

'I know it must be cold. I'll put it in the fridge the day before.'

Bujare sat holding his hand until he seemed to be asleep. She watched him a little longer, then kissing him on the forehead, she took the long walk back along the corridor to the lift. She was surprised to find it was raining. She waited under the awning at the entrance to the hospital until the taxi came.

***

Erag showered and dressed. He put on his jeans, chose a short-sleeved black sweatshirt. He didn't tuck the sweatshirt in; it hung loose, long enough at the back to cover the knife he always carried, strapped to his waist. He was waiting in the red SUV, outside Rumesh's flat at seven thirty.

Getting into the car, Rumesh immediately lit a cigarette. When he reached for his seatbelt, Erag noticed the new red hair band around his ponytail. Rumesh found the seat belt buckle, straightened up and noticed Erag's heavily bandaged left elbow. He sneered when Erag told him he'd hurt it lifting weights.

Rumesh wanted to use the directions that Albert gave him. He read from the piece of paper; they followed the main road for three miles before turning off into the side streets. Erag followed his instructions, driving with his window open to let the cigarette smoke out.

When Erag asked, Rumesh told him he didn't know what was in the parcel they had to collect or what they had to do with it. 'Albert said I should phone him when we have the parcel in the car. He'll tell us where to deliver it. Turn right here, then we want the third street on the left.'

The third street on the left needed resurfacing. Rumesh was thrown forward and cursed when they went over a pothole. Most of the small front gardens were overgrown; in one of them, a shopping trolley with no wheels lay on its side. Several of the houses were boarded-up, broken windows stood out in the ones that weren't. They parked in front of the last house in the street.

What had once been a front garden was now an expanse of cracked paving stones, with weeds sprouting where the grouting had disintegrated. All the windows were boarded up. A notice in large red letters, stuck to the front boarding read 'VACATE, DO NOT ENTER'.

Standing in front of the house they read the rest of the notice. "The Department of Buildings has determined that conditions in these premises are imminently perilous to life". There was also a warning that violators of the VACATE ORDER were subject to arrest. The notice was from the Building Commissioner.

Rumesh was holding the bolt cutter. He turned to Erag.

'This is the house. Albert told me it's condemned. It will be demolished. The parcel is in the back room.' Walking up to the front door, they saw that in place of the normal lock the door had a hasp fitted with a strong looking padlock. The padlock looked new. Rumesh cut the padlock with the bolt cutter. Pushing the front door open he entered the house. Erag followed him in.

The boarding covering the window in the back room was half off. There was just enough light for them to see the cardboard box, bound with heavy tape, in the far corner of the room.

'That must be Albert's parcel,' Rumesh said, looking at Erag. 'Let's get it in the car. And then I'll phone him.'

Erag nodded, walked forward, and bent down to pick up the box. He winced as he felt the weight. Stepping back, holding his bandaged elbow, he said, 'I can't pick it up. It's too heavy for my elbow.'

Rumesh cursed, shook his head, and pushed past him. He bent down to get both hands on the bottom of the box. As he straightened up, holding the cardboard box, Erag, standing behind him, took a step forward. His left hand grabbed Rumesh's ponytail and yanked his head back. With one swift movement, the knife in his right hand, he slit Rumesh's exposed throat.

Lowering the body slowly, so that Rumesh was lying on his back on the bare floor, he stepped around the body to face him. Rumesh's eyes were still open. Erag thought there might be some life left in him. He crouched down, stared into those eyes, plunged the knife into Rumesh's chest and flexed his biceps.

Blood flowed onto the cardboard box. He wondered if it would seep through to the twelve 1.5 kg bags of flour he'd bought in the supermarket. Eighteen kilograms had been heavy enough for Rumesh to have to use both hands to lift the box.

Taking the small gun from Rumesh's waist, he picked up the bolt cutter, went out of the front door and closed the hasp. He felt in his pocket for the second heavy duty padlock, identical to the one he'd put on earlier. It wasn't there. He swore, went back to the car and looked for it. He was still searching when he noticed two boys coming up the road towards him, two girls walking behind them. The boy in front was holding a football. Erag slipped into the car, did a slow three-point turn and drove away from them, not rushing, not wanting to attract their attention.

When he was well away from the area, he stopped in a side street, pulled off the elbow bandage, and rang Albert.

'I've done it,' he said. 'Rumesh is dead.'

'Good,' Albert said. 'When will you see to the girl?'

'Tomorrow, I will go to the farm to see the girl. She is in the punishment block.'

Once outside his flat, Erag searched the car again, using the torch on his phone. The padlock had fallen out of his pocket, slipped down in the narrow space between the two front seats. He had to slide the passenger seat back and move the padlock along with the tips of his fingers before he could fish it out.

Chapter 34

Roxanne was in Milton Keynes when Angie phoned her. 'I sold the Audi,' Roxanne said. 'I've come here to get some fresh clothes and to square things with my GP partners. I'll be back in Birmingham tomorrow morning.' She paused. 'Are you ringing to see how I am or is there another reason?'

'Both. I wanted to see how you were coping, But I do have a question for you.'

'Fire away,' Roxanne laughed.

'It's just that I thought you told me Walter was waiting for a reconditioned iPhone. And that he didn't have a landline.'

'Right on both counts,' Roxanne said. 'I bought him a new iPhone for his birthday three months ago and then we had to have a bloody great row before he finally agreed the land line was superfluous to his needs. What a technophobe! It took him a while to get used to the iPhone, and then he dropped it getting out of his car – twice! He wouldn't let me buy him another new one, so we settled for a reconditioned one. But he was slow in trading in the new one – I'm expecting the reconditioned one to be delivered any day now.'

'The thing is, we have someone who says Walter phoned her at 9.30 a.m. on the day he died. She thinks he made the call from home.'

'Not possible. Maybe he used a neighbour's phone. Have you checked that?'

'Not specifically, but we have interviewed them all at least once. No one mentioned Walter using their phone.'

'Maybe they delivered the reconditioned one earlier than expected,' Roxanne said, her voice trailing off.

'Okay, thanks. We'll think on.'

'Me too. I'll let you know if I solve the mystery.'

Angie put her phone away, told Ross and Bridges what Roxanne had said.

'Well, we've already agreed he couldn't have had his mobile,' Bridges said. 'Otherwise, he'd have used it to make the second call to Theresa Vines.'

Ross nodded, turned to Angie. 'I phoned the Dyfed-Powys Police earlier, while you were clearing your head. Reminded them the van stolen in Aberystwyth is involved in a murder investigation and told them we now think it might be somewhere in their area. I've advised them the occupants are involved in organised crime and are highly dangerous. That if they see the van, they should follow but under no circumstances approach.'

Bridges stifled a yawn. 'Sorry, the early morning start is catching up with me.'

'Let's call it a day,' Ross said. 'We'll see what tomorrow brings.'

Angie nodded. 'We might find Rumesh Zeka.'

***

She waited outside the station for Philip. When she got in the car, he looked at her and turned off the engine.

'You look whacked. Hard day?'

'It's the hours looking at ANPR footage. It takes a lot of concentration.'

She saw his quizzical look. 'Automatic Number Plate Recognition. We've been searching for the white van.'

'Any luck?'

'Two sightings on the M6 the morning after Walter was killed. We think they took the M54 to Wales. The van was stolen from a builder's yard in Aberystwyth, so there's a Welsh connection. They might have had the girl in the back of the van and are now keeping her prisoner somewhere in that area.'

'Or she might be dead.'

'Yes, they might have killed her, hidden the van, and picked up another vehicle. We've alerted the Welsh police – they're on the lookout in case they try to move the van, but I doubt they'd do that.'

She told him about the mystery of Walter's phone calls and what Roxanne had said about them arguing over the landline. Philip started laughing, his shoulders shaking.

'What's so funny?'

'It's the picture of Walter and Roxanne arguing about him getting rid of his landline. I can just visualise it. Walter was fond, even proud of that landline. Or more accurately, of the use he made of it.'

'Enlighten me.'

'I got to see Walter close up when I lived with him,' Philip said. 'Angie, I saw aspects of him we couldn't see as students. Even though we met and shared those conversations over the seven years he mentored the two of us.' He turned to face her.

'Walter was a technophobe, Angie. He wouldn't even buy a dishwasher. Not far off being a modern-day Luddite. That's why he wrote everything down in those green notebooks. But the exception was the new handset he bought for his landline. He asked me to go with him to choose one. We ended up with one that had several features. I had to show Walter several times how to make use of them, but eventually he mastered it. I can still see the smile on his face. You'd have thought he'd won the lottery.' Philip chuckled. 'I suspect Roxanne is not exaggerating when she says they had a bloody great row before he let the landline go.'

'I never knew Walter had such a dislike of modern technology,' Angie said, shaking her head.

'More a distrust than a dislike.'

They were driving through Selly Oak, approaching the university. Indian restaurants and take-aways of every kind jostled with each other on both sides of the street.

'I don't feel like going home and cooking,' Philip said. 'Do you fancy stopping for a quick curry?'

Angie nodded. 'Okay. And then I think an early night beckons.'

Philip found a parking space just off the main road. Three Indian restaurants, side by side, faced them from across the road. They looked at each other, laughed as they both said, 'Middle one'.

They had a Cobra beer while they waited for the food. Philip told Angie about his visit to the crematorium, told her he had talked to Walter about the theft and asked for his forgiveness. And then he told her about his conversation with Roxanne in the café.

'So, Walter knew all the time about the theft. And Roxanne asked you to be a pall bearer, even though she knew too.'

'Yes.'

'Don't you see?' Angie said. 'Roxanne must have known Walter had forgiven you, that he would've wanted you to be a pall bearer. She wouldn't have asked you otherwise. Isn't that what you wanted to know?'

Philip nodded, then told her what Roxanne had said about Walter regarding him almost like a son. He paused while the waiter put the curry dishes on their table before continuing. 'She told me something else too. That before he was married, Walter and my mother had a six-month relationship.'

'What! How did they meet?'

'They were both at the same school for a while.'

'And you never suspected?'

'Never. I didn't pick up on any unusual vibes, either at parents' evenings or when he came to visit.' He laughed. 'It would seem I lack the observational powers that a good detective needs!'

Angie paid the bill; she told Philip it was the least she could do for being chauffeured. They were both tired, spoke little on the drive to her flat. Pulling up, he asked what time she wanted him in the morning.

'Roxanne is coming back from Milton Keynes early tomorrow morning. I'm going to go and see her about ten o'clock, but I'll get a taxi and she can drop me at the police station afterwards. You've got enough to think about at the moment.'

'I know,' Philip said. 'But I'm still going to pick you up in the morning. I want to help you find Walter's killer, and this seems to be the only way I can help. Driving you around makes me feel I'm contributing.'

They agreed he would pick her up at 9.30. Philip drove off, looked in the rear-view mirror.

Angie was still standing on the pavement, staring after him.

***

Back in his flat, Philip opened a bottle of red wine, switched the television on and then changed his mind and switched it off as the screen came to life. He put on a John Lennon CD instead and sat back on the sofa. The emotional roller-coaster of recent events was taking its toll. He had awaited his dinner date with Walter with mixed emotions – relieved that he had at last found the courage to confess to the deed that had preyed on his mind for so long, fearful of how Walter would react. And then the chance to meet Walter had been snatched away from him, replaced by the shock of Walter's death and the way he had died.

Meeting Angie again after so many years was an unexpected joy, but it had raked up old and painful memories of his mother's death. And today Roxanne had told him Walter and his mother had been lovers before he was born.

In the background John Lennon sang 'Imagine'. Philip refilled his glass and his thoughts turned to his conversation with Anna. He was more worried about the fraud investigation than he had let on to Angie. Anna's warning remarks about what could happen in a court case had struck home. If he was convicted of fraud, it would be the end of his career – no other college would employ him. Prison would follow. Philip shuddered at the thought, wondered if he would survive. Would the depression return? And, if he did survive, what kind of person would he be? Prison would change him, would leave its mark on him. The thought crossed his mind that it was punishment for what he'd done fifteen years ago. Maybe he deserved a spell in prison.

Too many dark thoughts. He had to snap out of it. Turning the volume up, he sang along to "Woman" to stop himself doing any more thinking. He thought he heard a faint ringing in the background, turned the volume down and listened. His doorbell was ringing. Philip sighed, opened the door to apologise to the young mother in the adjacent flat for the loud volume. But the person in front of him, with her head down, was his PA.

'Becky?'

'Hello, Philip,' she said, raising her head. He stared at her, took in the cut lip, the bruising on her cheeks, and the one eye that was half-closed.

'Could I come in, please?' Becky said. 'I need to talk to you.'

***

The four thirteen-year-olds – the two boys and the two girls – were in the same year nine class. After a private discussion the boys had decided it was time to make what they called "a move" on the two girls. They thought both girls looked good, and they didn't want to fall out with each other, so they tossed a coin. The taller boy won and chose the taller of the two girls; he had seen her playing netball and liked what he saw. His friend was secretly pleased – he was conscious of his height, and on balance he thought the shorter, red-headed girl who made him laugh in class would suit him better. Unknown to the two boys, the girls too, had had a private discussion; they knew what the boys were thinking but hadn't made up their minds yet how they would respond.

The four of them had spent the last hour in the park, walking around, talking and joking with each other. The boys had brought a football with them; the girls agreed to take turns in the makeshift goal while the boys took penalty kicks. Now, in the fading evening light, they were walking home. They'd enjoyed each other's company. But the boys just hadn't found the right moment to make their "move". They shared a glance with each other, silently agreed it would have to be another day.

They'd talked a bit about school. The four of them, who were seated at the same table for their English lessons, agreed they all liked English. They liked the teacher: he was young, with a sharp sense of humour and he gave them interesting exercises to do. The last one had been to write a short story in twenty minutes, exchange with another pupil and then in the next five minutes see how many words they could change without altering the meaning of the story. He'd given them an example – you could change "he walked quickly" to "he hurried".

'That's just stupid,' the tall boy said. They looked where he was pointing, at the notice outside the boarded-up house. 'It says "VACATE". It should be "VACANT". You'd think they could spell!' The short, red-headed girl, the smartest of the four, chewed the inside of her mouth while she looked. 'It's two different words,' she said. 'They're not telling people the house is empty, they're telling them to get out. To leave. That's what "VACATE" means.'

'It's a condemned house. That means it's going to be demolished,' the shorter of the boys said. His father was a builder. 'It could be the foundations, or it could be what they call black mould. That's why it's all boarded up and locked.'

'It's not locked,' the red-headed girl said. 'There's no padlock.'

They all stared at the door. She was right. There was a hasp that was closed, but there was no padlock through it.

'Let's go in,' the tall boy said. 'See if they've left anything behind.'

The girls shook their heads. 'I'll come with you, but I'm not going up the stairs,' the builder's son said. 'My dad says the staircase can give way sometimes.'

The girls watched as the boys walked up to the door, pulled the hasp back, and pushed. The door swung open. The two boys hesitated, looked at each other.

'Come on,' the taller one said. 'Just a quick look downstairs.'

He went in. His best friend followed.

The girls decided not to wait.

Chapter 35

Bujare reached behind the magnum of champagne and took a bottle of red wine from the cupboard. She was pleased it had a screw top; she felt too tired to do battle with the corkscrew. Reading the label, she saw it was a bottle of Shiraz. She poured a glass, sat at the kitchen table and smoked a cigarette, trying to work out what she would say when Rumesh and Erag returned to the farm. She didn't know when that would be; sometimes they rang Pavel to tell him they were coming, but sometimes they had just turned up. As if they were trying to catch them out.

They would expect to see Pavel, would want to know where he was. If she told them the truth, they might send another man down to be with her. The thought made her shiver. If they came in the day, she could tell them Pavel had taken the car to the garage to have the clutch repaired, that it was a big job, and he would have to wait several hours. But they might come in the night, like they had last time when they'd brought the man who was now in the punishment block. What would she say then?

How long would Pavel be kept in the hospital? They'd told her it was too early to say. Maybe five days if he made a good recovery, but it might be longer. He would still need to be looked after, would require lots of care when he came home. She'd told them she would look after him.

She smoked another cigarette, then took the bottle to her bedroom, and sat for a moment on the big four-poster bed before changing into her nightdress. Her wedding photographs were arranged in an album, which she kept on the shelf above the headboard. Pouring another glass of wine, she fluffed the double pillows, sat up with her back against them, and opened the album. Turning the pages slowly, looking at the photographs, remembering how happy she had been that day, she soon fell asleep; the album lay open on Pavel's side of the bed.

Bujare slept deeply. She dreamt her mobile phone was ringing, ringing… she opened her eyes, saw the lit display screen, and heard the sound coming from the phone on her bedside table. In the reflected light from the phone, the face of the alarm clock was showing 3 a.m. She sat up quickly, snatched the phone.

'Yes?'

Pavel's voice was loud, barking at her. 'Bujare! Come now! They're trying to kill me.'

Bujare's heart pounded. 'Who is trying to kill you?'

He was still barking at her. 'Don't ask stupid questions. The doctors and the nurses. They are trying to kill me. You must come straight away!'

'I'm coming!' Bujare said. 'I'm coming now.'

'Hurry!' he said, and the line went dead.

Scrambling into the clothes she had discarded three hours earlier, she rushed to the bathroom and wiped her face with a hot, wet, flannel. Then she rang the taxi company. The phone rang for a long time before an answering machine told her to call back after 6 a.m. She remembered the taxi service did not operate after midnight.

She sat on the edge of the bed, her head in her hands, her heart still pounding. Pavel needed her. She couldn't wait until the taxi company opened at 6 a.m. Pavel had said she must come straight away. She lit a cigarette, puffed at it while she paced up and down.

The white van! She remembered the white van parked in the shed, the one they'd brought the girl in. They hadn't wanted to drive it back. They had taken the red SUV instead and hidden the van under a dust cover. Rumesh had told Pavel that the van was not to be used. But it was their fault that Pavel had to drive the SUV with the bad clutch, it was their fault he was lying in hospital. And people were trying to kill him. Pavel had told her to come at once.

Bujare decided she would use the van just this one time. They wouldn't know. She searched for the keys to the van in the kitchen drawers, then ran to search the drawers in the dining room, but they weren't there. She felt the panic, made herself take deep breaths while she tried to think where Pavel would have put the keys. She ran to the bedroom, found them in the drawer of his bed-side table.

She shivered in the cold night air when she stepped outside. And it was pitch black. Stepping back in, she pulled her coat off the hook and grabbed the heavy-duty torch from the side shelf. She ran to the shed, holding the torch in front of her. She pulled frantically at the dust cover over the van but found she needed both hands. Swinging the torch around the shed, she saw the empty barrel in the corner and rolled it over nearer the van. She put the torch on it, pointing it so the beam gave her the light she needed to get the dust cover off.

The van started straight away. She found the headlights switch and managed to find the reverse gear on her third attempt. And then she was off, down the rutted track that led from the farmhouse to the road. The world was asleep; there were no lights showing as she drove through the village of Pennal. Bujare drove at a good speed, but kept within the speed limit, remembering she should not attract attention to the van. She shuddered as she came to the right-hand turn at the bridge; the police had told her that was where Pavel had almost died.

After the bridge, it was a straight road. She left one hand on the wheel, put her right hand over her breast. Her heart was still pounding. Who was trying to kill Pavel? She must have misheard when he said it was the doctors and the nurses. But why were they not protecting him? The questions in her head would not go away.

Over the whole twenty-five-mile journey, no headlights appeared in her rear mirror. Only three cars passed her, going in the opposite direction. There was no problem finding a parking space at the hospital. She ran to the main entrance, pushed the door. It was locked. Taking a step back, confused, she looked through the glass doors to see if there was anyone she could call. There was no one. Then she noticed the sign with an arrow pointing towards a night door. She followed the arrows around to the side of the building until she came to the night door.

Going in through the door, she found herself in a completely different part of the hospital to the main entrance. A long, empty corridor stretched before her. Bujare was getting out of breath. Panting, she hurried along the corridor, looking for a lift to take her to the sixth floor, to where Pavel was. There was no lift, just corridors branching off either side of the one she was on. There was no one to ask. She took the right-hand corridor which stretched into the distance. She kept walking and was on the verge of tears, when a doctor, on his way out, directed her to the lift.

When she arrived at Pavel's bedside he was lying in his bed, the morphine drip still in his arm.

A doctor and a nurse were standing at the foot of his bed. Bujare didn't recognise either of them. Pavel saw her come in, beckoned her over urgently. She leant forward to give him a kiss on his cheek, but his left hand pulled her head down close to his mouth and he hissed in her ear.

'They're trying to kill me.'

She started to raise her head up, but he hissed again.

'Don't use your phone. They've got our phones bugged. They'll know what we are saying.'

Bujare stepped back, bewildered, and looked at the young doctor.

'He's been like this since he woke up,' the doctor said. 'And he won't let the nurse give him his pill.'

Bujare took a few deep breaths, exhaled slowly, 'Let me see if I can talk to him.' She took Pavel's hand in one of hers, stroked his cheek with the other, whispered, 'They're not trying to kill you, Pavel. The nurse just wants to give you a pill to help you.' Then she added, 'And our phones aren't bugged.'

Pavel stared at her wide eyed. 'I thought you were on my side,' he hissed bitterly. 'I thought I could trust you.' He pushed her away.

She looked helplessly at the doctor. 'I don't understand. Why is he like this?'

'It must be the morphine drip,' the doctor said. 'Some people react adversely to opiates. Morphine induced hallucinations are more common than most people realise.' He turned to the nurse. 'Let's see if we can take the drip out.'

The nurse approached Pavel, but as she put her hand out to the drip, he grabbed hold of her forearm. She tried to free herself, but he held her in a vice like grip. The young nurse stood still, unsure what to do. Bujare watched with her mouth open. Three minutes later, Pavel still had hold of the nurse's forearm. Her face was red, the skin on her forearm was becoming mottled. She looked at the doctor, but he didn't move. Bujare looked from the nurse to the doctor, realised he was not willing to use physical force. At least not in front of her.

'Let me do it,' she said, walking around to the other side of the bed where the nurse was being held. She put her hand on Pavel's hand where he gripped the nurse and said, 'Let her go, Pavel.' When he didn't respond, she moved around a bit more so she could get both of her hands around his fingers. It took all her strength to prise his fingers back enough for the nurse to withdraw her arm.

'Let me try to give him the pill,' Bujare said.

She held out the pill and a glass of water. 'Take this pill, Pavel. It will help to make you better.'

He pushed her hand away. 'It's poison. I told you they're trying to kill me.'

Bujare left the room, walked out of the ward. She paced up and down the long corridor, trying to gather her thoughts, to keep herself calm. When she returned to the ward, the doctor was at the central desk.

'How long will he be like this?' she asked him.

'We'll take the morphine drip away when he falls asleep. He might be back to normal when he wakes up. Or it could be another forty-eight hours before the effect of the morphine wears off.'

Bujare sat by Pavel's bed. He stared at her, but she remained silent, not knowing anymore what to say to him. After an hour had passed, he fell asleep. She watched him for another ten minutes. Then, as she stood up to leave, he opened his eyes and stared at her. She leant forward to stroke him, but he pulled his arm away as soon as he felt her touch and glared at her fiercely. So, she just sat and waited and tried very hard not to cry.

After another half hour, he closed his eyes, and when they were still closed fifteen minutes later, she slipped away and went to find the doctor. She told him Pavel was sleeping and that she would be back in the evening. Before she left the ward, she searched for the nurse, found her talking to another patient. Bujare waited until she was free.

'How is your arm?'

The nurse held up her arm. Bujare shook her head when she saw the bruising that would turn black and blue.

'I'm so sorry,' she said. 'My husband is normally a gentle man. I've never seen him like this.'

It was just before seven in the morning – the large car park that had been empty when she arrived, was now filling up. She tried to remember

where in the car park she had left the white van.
When she found it, she breathed a sigh of relief.
She started the engine, then remembered her seat
belt. She had trouble locking the seat belt in place,
could feel the tiredness overtaking her. She
decided to rest her eyes for fifteen minutes.
Turning the engine off, she moved the seat back to
make herself more comfortable.

She was awakened by a sharp sound; a nurse in
uniform was rapping on the window with her car
keys. Bujare took a moment to lower the window.

'Are you okay?' the nurse looked concerned.

'Yes, I am fine. I was just having a rest,' Bujare
said. 'Thank you.'

The nurse, who was just starting her shift,
smiled understandingly. Watching her go through
the main entrance of the hospital, Bujare wondered
if she would be on Pavel's ward. She looked at her
watch and was startled to find she had slept for two
hours.

This time, she had no trouble with the seat belt.
She started the van and took the road to
Machynlleth. It had rained while she was asleep;
the road surface was wet, but the traffic was
relatively light. She drove slowly, her mind in a
whirl, trying to put together what was happening
to her.

The white BMW that she first noticed in her
rear-view mirror as she drove past the clock tower
in Machynlleth was still there after she crossed the
bridge and turned left. She went through Pennal,

slowed down, and signalled to turn left into the track leading to the farm. As she did so, the white car overtook her and disappeared into the distance.

Chapter 36

Ross got the phone call just after 2 a.m. It was Armstrong, the same inspector who had been on duty the night Walter Price died. 'I think we've got your man,' he said. 'The photograph you circulated, the man with the ponytail. We've found him.'

Ross jumped out of bed. 'His name is Rumesh Zeka. I'm on my way. Where have you got him? I want to interview the bastard.'

'You won't be able to do that. He's dead.'

Ross swore, paced the bedroom. 'Dead? How?'

'His throat has been slit,' Armstrong said. 'And there's a stab wound in his chest. Not sure of the sequence, but the stab wound is like the one from your victim in the car park. The knife dragged across his chest, blood everywhere.'

'Where did you find him?'

'Some kids found the body – two thirteen-year-old boys. They entered a condemned house that's waiting to be demolished and stumbled across the body. That was earlier this evening, but they didn't tell their parents until an hour ago – they were scared they'd be in trouble for going into the house.'

'Where's the body now?'

'It's at the morgue; we moved it out quickly because of the building being unsafe.'

'Okay, I'll meet you at the morgue. I'll need the addresses of the kids who found the body. They'll have to be interviewed with their parents present.' He cleared his throat. 'Have you told anyone else?'

'No, I haven't. I phoned you as soon as I recognised him from the photograph.' There was a slight pause, then Armstrong added, 'I've heard on the grapevine that your investigation is being handed over to Cunningham. But until the handover has taken place, as far as I'm concerned, it's still your case.'

'Thanks,' Ross said, ringing off.

He phoned Bridges, told him about Armstrong's phone call, said he'd meet him at the morgue. Then he rang Helen Jackson and counted; she answered on the thirteenth ring.

'Another sleepless night?' she said. 'I don't suppose you're ringing in the middle of the night for a chat, so it must be work. What do you want?'

Ross explained.

'It's my day off today,' she said.

'Armstrong says the chest wound looks very similar to Walter Price's wound,' Ross said. 'And you did the autopsy on him. Be good if you did this one too. It's urgent.'

'It always is with you.' There was a long pause followed by a heavy sigh.

'I'll be there in an hour,' the pathologist said.

Angie was surprised when her doorbell rang at 9 a.m. and Philip announced his presence through the intercom. She buzzed him through, was waiting at her door when he came up the stairs two at a time.

'No Sunday lie-in?' she greeted him. 'And why the wide smile?'

'I have good reason to smile,' Philip said. 'It looks like I'm not going to go to prison after all.'

They sat in the kitchen. Angie put the percolator on while Philip told her about finding Becky waiting outside his flat and the state of her face.

'She's been in a relationship with a much older man for the last year. She said they're both mad keen Aston Villa fans – she met him when they were on the same supporters coach going to an away match. I've never met him, but I have noticed bruising on her face a few times in the past. It turns out he hits her – usually when he's been drinking; she says he's always apologetic when he sobers up.'

Angie grimaced, 'Why does she stay with him?'

'Strange as it seems, the football has got a lot to do with it. Becky says she really enjoys going to home matches with him or going to the pub if an away game is being televised. She stops over at his flat on Saturday nights and during the week if there's a midweek match on television.'

'My dad used to have a season ticket for Aston Villa. I still keep an eye on their results. They won last night, didn't they?'

Philip nodded. 'Yes. And Becky had her interview with the auditors yesterday. She said she was dumfounded when they showed her the fraudulent claim forms with my signature. She knew she and I are the only ones who have access to my electronic signature, and she was always careful to log out of her computer if she left her desk.'

He took the cup of coffee that Angie held out. 'Becky said she was upset; felt she must have slipped up somehow. Then she remembered Graham – that's his name – picked her up from work once when they were going to an early evening match. She'd left him in the office while she got changed, only logged out when they were leaving. She realised he'd been alone in the office with the computer while she was getting changed.'

Angie nodded. 'And she met him last night because the Villa match was being televised?'

'Yes. They were going to watch the match at the pub. She told him there was a problem at work and reminded him of the time she'd left him alone in her office. She asked him if he'd interfered with her computer. And that's when he went ballistic, said he wouldn't stand there and be accused. He started hitting her. She ran out of the flat; he chased after her, but she made it to her car and drove away.'

Angie looked at Philip quizzically. 'All that proves is that she's with the wrong man. How does that help your case?'

'Because Becky knew Graham would go to the pub to watch the match. She waited until the game had started and returned to his flat. She had her own set of keys, so she let herself in and searched his bedroom. She found a sheaf of blank claim forms with my signature on them. She took one of the forms with her and went back to her flat. But she couldn't settle. So she drove to my flat – she knows my address. I was about to go to bed when she rang my bell.'

'Now I understand why you're upbeat. What did you do?'

'I phoned Anna, our principal, and told her what Becky had said. She asked Becky to come to her house and bring the blank claim form with her. Anna rang me afterwards to say she had contacted the police.'

'So, you're in the clear.'

'I think so,' Philip said. 'I'm hoping the police can get a confession out of Graham. But yes, I'm feeling a lot better today. In fact, I feel like celebrating. How about you join me for dinner tonight?'

'Dinner sounds good, but let's wait and see how our investigation goes today.'

She cocked her head to one side, listening. 'Hang on. My phone is in the bedroom. I think I can hear it ringing.'

It was Roxanne. 'I've been back in Birmingham an hour. When were you planning to come over?'

'10 a.m.?'

'Good timing!' Roxanne said. 'I think I've solved your phone mystery.'

'What! How?

'I'll have to show you,' Roxanne said, ending the call.

Chapter 37

Roxanne was on the phone when they rang the front doorbell. She kept the phone to her ear, opened the door with one hand, and gestured for them to go into the lounge before disappearing into the kitchen to continue her call.

'That was the Practice Manager, warning me our senior partner is going to be phoning me,' she said when she came back in. 'Apparently, he's not a happy man.'

'Not happy with you?' Angie asked her.

'Yes. We don't really get on. I'm the newest partner, so I don't know what he was like in his younger days, but I feel he's far too focused on the bottom line. Probably something to do with the fact he's due to retire in a couple of years. The Practice Manager says he's concerned about the number of days I've had off. He doesn't understand why I'm not back at work now that the funeral is over.'

'Is he aware of the circumstances?'

'I haven't told him personally, but I'm sure the others have. Anyway, we'll discuss it when he phones.'

Smiling, she looked from one to the other. 'I've got a present for you, Philip. And one for you, too, Angie. Well, sort of presents. But before that, do you want tea or coffee?'

She went to make the tea, came back with her hands behind her back while the kettle was boiling.

'This is for you, Philip.' Roxanne held out her hand. It was a framed photograph of a younger Philip with Walter. They were sitting in a restaurant, side by side, holding champagne glasses aloft, and smiling at the camera. There was a cake on the table in front of them. Philip held the framed photograph in his hands, turned away for a moment before turning back to them.

'It was taken on my eighteenth birthday. Walter took me out for dinner at an Italian restaurant in Acocks Green. He was friendly with the owner; he'd asked him to bake a cake for me.' Philip fell quiet as he remembered.

'I found it with some other old photographs in his bedroom,' Roxanne said. 'And thought after our conversation, you'd want to have it.' She looked at Angie. 'I'm assuming you're aware of our conversation?'

'She is,' Philip said, as Angie nodded.

Roxanne hugged Philip, stood back and met his eyes. 'Put what happened behind you now, Philip. Get on with your life. Dig deep. That's what he would want you to do.'

Turning to Angie, she held out an iPhone. 'This is the reconditioned mobile phone that was delivered this morning. I don't want it. It'll only remind me of what happened.'

Nodding, Angie took the phone from her outstretched hand with a puzzled look. 'Thanks. But this doesn't solve the mystery?'

'No. But your second present does. I should be angry, but in truth I didn't know whether to laugh or cry. Look behind the sofa you're sitting on.'

Angie looked. She saw a black handset in its base, and an answering machine with a small oblong box attached to it. She turned back to Roxanne as understanding dawned.

'Walter didn't get rid of all the handsets for his landline?'

'No, he bloody well didn't,' Roxanne said. 'I can't believe he lied to me. He got rid of the three downstairs handsets but kept this one in his bedroom. I found it when I was searching for Philip's photograph. It was plugged in to the same old socket, but he'd pushed it under the bottom shelf of his bedside table, so it wasn't visible. Crafty old devil!'

Philip was looking at the handset, laughing. Roxanne looked at him with raised eyebrows.

'It's the same landline setup he had when I lived here,' Philip said. 'The one I helped him choose. He was proud of the fact he learned to use its functions. I told Angie he'd find it hard to get rid of it, even after he retired.'

'You were with him when he bought this?'

'I was. Do you want to hear the story behind why Walter bought this handset?'

'Yes,' Roxanne said. 'I'd really like to know what was so bloody special about it!'

'Do you remember a girl called Natalie James?' Philip asked Angie. 'She committed suicide when she was in year 9. Walter held a special assembly in the term before I came here to live with him.'

Angie nodded. 'Yes, I remember.'

'Well, one evening, Walter told me he believed Natalie James had committed suicide because she was being abused by her stepfather. The family were being supervised by Social Services and Walter said he'd shared his suspicions several times over the phone with the social worker. But when there was an enquiry, the social worker denied Walter had ever voiced his suspicions. There was nothing in their files. Walter showed the investigating panel the notes he's made in his green notebook, but they said there was no corroboration.'

'What's the link with the landline?' Roxane said, lips pursed.

'I told Walter the inquiry panel would have believed him if he's recorded his telephone conversations. He said he didn't know that was possible and was amazed when I told him he could do that at home – if he had the right landline setup. So, he asked me to go with him to get the right setup. We went to an electronics shop, told them what we wanted. We bought four handsets, an answering machine and that little oblong box that made it possible to record conversations when it was attached to the answering machine. Walter was over the moon.'

'Did he ever use it?'

'Yes. We set it up in his study,' Philip said. 'Social Services had agreed to Walter taking me in, but only if he consented to a weekly phone check-up, and a monthly home visit. Every time the social worker phoned, Walter had to speak to her first. Then he would leave the room and I had to speak to her. We recorded both conversations every week. I showed Walter the sequence of buttons the first few times, but eventually he got the hang of it. He was very pleased with himself. It was his one and only technological triumph.'

Roxanne sat back in the sofa, staring into space. Philip saw the tear escape, gave her a moment.

'Did he ever explain any of this to you?'

'No,' she said. 'We never talked technology. Every time I tried, he changed the subject. Even if it was about the benefit of having a dishwasher. I guess he felt I was bent on changing his lifestyle.' She stood up from the sofa. 'Maybe I should've been more accepting of the way he was. Of what he felt comfortable with.'

She'd left her phone in the kitchen; they heard it ringing.

'That's probably the senior partner,' Roxanne said. 'I'd better take it.' She headed off to the kitchen and closed the door behind her, leaving Philip and Angie in the lounge.

Philip saw Angie staring at the handset. 'What are you thinking?'

'This must be the phone Walter used to make the first call to Theresa Vines – the one early in the morning.'

'And?'

'The men who killed him knew about the green notebook, knew to look in the study. We think Walter turned to someone he believed he could trust for advice or even help. Somehow the information was passed to the Albanians.'

Philip looked at her, 'You're wondering if Walter used this phone when he asked for help?'

'Yes.'

'Walter had a cautious side to him,' Philip said. 'If he thought he'd come across highly sensitive information, I doubt he would have revealed it over the telephone. It's more likely he would've gone to see the person.'

'That makes sense. But he might have made a phone call to arrange a meeting.'

Philip nodded, 'Do you want me to see if I can get the last number he dialled?' He was moving as he spoke, knowing what her answer would be. The connection was on the other side of the room, on the wall, by the larger sofa. Philip plugged the handset in, got the dialling tone, pressed one of the symbols, and showed Angie the handset.

'The number showing on the display is the last one dialled on this handset. Do you want me to dial it?'

'Yes.'

They heard it ring once, then go straight to voicemail. An automated voice told them the office was closed and would reopen at 9 a.m. on Monday morning.

'Does it tell you what day and time Walter dialled the call?'

'No,' Philip said. 'If I remember correctly, it does that only for the last received call.'

'Try that. Let's see who the last person was to phone Walter. Maybe it was the person who he'd phoned, returning his call.'

Pressing the button to put the speakerphone on Philip dialled 1471. The operator's voice was loud: she gave the number of the last person who had called and the date and time that the call was received.

'It's the same number Walter dialled – the one that went to voicemail,' Philip said.

'And it was made at 4.50 p.m. on the day that Walter died,' Angie said. 'We know from the CCTV that Walter left the Refuge at 3.55. He would have got back to this house about 4.25. If he phoned someone who he thought could help him, that could well have been about 4.45. And then that person phoned him back five minutes later.'

'It fits. Sounds like the right sequence of events,' Philip said.

Angie leant forward. 'I wish I knew what was said. I've got a feeling it was this conversation that led to Walter being murdered.'

They sat without speaking. Then Angie stood up. 'Let's go. At least we can trace the number.' She put her head around the kitchen door, but Roxanne still had her phone to her ear. Angie indicated they were going, and Roxanne gave her a thumbs up, signalled she would phone her later.

Philip was still sitting down when Angie walked back into the lounge.

'I've been thinking,' he said. 'Wondering if Walter would have recorded this last conversation. It's the sort of thing he might do if he was worried.'

Angie stared at him. 'Do you know how to find out?'

'It's the same set-up we used to record our conversations with my social worker. I know how to play it back if he recorded it.'

Philip knelt, attached the answer phone to the handset and the little oblong box to the answer phone. 'Here goes,' he said.

Angie felt her heartbeat increase as she waited. They heard the ringing, then Walter's voice answering, then the other person responding. They listened in silence to the conversation until Walter ended it. Angie sat back in the sofa, her head spinning. She didn't move for a full minute while she replayed in her head what she'd just heard. Then she stood up, felt in her pocket for her phone, frowned when she couldn't find it. Philip was still sitting, staring at her, wide eyed.

'Thank you, Philip,' Angie said. 'Can you do that again so I can see the sequence. Then can you disconnect this set-up – I've got to take it back to the station for Ross and Bridges to hear.'

They were just opening the front door when Roxanne appeared. 'I thought you'd gone,' she said.

'Just leaving.' Angie pointed to the plastic bag Philip was holding. 'We'd like to take this landline set-up with us, see if we can learn anything from it. Is that okay?'

'Be my guest. I don't really want to see that bloody thing again.'

'Thanks,' Angie said. 'How did it go with the senior partner?'

'Helpful. We had a clear-the-air type conversation. He was more understanding than I expected, told me his own father had died suddenly a couple of years ago. But one of our other partners has taken ill, and she's got a full appointments book for Monday morning. I've agreed to cover for her. I'll be back here the following weekend.' She followed them out of the door, tapped Angie on the shoulder until she turned around.

'I know you won't give up until you find the man who murdered my father,' she said. 'I just wanted to thank you for the support.'

Angie squeezed her hand gently. 'I've been meaning to ask you since you mentioned him. My PCC – George Kershaw – who gave the eulogy at Walter's funeral. Was he the tanned, athletic looking man who was one of your pallbearers?'

'That's the one,' Roxanne said. 'I think the tan is genuine. Apparently, he's got a house in Majorca, goes there for weekends. In fact, he told me at the funeral that he was going there this weekend.'

Back in the car they found Angie's phone under the front seat. There were three missed calls from Ross. She started to phone him but changed her mind, and asked Philip to take her to the station.

Neither spoke during the drive, but as he pulled up outside the station, Philip said, 'One question. Did Walter know your Chief Constable?'

'I don't know.' Angie said. She got out of the car and leaned in through the window. 'I'll go and find Ross. He'll know what to do.'

But Ross was not in his office. And Bridges was nowhere to be seen. Putting the plastic bag on Ross's desk, she took out her mobile phone, and saw that as well as the three missed calls, she had a voicemail.

Chapter 38

Erag always slept in the nude. In the morning he had woken to find the sheet wet with his semen. He smiled as fragments of the dream about Elira came back to him. He smiled too, because he was free from Rumesh telling him what to do. No more orders. And no more cigarette smoke.

Waiting outside when the doors of the gymnastics centre opened at 8 a.m., he'd spent the first hour on the special mat, starting off again with backward somersaults from a standing start. Two other early morning gymnasts stopped their routine to watch him. The second hour he exercised with the free weights.

Now, back in his apartment, looking in his bathroom mirror, he stroked his face with his fingertips to check the fresh razor blade had given him the smoothness he wanted. Satisfied, he spent the next five minutes with the concealer tool, holding it like a pen, dabbing the pock marks on his cheeks one at a time, rubbing each one gently with the tip of his index finger to blend in the cream. The pock marks were the legacy of the bad acne from his teenage years; the concealer pen made a difference, but he only used it on special occasions.

Holding a rolled-up hand towel in front of him at waist height, he squeezed and twisted it, watching his upper body muscles rippling. It gave him confidence, made him feel good about himself to see the strength of his upper body: pecs, shoulders, biceps, triceps – the muscles he had used when he worked through his daily routine on the rings.

He'd tried the pommel horse, preferred it at first. But the trainer had told him he was too short at five foot five to excel at it. 'The best ones on the horse will always be the tall ones,' he said. 'Focus on the rings. You are more suited to them.'

It was his grandmother who had taken him to the gymnastics club when he was five; he'd gone to live with her when his mother ran away with another man. Erag won many junior competitions on the rings, regional competitions too. It was only when he got to the finals of the national competition but no further, that he realised there were others better than him. After that, he'd lost heart and given up the competitions, despite his grandmother's pleading.

He had seen others his age, driving around in big cars, flashing rolls of banknotes in the bars. Welcomed into one of the gangs, Erag got noticed in the fights against their rivals by the boss man, who took him under his wing. The first time he used a knife, he'd felt a rush of blood as the blade pierced the skin of his victim. He'd tried a gun once but found it too impersonal. He didn't get the same buzz. So he stuck to the knife, enjoyed watching the faces of his victims as the blade went in.

Putting the hand towel back on the rail, he reached for the bottle of aftershave. He wanted to smell good for the girl. And look good. The new designer polo top he had bought earlier was light blue with a darker blue collar and blue edging around the chest pocket with the button. It was short-sleeved; you could see the muscles of his biceps and if he left the top two buttons undone, you could glimpse the contour of his pecs. He thought the girl would like that.

Erag had been with many girls, but never had an actual relationship with one. They were prostitutes or girls his friends passed around. They gave him the sex he needed but no more. He didn't understand why some of them seemed scared of him. But this girl in the punishment block on the farm was different. She was respectable. He thought Elira was the most beautiful girl he'd ever seen. He wanted her to like him. To want him.

Albert had told him to kill both Rumesh and the girl – the police knew what they looked like and were searching for them. Erag had enjoyed killing Rumesh, but he didn't think Elira had to die. Albert just wanted to stop her from talking about what she had overheard. Erag thought he could keep her at the farm, visit her once or maybe even twice a week; it wasn't that long a drive to the farm from Birmingham. He would take her presents and they could drink wine and sleep together overnight in the farmhouse. He could even take her nice clothes and shoes for her to wear when they were together.

He would tell the old woman to give her better food during the week. Grateful that he was sparing her life, overtime, the girl would grow to like him. They could have a proper relationship, talk to each other; he could tell her what it felt like to be up in the air on the rings during the tournaments, hearing the audience applauding his skill and his strength. He still missed that.

Opening the wardrobe door, he checked his sideways profile first in the full-length mirror on the inside of the door, then turned to face the mirror. The new polo shirt went well with his black leather trousers and his new trainers. Erag liked what he saw, thought the girl would too.

It was 11.30. He'd planned to leave at noon, arrive at the farm about 2.30. But as he stood there, thinking about the girl, the hardness between his legs growing, Erag had another idea. He would go into the city centre first, to the jewellers in the Bull Ring. He would take a present for her. She would like that.

***

Angie waited impatiently for Ross and Bridges to return. She'd located the phone socket in Ross's office and attached the phone set-up from Walter's house. She felt again the slow burning anger that had overtaken her on the drive back from Walter's house to the station, as she worked through, in her mind, the implications of what she had heard. It was partly Walter's death. But it was also the betrayal of trust by someone he had befriended in the past and turned to when he needed help. And the undermining of her belief in the integrity of a justice system she considered herself part of. She felt tainted.

She dealt with her impatience by getting a cup of coffee from the canteen and forcing herself to read the National Crime Agency reports on organised crime. There were copies of press coverage of a lap dancing club in Broad Street that had been closed down. There was a photograph – the sign outside read "Gentleman's Club". Men out for a good time were encouraged by scantily clad girls to drink themselves into a stupor; their credit cards used while they were unconscious. Customers paid more if they wanted to avail themselves of the extra services offered by girls in the VIP booths. NCA reported that the business interests behind the club were Albanian.

The NCA also reported that Balkan criminals were moving away from their traditional smuggling of heroin because of their location being on the opium trail from Afghanistan to

Europe; instead, they were now focusing on the trafficking of cocaine, which was far more profitable.

Ross and Bridges came back just before 12 noon. They had been interviewing the two boys who discovered the body. 'We've had an eventful morning,' Bridges said. 'Did you get Ross's message?'

Angie knew from Ross's voicemail that Rumesh Zeka's body had been found in a condemned house. 'Yes, I got the message. Do we know how it happened?'

'We have our suspicions,' Ross said, 'but let's wait for the pathologist's report.' He ignored Bridge's smile. 'Helen Jackson should phone us soon. I can fill you in on how the body was discovered.'

'Okay, but first I've got something you need to hear.'

The excitement in her voice alerted them. Their eyes focused on her. 'You were going to see the daughter – Roxanne – to see if we could get to the bottom of Walter's phone calls,' Ross said. 'I take it you've solved the mystery.'

Angie nodded as she took a mobile phone out of the plastic bag by her feet and placed it on Ross's desk. 'That's the reconditioned mobile Walter sent for. But they only delivered it this morning. Roxanne thought Walter had got rid of all four of the handsets from his landline, but he hadn't. He got rid of three but kept the fourth one hidden in his bedroom. That was the phone he used when he made the morning call to Theresa Vines. He used it again, later on Wednesday, right after he returned from the refuge. The person he phoned was with someone, but he phoned Walter back a few minutes later. Walter confided in him, asked for his help.'

Angie had their full attention now. She had moved so she was standing with her back to the window. Bridges remained standing, his back to the door, his eyes fixed on her face. Ross, sitting at his desk, swung around in the swivel chair to face her, spoke quietly.

'Do we know who that person was?'

'Yes, we do. The last number dialled came up on the screen of the handset. We dialled it and it went straight to voicemail.'

This time it was Bridges speaking quietly, 'Whose voice mail?'

'The office of George Kershaw, the Police and Crime Commissioner. Our PCC,' Angie said, struggling to keep her voice on an even keel.

There was a long moment of silence while they processed that. It was Bridges who broke it. 'Why would he phone the PCC? Did he know him?'

'Walter knew him from when they were both headteachers. Roxanne told me Walter used to mentor George Kershaw, that he would come to their house, they would spend time in his study. They played golf together. He did the eulogy at Walter's funeral.'

Ross cleared his throat. 'So, Walter phoned the PCC's office, and someone from the office phoned him back. But we don't know for sure who that person was. And we don't know what was said. So it's speculation when you say that Walter spoke to the PCC and confided in him. Even if it was the PCC, the conversation might have been about golf. Right?'

Without waiting for her answer, he turned to Bridges. 'I could murder a coffee.'

Bridges was halfway out of the door when Angie said, 'It's not speculation. We have a recording of the conversation.'

Bridges came back into the room, closing the door behind him.

'Did you just say you have a recording of the conversation?'

'Yes.' Angie told them about Walter's bad experience with Social Services, and the phone set-up he bought afterwards. She told them a little about Walter taking Philip in to stop him being taken into care and the recorded conversations with Social Services. And then she told them that, with Philips's help, they'd checked and found Walter's recording of his last phone conversation.

Angie had copied the recording on to her phone while she was waited for them to return. She put her phone on speaker and they listened to the conversation between Walter Price and George Kershaw. Ross and Bridges listened in utter silence, but she saw the range of emotions play across their faces. The recording ended.

'What a bastard!' Bridges looked pointedly at Ross. 'Now we know why they only searched the study. And how they found out Walter had taken the girl to the refuge.'

'Roxanne says the PCC is in Majorca for the weekend,' Angie said. 'He's not back until Monday.'

Ross stood up and walked over to the window. He stood still with his back towards them, his hands in his pockets, as he stared out over the boating pool.

Bridges moved his head, beckoning to Angie to follow him. 'We'll get those coffees,' he said out loud as she followed him out of the office.

She caught up with him on the stairs. 'What do you think Ross will do?'

'He needs some thinking time. We're heading for a media frenzy that will undoubtedly damage our credibility with the public. A decision like this is well above Ross's pay grade. Procedure would be he passes it upwards to the Deputy. But I doubt he's going to do that.'

Ross was sitting at his desk, finishing off a sausage roll, when they took the coffees back.

'You're sure Roxanne told you the PCC is away for the weekend in Majorca, back on Monday?'

'Yes, she said he's got a house on the island.'

'Right,' Ross said. 'For the time being, we keep this to ourselves.'

He took out his mobile phone, held it out to Angie. 'I'd like a recording of that conversation on my phone.'

Chapter 39

Ross filled Angie in on what they knew about Rumesh Zeka's murder. 'The two thirteen-year-old boys who discovered the body in the condemned house around 8.30 p.m. ran straight home but didn't tell their parents; they were frightened they would be in trouble for entering the house. No surprise that the boys were terrified, couldn't sleep. They kept texting each other until finally, well after midnight, they agreed to tell their parents at the same time. The parents rang each other, then they rang the police. Armstrong was the Duty Inspector. He went to the address, found the body, recognised Rumesh Zeka from the photograph we had circulated and rang me. They had to get the body out immediately because of the state of the building.'

'You think Rumesh Zeka fell out with his partner and was killed during a fight?'

'That's one possibility. More likely there was a leak. If they found out we'd circulated his photograph and were actively looking for him, they might have decided killing him was the safest option. Dead men can't talk.'

Bridges said, 'Given what we now know, the leak could have come internally from the PCC.'

Ross nodded. 'Or from Interpol. It wouldn't be the first time.'

'You said the house was due for demolition,' Angie said. 'Was he killed somewhere else and then the body moved to the house?'

'Probably not,' Ross said. 'There was a lot of blood at the scene and a cardboard box with 12 bags of flour next to the body. Forensics are going over it. It's possible he was lured to the condemned house under the pretext of picking up a box full of cocaine.'

Ross's phone rang. He took the call and listened, 'Thanks, Helen, I owe you another one.'

'That was Helen Jackson. The body hadn't been lying there long – less than five hours. She doesn't think the body was moved – she says the amount of blood confirms he was killed where they found the body.'

'What about how he was killed?'

'His throat was slit. She thinks, judging from the angle of the wound that his head was pulled back to expose his throat, probably by a shorter man from behind, yanking his ponytail. She says the chest wound is gratuitous violence – he would have died from the throat wound. She confirms there is a marked similarity between Walter's chest wound and this one. She's pretty sure they were done by the same person, using the same knife.'

'We might be dealing with a psychopath here,' Bridges said. 'He enjoys the act of killing.'

Ross's phone rang again. He answered, sat up straight, then gestured with his free hand that they should leave the room.

Angie followed Bridges out of Ross's office. Bridges turned to speak to her, saw the look on her face. 'You're wondering why Ross ordered us out?'

She nodded silently.

'Ross is breaking the protocols; that's why he doesn't want you in the room. This is heading for a disciplinary and he's trying to protect your future career as best he can. As far as you know, he's following procedure. You're following orders.'

Bridges gave her a moment, then he said, 'How about stepping outside for some fresh air?'

They went out into the car park. Bridges patted his pockets, produced a packet of cigarettes.

'Fresh air?' Angie smiled at him.

'Almost stopped. Just an occasional one in the car park. My new love doesn't like it and I aim to please.' He held the packet out to Angie who shook her head. He took out a lighter. 'Ross will be gone soon. I've got just over five years left. We've done our bit. The future of the force lies with people like you. And from what we've seen, both Ross and I think that, given the chance, you've got a bright career ahead of you.'

'Thank you,' Angie said, moved by his words. 'I hope I get the chance to prove you right.'

Bridges pursed his lips, blew a smoke ring, and gazed at Angie steadily. 'Feel free to tell me to mind my own business. You've never said what happened in Iraq. We've been wondering, but not wanting to ask.'

Angie turned away, stared into the distance, remembered the psychiatrist's warning: '*You'll chose when the time is right. You'll know when you feel strong enough to talk about it. It will be a major step forward. But only do it when you feel ready.*'

Was she strong enough now? Was she ready?

She turned to face Bridges but looked past him as she spoke quietly in a matter-of-fact tone. 'There's been a relationship between the British and Iraqi police forces since our officers went over to help with their training after the Iraqi war. They have all female classes now at the Baghdad Police College. I don't know how I was chosen, but I received an invitation from our Police Leadership College to represent them at last year's graduation ceremony. Two of us flew out – I went with a female DI from the Metropolitan Police. It was supposed to be a five-day visit.'

Angie paused, took a deep breath and exhaled slowly before continuing.

'I spent the first two days with the female trainees at Baghdad Police College, talking them through some of the investigations I'd been involved in. They learn English as a second language, so it was useful language practice for them as well. One of them, Wafaa, invited me to have dinner with her family on the second evening. I played with her six-year-old twins.'

She paused again to control her breathing. Bridges stubbed his cigarette out on the wall, but held on to the stub, waiting for her to continue. Angie shifted her gaze to make eye contact with him.

'The graduation ceremony was on the third day. The women wore their blue uniform shirts. They looked so proud of what they'd achieved. The Police Academy is in a fortified compound with security barriers. When they were leaving at the end of the ceremony, as the crowd stepped out onto the road, a suicide bomber driving a car rigged with explosives careered into them, causing an explosion. I was in the compound, but the blast still blew me over and I had minor injuries. When I opened my eyes, Wafaa was staring at me. Just her head on her torso. There were bits of bodies all around me. Nineteen of them died.'

Bridges put his hand gently on her shoulder.

'They flew me back the next day and told me to take two weeks off. I thought I'd get over it, but the flashback of Wafaa's torso and the carnage kept recurring. And sometimes a picture of her twin boys. I went back on duty after the fortnight, but I wasn't functioning properly – sudden outbursts, socially withdrawn and panic attacks. They diagnosed PTSD and signed me off. It's taken a good nine months. There was talk of me accepting a desk job or changing career, but I wouldn't have that; I've always wanted to be a detective. They finally agreed a trial period and told me to report to Ross.'

Bridges was on his second cigarette. He blew another smoke ring, watched it lose its shape. 'I didn't realise how far you've had to travel to get to where you are now. From where I'm standing, you've made the journey. Don't believe anyone who tells you you're not fit for active duty.' He stubbed the unfinished cigarette out. 'Ross should be done by now.'

They went back in as Ross was coming down the stairs, looking for them. He turned around and they followed him back into his office.

'The call I took was from a Dyfed and Powys DCI. One of their unmarked cars picked up our white van going through Machynlleth at around 9.30 this morning. They followed it until it turned down a farm track just past the village of Pennal. The description is that the driver was a middle-aged female. There was no one in the passenger seat.'

'It's been three hours since they spotted the van,' Bridges said. 'Why didn't they inform us earlier?'

'The detectives who spotted the van were at the end of their shift; they passed it on, but then there was a major domestic incident resulting in the message getting shuffled back. Many apologies, but they've now deployed two detectives to watch the turn off to the farm track. They'll follow the van if it leaves.'

'I don't think our man is at the farm,' Bridges said. 'My guess is that he's hidden the van there and changed vehicles. But we might find the girl if they haven't already killed her.'

Ross nodded. 'The only entrance to the farm is along the track off the main road. There's a pub car park about two hundred yards before the turn off. Dyfed and Powys police are going to meet us there.'

'What did you get from them?' Bridges asked.

'The DCI happened to be someone I know from the past. I told him what I wanted. He gave me some advice before putting me through to their superintendent. Not an easy conversation but he's given the approval for two armed officers to meet us in the car park. They'll take the lead when we go into the farm.'

Ross turned to Angie, 'Bridges and I will go. You stay behind, check the CCTV footage between 6 p.m. and 9 p.m. in the streets around the condemned house, see if it throws up anything.'

'I want to come with you and Bridges to the farm,' Angie said determinedly.

Ross hesitated, looked at the cast on her hand. 'Are you Taser trained?'

'Yes, I had Taser training before I went to Iraq.'

Ross looked at Bridges. Bridges nodded. 'She's earned the right.'

'Okay,' Ross said. 'You can come with us to the farm.'

***

The main street of Machynlleth was busy for a small town. It was a sunny autumn day; the pavements on both sides of the main street were crowded with a mixture of residents and tourists drifting contentedly in and out of the antique shops and the small independently owned shops that gave the Welsh town its character. Cars in search of parking crawled along searching for a space on the street, most of them eventually turning into the council car park that was pay and display.

It was gone 3.30 p.m. when the red SUV came down the main street past the antique shops and turned right at the clock tower. Erag had taken his time. There was no need to rush; the girl would be there, waiting for him, whatever time he got there. He patted his leather jacket, felt the little red velvet box with the ring he'd bought for the girl. It was a simple ring – a band of silver with a green stone inlaid. He'd remembered that the girl's eyes were green.

Driving past the town's only petrol station, he turned left towards Pennal and Aberdovey when he came to the bridge. The road ran alongside the river for the next three miles before he came to the village of Pennal.

It was a small village with a church off to the right as the road curved to take you across a humpback bridge. The small grocery shop that used to be just before the curve had closed but the gastro pub on the left, immediately before the bridge, was known for both its range of gins and its Sunday roasts. Erag noticed the busy car park as he drove past. Two hundred yards past the humpback bridge, he took the turning down the farm track. The workman, trimming the roadside hedge a hundred yards further along, saw the red SUV make the turn and reached for his phone. His companion, sitting in the unmarked car in the pub car park, answered the call.

Chapter 40

Bridges was at the wheel of the unmarked Mondeo; Ross was in the front passenger seat. Angie sat in the back with the tasers. The satnav showed one hundred and twelve miles to the farm and 4.10 p.m. as their "arrival at destination" time. Road works at the roundabout that took them on to the motorway held them up, but on the M5 itself the traffic flowed smoothly. Bridges drove steadily, overtaking when the opportunity arose but not forcing it. After six miles, the M5 took them on to the M6 and the traffic flow slowed: one lane closed, and the other two lanes dominated by container lorries.

They drove without speaking, letting Bridges concentrate because he couldn't see past the container lorries in front of him. It all changed when they left the M6 and joined the M54. There were few cars and only the odd container lorry. 'Twenty-two miles and must be up for the quietest motorway in the country,' Bridges said, relaxing into his seat. 'Twenty-two miles of driving pleasure.' Ross merely grunted. Bridges glanced across at him. 'Tricky with Dyfed and Powys, was it?'

Ross didn't answer straight away, seemed to mull the question over before answering. Angie, sitting in the back leant forward to catch his words. 'It helped I knew their chief inspector who covers the Machynlleth area. Vince Evans is as solid as they come; we were at Police College together. He had to refer it upwards when I asked for armed support, but he advised me to use a phrase from their manual on inter force collaboration. So when I spoke to his superintendent, I argued that our involvement was desirable because "our intimate knowledge of the case and the individual we were looking for would assist in reducing risk and the level of force potentially required".'

They were on the A483 when Ross's phone rang. He looked at the screen, held the phone close to his ear to cut out the road noise. He listened, held the phone away, turned to Bridges, 'How long before we get there?' Bridges pointed at the satnav display. Ross put the phone back to his ear. 'The satnav is saying thirty minutes. I'll phone you if we get held up.' He put the mobile down on his lap. 'That was Vince Evans. A red Toyota RAV4 turned down the farm track five minutes ago. One male driver on his own.'

Bridges nodded, didn't need telling to get a move on. For the last half mile, they'd been behind a tractor towing a trailer loaded with bales of hay. He gave one long blast on his horn and overtook the tractor. An oncoming car flashed them. The tractor driver gave them the finger as they went past.

***

Bujare had fallen asleep on the bed after she came back from seeing Pavel. She awoke with a start. It was gone 3 p.m. She lay there with her eyes open and her mind in a whirl as she remembered her visit to the hospital. The doctor had said they would take Pavel off the morphine drip. Maybe his crazy behaviour would have stopped by the time she went tonight. Maybe he would just be the Pavel she knew and loved. She would order a taxi to take her to the hospital.

And then she remembered the girl. She had to free Elira. Her niece. Altina's little baby who had grown into such a beautiful girl. She would have to do it on her own. Without Pavel's help. But how?

Bujare suddenly felt wide awake. She sat on the side of the bed and made her plan. It would have to look like Elira had escaped. She could say that when she took her food across, the girl was lying on the floor of the cell, not moving, so she had gone into the cell to see to her. But then the girl had sprung up, pushed her hard against the wall and run out while she was dazed.

She and Pavel had money hidden under the mattress in the bedroom – over £500. She would give it all to Elira. There were trains from

Machynlleth to London – she could get one of them. Bujare remembered she had come across an old train timetable in one of the kitchen drawers. Springing up from the bed, she rushed to the kitchen and sat down with the timetable. There was a train from Machynlleth to Paddington leaving at 6.05 p.m. Elira could get that one. The taxi to the hospital would be going past the station; she could come in the taxi with her. But what would they do when they found out the girl had escaped? Bujare tried not to think about that. She decided to make herself a cup of tea and go over her plan.

The kettle had just boiled when she saw the red SUV coming down the track. She stepped back from the window, watched the SUV swing around and park in front of the shed. She felt the tightness in her chest and her throat, and thought she was going to faint. Why had they come? What did they want? What would she say about Pavel? What about the girl?

Filling a glass of water from the tap, she drank it in one go, and took a deep breath to ease the thumping of her heart. Erag got out of the driver's door; she noticed he was dressed differently. She waited for Rumesh to emerge from the passenger door, but it didn't open. Erag had come on his own. Her hand was trembling.

She watched him take a step towards the farmhouse, then turn around and stare at the van. And then she realised he wasn't staring at the van;

he was staring at what was lying next to it. The dust cover. She hadn't put the dust cover back on. He would know the van had been used. He walked around to the front of the van, put his hands on the bonnet. *He's feeling if the engine is warm. Pray God it has cooled down.* Bujare, her knees knocking, looked around wildly, spied the bucket in the corner of the kitchen. She grabbed the bucket, ran with it to the sink and turned on both taps fully. She looked again. He was putting the dust cover back over the van.

She went out of the farmhouse door, started walking towards the shed, her head down. He finished putting the dust cover in place, saw her as he turned around. They met halfway between the farmhouse and the shed. She acted surprised to see him, forced a smile. He didn't return her smile.

'Why is the dust cover off the van?' His tone was harsh. Suspicious.

'It's dirty,' Bujare said. 'Pavel said I should wash it. I was just about to start.'

She had her Wellingtons on, was wearing rubber gloves, had put down the big bucket filled with hot soapy water. She held a thick sponge in her other hand.

He stared at her, at her rubber gloves and the sponge in her hand. After a long moment, he said, 'It doesn't need to be cleaned. Don't take the dust cover off the van again.'

Bujare nodded.

'Where is Pavel?'

'He's taken the old SUV to the garage in Aberystwyth that's open on Sundays. There's something wrong with the clutch. He has to wait while they fix it. They said it could take a few hours.' She'd expected him to be angry that Pavel wasn't there, but he just nodded, looked almost pleased.

She worked up her courage. 'Why isn't Rumesh with you?'

'He's sick.'

'What's the matter with him?'

'Don't ask so many questions.'

He showed her his hands. They were dirty from the dust cover and the bonnet of the van. 'I need to wash my hands.'

She emptied the bucket on the grass. He followed her back into the farmhouse.

Back in the kitchen, she pointed at the sink. 'There's soap underneath.'

'I want to use the bathroom. The one in your bedroom. I'll wash my hands there.'

Bujare hesitated, then led him down the corridor and stopped outside her bedroom door. She did not want to go in with him. 'This is my bedroom. The bathroom is on the far side.'

Erag closed the bedroom door behind him. She waited outside, not liking him being in her bedroom. Why was he dressed like that? As if he was going to a party. She had smelt his aftershave. And noticed he'd tried to cover up the pockmarks on his face. She thought of Elira in the punishment block, remembered how he had fondled her breasts when she was unconscious. A feeling of dread overtook her.

When he came out of the bedroom and walked past her, she stole a quick look as she pulled the door shut. The drawer where she kept her gloves and scarves was still partly open. She kept her towels in a cupboard in the bathroom. There was one lying at the foot of the bed.

'We have to get the girl,' he said. 'I need to talk to her.'

'We don't have to bring her over here,' Bujare said. 'It would be less trouble if you just talked to her in the cell.'

Erag stopped and stared at her. 'You talk too much for an old woman. Just do what you're told. Otherwise, there will be trouble.'

Then he said in a softer voice. 'Things are changing. We need to treat the girl better. I want to tell her how things will be different.'

'Different?'

'Yes. A lot different.' She saw the sly smile. 'I've even brought her a present.'

Bujare followed him over to the punishment block, her heart thumping in her chest. Elira spat at Bujare when she came out of the cell and found Erag waiting. After that, she caused no further trouble, walking behind Bujare with her head down. Erag walked behind the girl. Wiping the saliva off with her sleeve, Bujare took slow steps on the short walk back to the farmhouse. She was filled with a sense of foreboding.

Elira hadn't been in the farmhouse before. She followed Bujare past the kitchen, spoke for the first time when Bujare opened the bedroom door.

'Why have you brought me here?'

Elira moved into the room as Erag crowded her from behind. He stood between the girl and the door, pointed at the towel on the bed. 'It's so you can have a shower. You must want to have a shower.'

Elira felt dirty. She wanted to have a shower. She looked at Bujare, but Bujare had her head down, staring at the carpet. The girl didn't move.

'I need to talk to you,' Erag said. 'The ship comes in tomorrow, so what you overheard doesn't matter anymore. Things can be different.' He held out the towel to her. 'Have a shower first. Then we'll talk.'

Elira raised her head and looked at him for the first time.

'I'll wait outside,' he said, holding out the towel again.

Elira finally took the towel and waited.

Erag nudged Bujare, followed her out into the passageway, closed the bedroom door behind him.

'I'll wait here. Bring me a bottle of wine and two glasses.'

'I'll wait with you,' Bujare said. 'In case she wants anything.'

Erag turned to face Bujare, put both hands around her neck, and squeezed while he watched her; she saw the gleam in his eyes as she struggled to breathe.

'Do what I say, old woman,' he said in a low voice. 'Or things will go badly for you.' He took his hands away from her throat.

Bujare gasped, put her hand to her throat as she tried to get her breath back.

'Get the wine,' he said. 'And two glasses.'

In the kitchen, standing bent over the sink, she thought was going to vomit. She waited until the feeling passed. Her throat was sore. She took out her mobile phone, intending to ring Pavel, to ask him what she should do. But then she remembered there was no point.

She put her head around the door, looked along the passageway. He was still standing outside the bedroom door, his back towards her. The keys to the van were in the kitchen drawer. She could run to the van, drive off and get help for Elira. She looked out of the kitchen window to where the van was, but the dust cover was now back on. He would catch up with her before she could get it off. What else could she do?

She put her head around the door again, saw with beating heart that the passageway was now empty. He was not outside the bedroom door. She heard Elira screaming. Loud, piercing screams that jolted Bujare's body like an electric shock. She heard the screams again. And then there was silence. She ran to the cabinet with the wine glasses, reached up for the two nearest ones. The bottom cupboard full of the wine bottles she had rearranged, was on the other side of the kitchen. She reached down into the cupboard; her hands closed around the first bottle they touched. She straightened up, felt the weight, and realised it was the magnum of champagne she was holding.

Grasping the glasses and the bottle, Bujare hurried along the passageway and listened outside the closed bedroom door. She heard his voice. She wanted to burst into the room, to see that the girl was safe, but she remembered what he had done to her neck. She knocked on the door, was about to knock a second time when he flung the door open.

His eyes had gone unnaturally bright. He had deep scratch marks on his face where the girl had raked him with her nails. Blood, oozing from both cheeks, had dripped on to his polo shirt. He stood with the door only half-open, his body partly blocking her view. But beyond him, she glimpsed Elira lying on the bed, her hands tied by scarves to the brass bedposts, a gag in her mouth. She was naked.

He saw from the expression on Bujare's face that she'd seen the girl. He put his hands on her throat but didn't squeeze.

He stared into her eyes. 'Don't forget what I told you.'

She nodded.

'Put the bottle and the glasses on the dressing table. Then get out. Do not disturb us.'

Bujare couldn't bring herself to look at Elira. She walked to the dressing table that was at the far end of the bedroom, put the glasses and the bottle on the dresser, keeping her head down as she turned around. She had reached the door when she heard him snarl.

'What's this?'

She turned back. He was holding the magnum of champagne, looking angrily at the top.

'It's champagne,' Bujare managed to get the words out.

He scratched impatiently at the gold foil, feeling the wire cage underneath that protected the cork. She noticed blood was still dripping onto his blue polo shirt. He saw her staring, glanced down at his shirt, and cursed.

He handed her the magnum of champagne. 'Open it! Then get out.'

Taking the bottle from him, keeping her back to the girl, Bujare scratched at the gold foil. She used her nails to get it off the neck of the bottle, found the little ring to twist and loosen the wire cage protecting the cork. Her hands were shaking. She managed to grasp the little ring between her thumb and first finger. Started twisting.

Chapter 41

The two unmarked police cars were in the pub park when they got there. DCI Vince Evans got out of his car to greet Ross. 'Long time no see,' he said, extending his hand. Ross shook it, introduced Bridges and Angie. Vince Evans's glance took in the tasers and Angie's cast.

'Armed back up is on its way,' he said. He gave Ross a knowing look. 'A bit of a bureaucratic holdup. Two armed officers should be here within twenty minutes.'

'Appreciated,' Ross said. 'We're not sure what we're going to find there. The van that your men reported turning down the farm track has been used in a murder. There were two men involved. One of them is dead. We're not sure where the other one is. And there's a missing girl – they might be holding her there if they haven't already killed her.'

'Why hide the van up here and then drive it in the area it was stolen from?'

'We were surprised, too. But the license plates your men reported matches the van we've been looking for.'

'You said there were two men and one of them is dead,' Vince Evans said. 'Do you think the other one is holed up at the farm.'

'I don't know. But if he's there, your men need to know he's a knife-wielding psychopath.'

'The red SUV that your officer reported turning into the farm an hour ago,' Bridges said. 'Did he give a description of the man driving it?'

'No, he just glimpsed the side of his head after he made the turn,' Vince Evans said. 'He'll alert us if any vehicle tries to leave. The first hundred and fifty yards of the track is straight, so he's got a good line of sight.' His phone buzzed. He took the call, listened, then put the phone away.

'Armed support is fifteen minutes away. They'll come here and then we'll follow them in.'

'I'll wander up and talk to the watcher,' Angie told Ross. 'Go over what he saw of the driver of the red SUV.'

Ross nodded, 'We'll pick you up on the way in.'

The detective pretending to cut the hedge had moved back along the road to be opposite the turning to the track. He was Angie's age, with a beard. His eyes went from the cast on Angie's left hand to the Taser in the holster on her right hip.

'Expecting trouble?'

'Just a precaution. What did you see of the driver of the red SUV?'

'Not enough to give an accurate description.' He pointed up the road. 'I was a hundred yards further up, not wanting to attract attention. I saw him coming up the road when he came over the humpback bridge, but he didn't signal he was turning, so I didn't pay too much attention; I thought he was going straight down the road to Aberdovey. By the time I heard the engine change gear and looked up, he had made the turn. I caught the side of his face though – I'd guess he was younger than the two of us. I glimpsed a collar – I'd say he was wearing a jacket.'

'So not a workman or a delivery?'

'No. Not dressed like a workman. And a delivery man would have been back out by now.'

Angie nodded, looked across the road at the farm track. As Vince Evans had said, it ran straight for close to a hundred and fifty yards before disappearing to the right. She turned her phone off. 'Armed backup should be here soon,' she said. 'I'm going to wander halfway down the track, see what's around that corner. If you tell my boss, CDI Ross, they can stop for me on the way in.'

Crossing the road, she walked along the centre of the track, confident she would hear any approaching vehicle before they rounded the bend. Trees lined the track on the right-hand side, open fields lay on the left. She went into the trees as she approached the bend. Beyond that, the track straightened out again for over a hundred yards. She could see the farmhouse and a window to the left of a door. There was no movement. There was a block building on her left, an open shed on her right. A red SUV was parked in front of the shed.

The line of trees stopped fifty yards before the end of the track.

She came to the last tree, looked again at the window for any movement, then crouching low, covered the distance to the SUV in a run. Another vehicle was parked in the shed, a dust cover over it. Lifting the corner of the dust cover, she saw that it was the white van. She glanced at the watch on her right hand, thought the armed backup should arrive any moment. She waited in the silence.

Her head jerked around at the sound of a piercing scream. She was certain it was a woman's scream. Had it come from the block on her left or from the farmhouse? Angie spun around and stared anxiously up the track. Where was the armed backup? She shouldn't go in on her own. She spun around again at the sound of the second scream, could tell this time it came from the farmhouse, from somewhere to the right of the kitchen window. She took a deep breath. *The backup would appear in a moment, be right behind her.*

She made the dash to the farmhouse door, pushed against it with her knee, the Taser in her good right hand. It was open. Angie moved into the kitchen, taser at the ready. There was no one there. She stood still and listened. All was quiet. She moved silently along the passageway. A door on the right was slightly ajar, open enough for her to see a girl naked on the bed, tied and gagged. It was the girl from Margaret's portrait. From that angle, Angie could see no one else. She adjusted her grip on the Taser, pushed the door gently with her knee and crept into the bedroom.

A short, thickset woman, her back towards her, stood bent over a dressing table in the far corner. Angie glimpsed a bottle. The girl saw her, looked at her wide-eyed, started moving her head from side to side and up and down, trying to loosen the gag. Angie put her finger over her lips. The girl nodded and stopped moving. Angie crept silently to the top of the bed. Her left hand was useless in the cast; she could only use her right hand to untie the gag that was tied behind the girl's neck. She rested the taser on the bed next to the girl's head, leant forward to reach the knot behind her neck. As she did so, the woman at the dressing table sensed the movement, looked up, and saw her in the mirror.

The woman turned to face Angie. Her mouth opened and closed, but no sound came out. Her eyes filled with terror; she pointed behind Angie. Angie spun around and looked, saw the closed door in the corner of the bedroom opening. A short, heavily muscled, bare-chested man emerged, looking down at the wet, blue polo shirt he was holding. At that instant, he looked up. Their eyes met. Angie spun around, grabbed the Taser from the pillow in one fluid motion with her right hand, spun back with her finger already on the trigger and fired. But Erag had turned around, taken two steps back, and launched himself into the air, somersaulting high across the bed. The Taser's barbed darts were too low, aimed at the height he had been.

Angie felt him crash into her, felt the straight arm punch to her stomach. She collapsed. He laughed and shoved her backwards. She hit her head on the radiator against the wall as she fell, saw him through dazed eyes. He put her in a sitting position, propped against the wall, and squatted down in front of her so he was at eye level. Then he reached behind his back and showed her the knife. She saw the bright spark in his eyes. 'It's better for me if you have your eyes open,' he said.

She knew what to expect. What he would do to her body. *This is how Walter died.* She closed her eyes, waited for the impact.

She heard the sickening thud. But felt nothing. She opened her eyes. He was crouched lower than before, leaning forward as if he had lost his balance. The knife had fallen from his grasp. The short, thickset woman, the big bottle raised to shoulder height, brought it down on the back of his head a second time. And a third time. He twitched slightly then, and the bottle came down again. This time, Angie heard the crunch as the back of his head caved in.

Taking a deep breath, she put her good hand on the radiator to push herself up. The woman was still standing over the man, still grasping the raised bottle like a rounders bat.

'He's dead,' Angie said.

The woman appeared not to hear her. Angie took the bottle gently from her, was surprised at how heavy it was. She was still holding the magnum of champagne when the bedroom door burst open. Two men, dressed in black, were pointing their guns directly at her. Behind them, she could see Ross and Bridges.

***

Ross and Bridges led a trembling Bujare out of the bedroom. Angie stayed behind while the girl put her clothes on. Erag's leather jacket hung on the back of the door. She found the keys to the red SUV in the left-hand pocket. In the other pocket, she found a little red velvet box with a ring. Elira looked at the silver band with the emerald inlay, then at the bloodied head of the man.

'That one was a beast,' she said with venom. 'I'm glad he is dead.'

Angie stared down at the body of the man who had meant to kill her. And who had killed Walter. 'I am too,' she said.

Bridges came back in and took Elira into the lounge. Angie found Ross in the kitchen with a still trembling Bujare. He went to join Bridges while Angie stayed with Bujare. She made her a cup of tea, made herself one too. She waited while Bujare's breathing gradually returned to normal. Then she sat by her and held her hand. 'He would have killed me,' she said. 'You saved my life.'

Bujare nodded slowly, then spoke haltingly while a tear ran down her cheek. 'His name is Erag. He was an evil one. He was going to rape Elira.' She tried to get up, but her legs gave way, and she sat back down. 'Please,' she said, 'I must see Elira. It's very important. Where is she?'

Angie nodded, 'I'll get her.' She left Bujare sipping her tea and went to the lounge where Ross and Bridges were with the girl. Bridges was just closing his notebook. 'Just a preliminary,' Ross explained. 'We'll do a proper interview when we get back to the station.' They both gave her a long appraising look. 'Are you okay?' Ross asked, his eyes fixed on her face. Angie was touched; she realised they were looking out for her. Were concerned about her PTSD.

'Yes,' she said, 'I'm okay.' And as she said the words, she felt an adrenalin rush. It was true. After what she had been through, she felt okay. She was back on active duty, and she was coping.

'Are you finished with Elira? The woman – Bujare – is desperate to see her.'

Elira stood up, her head cocked slightly to one side as she looked at Angie. Angie thought what a good likeness Margaret's portrait was.

Bujare had spilt her tea. She tried to stand up as Elira followed Angie into the kitchen, but her legs gave way again. Elira remained standing, didn't sit in the empty chair next to Bujare. 'Please,' Bujare said to Angie. 'Could you leave us alone for a few minutes? Please.'

Angie left them alone for ten minutes. When she went back, they were both crying. Elira's head was buried against Bujare's chest; Bujare was stroking the girl and speaking softly to her. She looked up at Angie through her tears. 'She's my niece,' she said.

Ross phoned Birmingham, asked them to send another car to collect the man they'd found in the punishment block. Vince Evans phoned for an ambulance to take the body away. He said he would stay until the car from Birmingham arrived. Bujare told Angie about her visit to Pavel, asked if she could visit him one more time. Angie spoke to Ross. Ross had a word with Vince Evans. They were taking Bujare into custody, but it was agreed they would take her to the hospital first.

Elira sat in the back of the car with Angie. She fell asleep on the drive back to Birmingham. They were quiet in the car, not sharing their thoughts. But as they came off the motorway and joined the A38 to take them back to the station, Ross twisted around so Angie could hear him.

'We did it!' he said.

In the rear-view mirror, she could see Bridges smiling.

Chapter 42

They interviewed Elira back at the station, began by asking her why she hadn't gone to the Police. 'The man I was taken to have sex with was from the police. I saw the pass in his jacket pocket. And I knew he was an important man.'

Angie showed her a photograph of George Kershaw, 'Is this the man?'

Elira didn't hesitate. 'Yes.'

They asked her what she had told Walter Price – what details he had recorded in his green notebook. She asked them how they knew about him and when they told her, she was distraught. 'I thought he'd betrayed me,' she said. She wanted to know if he had a family, wanted to meet Roxanne when they told her he had a daughter.

Then she told them about the conversation she had overheard, the conversation she had relayed to Walter. When she had finished talking, they sat back in silence. Angie waited for Ross to speak. But it was Bridges who spoke first.

'You can't sit on this,' he said to Ross. 'You have to tell the Deputy.'

Ross sat still for a moment, then stood up. 'I can do better than that.'

He left the office, came back in ten minutes later, and spoke to Elira. 'I'm afraid you're going to have to do this again. Officers from our National Crime Agency in London want to interview you themselves.'

'When?' she asked him.

'Tonight. It's been classified as top priority. The NCA will have a car here with two officers in ninety minutes.'

So now they knew why Walter had been killed. The conversation the girl had overheard was about a shipment of cocaine. The name of the ship, the port it had sailed from, its destination and when it was expected. The Commander at the NCA had told Ross the timing fitted in with their intelligence that the Albanians were expanding into the Midlands. He thought it would be a large shipment.

'They almost got away with it,' Bridges said. 'If what the girl overheard is true, the ship is due to reach our shoreline sometime tomorrow.'

'They might still get away with it,' Ross said. 'That's why the NCA have responded so quickly; the Commander said once it reaches our shoreline, they could unload the cargo into smaller boats. The NCA aim to intercept the main ship before then, but he said sometimes it's almost akin to looking for a needle in a haystack. Apparently, they use smaller ships these days – the Commander said the last one with a big cargo from South America was a catamaran.'

They waited until the NCA officers arrived. The senior one had a brief conversation with Ross. They put Elira in the back of the car for the drive back to London. Before they pulled away, the senior officer lowered his window, nodded to Ross, 'We'll let you know how it goes.'

They went back up the stairs to Ross's office.

'Let's hope they intercept the drugs shipment. At least it would give some meaning to Walter Price's death,' Bridges said.

The adrenalin was fading. Angie felt the tiredness overtaking her. She wanted to sleep. 'I'll order a taxi,' she said, taking out her phone.

Ross had been watching her, 'Where is your flat?'

'Hagley Road. The taxi will only take twenty minutes.'

Ross took the phone out of her hands. 'I'll give you a lift,' he said. 'I'm going that way. There's someone I need to see.' Bridges looked at him curiously, but Ross didn't expand.

When they stopped outside her flat, Angie reached to unbuckle her seat belt. Ross put his hand on the strap. 'You know you should've waited for the armed backup. You should not have gone into that farmhouse on your own.'

'I didn't intend to go in on my own,' Angie said. 'It just happened. I'm sorry.'

'Learn from it,' Ross said. 'You were lucky this time.'

'Yes, sir,' Angie said.

'I saw you staring at the body.'

'Yes,' Angie said. 'I felt glad he was dead.'

Ross nodded, 'I can understand that. But that's not what I was getting at.' He turned to look her in the face, 'Be careful. You've had a near-death experience. It would be normal to have a reaction, to have the odd flashback. It might take a few days.'

Angie understood. 'Thank you,' she said. 'I've got my medication. It dampens down my body alarm systems, lessens the chance of them triggering a flashback.'

He nodded. '8 a.m. tomorrow then. I want us to be there by 9.15.'

'Where?'

'The PCC's office,' Ross said. 'He gets in at 9 a.m. We'll give him time to drink his first cup of coffee.' Angie stood and watched as Ross waited to join the stream of traffic. He hadn't said who he was going to see.

She had a quick shower and climbed into bed. The medication sat on her bedside table. She held the bottle in her hands, gazed at it but didn't open it. She examined her swirling emotions: deep satisfaction at finding Walter's killer; anger at the PCC's betrayal of Walter and of the justice system that she'd devoted her life to. But she also felt elated: she'd stared at the dead body of the man who had almost killed her and remained in control. Doing so hadn't triggered the kind of reaction she'd feared if she'd looked at Walter's body ten days ago.

It had been a long nine months of recovery. Maybe she was now finally over her traumatic experience. Maybe she didn't need the medication. She put the bottle back on the dressing table without opening it, lay back on the bed, was starting to drift into sleep when the psychiatrist's words floated into her mind: '*You must be emotionally literate if you are going to learn how to live with your PTSD.*' She sat back up in bed, reached over for the bottle. She would take the plunge. Not take her medication. But not yet. She couldn't risk a flashback. Not while there was unfinished business.

Angie woke up at 7 a.m. She took a few moments to reflect on the events of the previous day. And the night. She'd slept soundly. Her eyes strayed to the bottle on her bedside table. She wondered what would have happened if she hadn't taken her medication.

Chapter 43

It had rained heavily during the night, but Monday morning had improved to what the weather forecasters would call light rain and a gentle breeze. George Kershaw was in a good mood as he took the lift to his office on the ninth floor. Catching his reflection in the mirrored wall, he noted with satisfaction that his tan had deepened after his weekend in Majorca. He came out of the lift, pushed through the glass double doors to where his PA was already at work, winked at her as she looked up, gave a thumbs up for coffee, and carried on into his office. He opened his diary, looked at the screen, noted his first appointment was at 9.40.

The phone buzzed ten minutes later as he drank the last of his coffee.

'There's a Detective Chief Inspector here asking to see you,' his PA said. 'It's not in the diary but he's quite insistent.'

'Very well,' the PCC said. 'I've got fifteen minutes. Show him in.'

Pretending to be reading a file, he delayed looking up when he heard the door open. When he did look up, he was surprised to find there were three of them. The man standing in front of the others was tall, a little overweight, with a slight paunch. Behind him was another middle-aged man, shorter and in better shape, and next to him a woman with her left hand in a cast. The PCC thought she was a looker.

'DCI Ross,' the tall man said, holding out his hand. The PCC knew of Ross, had discussed him with the Deputy, but he had never seen his photograph. He came out from behind his desk, shook Ross's hand, glanced meaningfully at the other two.

'DS Bridges and DI Reeves,' Ross introduced them.

'I'm surprised we can afford such manpower,' the PCC said, forcing a smile. He indicated they should sit on the three-seater leather sofa. He took the leather chair opposite them.

'What can I do for you?'

'We're investigating the murder of Walter Price,' Ross said.

'Ah! DCI Ross.' George Kershaw paused, raised an eyebrow. 'My understanding is that you've been taken off that case. It's been handed to our newly promoted DCI Cunningham. Isn't that right?'

'Not quite,' Ross said. 'Cunningham takes over on the first of the month. Tomorrow. In the meantime, I'd like to ask you some questions.'

The PCC's jaw muscles tensed. 'Very well. What do you want to know?'

'How well did you know Walter Price?'

George Kershaw managed a sad smile. 'I knew him well when we were both heads of secondary schools. But that was some time ago.'

'I understand you did the eulogy at his funeral.'

'Yes,' the PCC said. 'His daughter asked me to do the eulogy. She wanted someone who could talk about the educational contribution he'd made to the city. I was honoured to be asked.'

Angie stood up and walked to the far end of the room, stood there feeling the return of the slow, burning anger. She faced the wall, listened with her back towards them.

'When did you last see Walter Price?'

'I saw him just over a year ago. We bumped into each other at a golf charity day.'

'And when did you last speak to him?'

'I just told you,' George Kershaw said, allowing a hint of sharpness in his tone. 'Just over a year ago.'

'That was when you last saw him,' Ross said. 'When was the last time you spoke to him on the phone?'

The PCC rubbed his chin, stared into space to indicate he was trying to recall. He shook his head.

'I can't recall any more recent conversation. Sorry.'

'His phone records show he phoned you a week last Wednesday. The day he was murdered.' Ross spoke quietly, his eyes fixed on the other man's face.

George Kershaw sensed the first sign of danger. 'Now you mention it, I think he did, but I was in a meeting and couldn't talk to him. I suspect it was probably an invitation to the annual golf charity day at his club.'

'Did you return the call after your meeting ended?'

The PCC shook his head slowly, added a note of regret to his voice, 'No, I meant to, but I completely forgot. I feel bad about that now, given what's happened.'

Ross nodded sympathetically. 'So you did not phone him back?'

The PCC shifted in his chair. 'No.'

Ross felt in his jacket pocket, took out his mobile phone, found what he was looking for. He put it on speaker, pressed the play button.

They heard Walter's deep voice answering the phone, then the unmistakable voice of George Kershaw. Walter telling him he badly needed some help and advice, that George was the only one he could think of because he'd promised not to go directly to the police, Walter telling him he'd stumbled across something very important that involved criminals from Kosovo, telling him about the girl and the Refuge, George asking for more details but Walter initially refusing to tell him more on the phone, asking for a meeting, George pressing him, saying he needed a bit more information before he could involve the Chief

Constable, Walter reluctantly telling him it involved a large shipment of cocaine.

'I've written everything the girl told me in my green notebook,' they heard Walter say. 'I can show you and the Chief Constable the notes if we can meet.'

Then George's voice. 'Come and see me at 8 o'clock tomorrow morning. I'll make sure the Chief Constable is here. You can tell him what you've told me. And you can give him the green notebook yourself.'

They heard the relief in Walter's voice, heard him thanking George Kershaw before ending the call.

Angie turned around. The PCC sat with his head down, rocking slightly, his fingers interlocked on his lap as he squeezed his hands together. Ross flicked through his phone, held out a photograph of Elira they had taken at the farmhouse.

'Do you recognise this girl?'

The PCC looked at the photograph but didn't answer.

'It's the girl who ran away from you in the hotel,' Ross said. 'She'll testify about the conversation she overheard.'

The PCC was still rocking backwards and forwards. He raised his head, 'I didn't know they were going to kill him. I swear it.'

Ross read him his rights. When Bridges stood up, he had a pair of handcuffs in his hands. The

PCC offered no resistance as Bridges cuffed him, then started to walk him slowly out of the room.

It was a spacious office. Angie had moved, stood halfway between the seating and the door. As George Kershaw went to walk past her, her right hand was a blur. She slapped him in his face. The anger that fuelled her force was so strong that he staggered. Regaining his balance, he looked at her in astonishment. The marks of her fingers stood out against his tanned skin.

'He was a good man,' Angie said fiercely.

She felt her hand twitching again, but Ross had moved swiftly. He laid his hand on her arm gently. 'Let it be,' he said quietly.

'All under control, Ross?' The voice was deep, measured, authoritative.

'Yes, sir,' Ross said. 'All under control.'

Angie turned around. A tall, broad-shouldered man with freckles and a receding hairline was framed in the doorway. He was in full uniform.

The PCC saw him, opened his mouth to speak, but was cut short.

'Don't bother, George,' the Chief Constable said. 'Ross came to my house last night, talked me through the investigation.' The Chief Constable took the five steps into the room that brought him face to face with the PCC. 'And I listened to the recording of your conversation with Walter Price. You used my name to lure a good man to his death.' He turned away from the PCC, held out his hand to Bridges. 'Thank you, DS Bridges.'

Then the Chief Constable turned to Angie, took in her cast, 'You must be DI Reeves.'

'Yes, sir,' Angie said.

'Ross has told me about the role you've played in this investigation. And he tells me detectives like you are the future of this force.'

Angie was stuck for words. 'I understand you're waiting to be returned to active duty at your current rank,' the Chief Constable continued. 'I don't see a problem there. You must be due a holiday. Ring my office when you're back and make an appointment. We'll sort that out and discuss your future in this force.' He paused, 'I wouldn't want you transferring somewhere else. Understood?'

'Yes, sir,' Angie said. 'Thank you.'

He held out a hand to Ross, turned to go, paused, and turned back to Angie.

'By the way,' he said. 'That's some right hand you've got there.'

He waited until she had looked up and seen his smile. 'My youngest son, John, started his teaching career at Walter Price's school,' the Chief Constable said. 'He's applying for Deputy Headships now. I don't think he would have survived his first year without Walter Price's support. Like you said, he was a good man.'

Chapter 44

The Chief Constable had asked Ross for a full report. Ross knew he would deal with the Deputy after he'd read it. Angie and Bridges were getting the coffees from the canteen – Ross was on his own when his phone rang. It was Helen Jackson, the pathologist, known for her straight talking.

'I seem to recall you owe me a few favours,' she said in her brisk voice. 'I'm calling them in.'

Ross was taken aback, 'What do you mean?'

'Dinner at Giovanni's in Harborne tomorrow evening. You're paying.'

Ross scratched his head with his spare hand. 'Fine,' he said. 'What time shall I book it for?'

'No need,' Helen Jackson said. 'I've done that. Eight p.m.' She rang off.

He still had the phone in his hand when Angie and Bridges came in with the coffees.

'Is that a smile or a grimace?' Bridges asked.

Ross stopped scratching his head. 'I think it's a smile,' he said hesitantly.

His phone rang again. It was DI Armstrong. He had interviewed the man from the punishment block. Ross listened, put his phone down. 'Armstrong and his men were waiting this morning when the minibus arrived to pick the men from the house up. They arrested the two men from the minibus and found eleven men in the house. All trafficked, kept and used as cheap labour. The men have told them of two other houses in the Midlands with the same set-up.'

Bridges nodded, then wagged a finger at Ross. 'You can be a cagey bugger sometimes,' he said. 'The Chief Constable turning up was a surprise – at least to me. I take it he was the someone you were going to see when you left us last night.'

'Yes,' Ross said. 'He came back from annual leave two days ago. One of those Alaskan cruises. I wondered how much our Deputy had told him. And the PCC had promised Walter a meeting with him when he knew he was on leave. Let's just say the Chief wasn't best pleased when he heard the recording.'

Ross turned to Angie. 'Bridges and I will finish this report for the Chief Constable. You had better go and see Roxanne, tell her what's happened before it's out there in the media.'

***

Angie's mobile phone was dead. She thought the battery had gone, then remembered she'd turned her phone off before she crossed the road to the farm track. She'd meant to phone Philip the previous night after she had taken her medication but had collapsed into sleep. When the screen came alive, there were five missed calls from Philip. She phoned him, apologised for the missed calls.

'We were supposed to meet up for dinner last night,' he said. 'What happened to you?'

'Quite a lot,' Angie said. 'I'll tell you when we meet up.' She asked him if he could drive her to Milton Keynes, told him she would explain all on the drive. But she couldn't restrain herself when he arrived in the car park. She asked him if they could take a walk around the boating pool before heading for Milton Keynes.

The only other person at the boating pool was a woman walking a greyhound. They were sitting on a bench watching the ducks when she told him they'd found Walter's killer. He asked many questions then; she answered as fully as she could. When she told him about Erag propping her up, squatting in front of her with the knife, he went very still. Then she told him what had happened in Iraq and about her nine months of recovery in Devon. And about being uncertain whether to take her medication the night before. That was when he put his arms around her, hugged her, and held her while she cried.

***

Angie had phoned ahead to let Roxanne know they were coming. Philip kept to the inside lane of the M40, content to adapt to the speed of the container lorries as he listened to Angie and asked more questions.

'So, Walter was killed because Elira told him about the drugs shipment?'

'Yes. They weren't sure how much she had overheard until they saw what was in the notebook. That's why they broke into the house first. To find out how much he knew. And once they read what was in the notebook, it was his death warrant.'

'Who made the decision to kill Walter?'

'The NCA told Ross it's controlled from London. But they've had no success so far in identifying who the top man is.'

'George Kershaw must know. It's probably the man the girl overheard him talking to.'

'Ross thinks the same. But he says the PCC knows he's a dead man if he talks. And he might be a dead man anyway if they *think* he might talk. Don't forget the NCA's report – the Albanian's rapid rise to dominate the cocaine market is because of their willingness to use extreme violence.'

'So, what will happen to him?'

'At the moment, he's charged with being an accomplice to murder. But Bridges said a top QC arrived to represent him. So we'll see how that one goes. If the NCA locate the ship before the cocaine has been unloaded, he'll be up on a drug smuggling charge too. Difficult for him to get out of that one if the girl testifies to the conversation she overheard.'

They were on the slip road exiting the motorway when Angie gave a start.

'I'm so sorry, Philip. I completely forgot about your own problem. About the fraud. The last thing you told me was that your PA thought her boyfriend was responsible and your principal was contacting the police. How did that go?'

'The police interviewed Becky. She gave them the claim form she had found in Graham's flat. When they arrested him and searched his flat, they found a pile of forms. It turns out he has a past conviction for forgery. Served a five-year sentence. They've also arrested the finance officer at the company that the money was paid to. Apparently, she and Graham have history together.'

'Poor Becky,' Angie said. 'She must be devastated.'

'That's not all. When the police searched Graham's flat, they found a quantity of cocaine hidden in a toolbox in his outside lock up garage. He's been dealing on the side. The Drug Squad are waiting their turn to interview him. They're keen to find out who his supplier is. From what you've told me it's probably the Albanians.'

Angie shook her head at the mention of cocaine, 'Anyway, all this must mean you're in the clear about the fraud.'

'Yes, I had my formal interview with the auditors earlier this morning.'

'Are you back at work from tomorrow?'

'No. I'm still officially suspended until the auditors have produced their report and it's gone to our Board. Anna says that will be at least another week. But the college will be cleared of any wrongdoing.'

Roxanne was just finishing her surgery when they arrived at the medical centre. They went back to her house, made her cups of tea, sat with her for two hours through her incredulity and anger, and shared her tears as they remembered Walter. Angie told her that Elira wanted to meet her, but she was still being questioned by the NCA.

Roxanne was opening a bottle of wine as they left.

Philip dropped Angie back at her flat. She invited him in, but he said Anna had asked to see him.

'I'm meeting with Ross and Bridges tomorrow night for a post investigation celebratory drink,' Angie said. 'They say it's a ritual. It will be their last one together before Ross retires. Do you fancy joining us and having dinner afterwards?'

'Love to,' Philip said. 'Where and what time?'

She told him.

Back in her flat, she opened a bottle of Merlot, took a glass with her to the lounge and lay on the sofa. She sipped the wine slowly, closed her eyes, tried to take stock of all that had happened – was happening – to her.

She'd returned to active duty, showing a brave face to the world but inwardly unsure how she would cope. It had been a rocky start, suddenly coming across Walter's photograph, but she had survived that, had survived the challenges she'd faced. More than survived. She had avenged Walter's death.

Ross's words on the drive from the farm came back to her. '*We did it!*' he'd said. She'd proved she could still work in a team.

The psychiatrist had been right. She was learning to live with her PTSD. If she took the necessary precautions, she was still an effective detective. And the Chief Constable had indicated she could return to active duty with her present rank. She would still be Detective Inspector Angie Reeves. Yeah!

And what about Philip…Their friendship had survived the years apart. But she wanted more than that. Did he feel the same? She'd been in the same situation before, fearful of the inevitable awkwardness if he felt different, not wanting to put at risk the closest friendship she'd ever had.

She opened her eyes, took another sip of wine and allowed herself a few more moments to consider what the future might hold. The Chief Constable had said she was due a holiday… She stood up from the sofa and sat down at the dining table. She opened her laptop, sipped her wine and smiled as she perused the holiday sites.

Chapter 45

They started the search at first light. Using the information Elira gave them, the National Crime Agency co-ordinated the search with the help of the Maritime Operations and Analysis Centre in Lisbon, the Irish Navy and the Irish Air Corps. It was three hours later when a helicopter from the Irish Air Corps finally spotted the catamaran off the south-west coast of Cornwall. It was nearing its destination; it had left Trinidad over a month earlier with its five-man crew.

The Demerara was intercepted by a Border Force cutter and escorted into Newlyn harbour near Penzance. The five crew members were taken into custody. Working with the NCA, specialists from the national deep rummage team, trained to find hidden compartments in vessels, boarded the catamaran. The search yielded hundreds of packets of cocaine – 1.6 tonnes in total with a street value estimated to be £250 million. The Commander from the National Crime Agency remembered his promise to ring Ross.

***

The crematorium was close to Solihull, on the opposite side of the city to where Walter's ashes lay. An old oak tree stood in the middle of a wide avenue of freshly mown grass, its branches spreading to provide shade during the summer for some of the commemorative plaques that lined both sides of the avenue.

Her black, marble plaque with a small white cross in deference to her Irish, Catholic heritage, was one in the shade of the oak tree; the inscription, with the dates of her birth and death simply said, 'Elizabeth Maddox'. Philip brought fresh roses because they'd been her favourite. He did the flowers first. Then sitting down on the grass next to his mother, he talked to her in a low voice. He told her about deciding to face up to his demons, of inviting Walter to dinner. About Walter being murdered before they could meet, and of the events that led to the death of the man who killed him.

He paused when a couple passed by, on their way to a plaque further along the avenue. Then he told his mother he knew about her relationship with Walter, and he now understood why they had moved from Devon. He said he was glad they had moved so he could go to Walter's school. And he told her Roxanne had said Walter would want him to move on, to leave behind the sense of shame that had haunted him for so long. He said he thought he could do that now.

Philip's mother had known Angie Reeves during the years she had been his best friend at secondary school; he told her what Angie was like now. And how he felt about her.

Chapter 46

They were meeting in the lounge bar of the Kings Head at 7 p.m. Ross and Bridges were already there when Angie arrived. And so was Simpson. He stood up and walked over when he saw her come in and glance around. Greeting her with a wide smile, he frowned when he saw her arm in a cast.

'Just a domestic accident,' she said, returning his smile.

'You got there in the end,' Simpson said, playfully punching her good arm. 'I knew you would.' He took a step back and gazed at her. 'Bridges told me what the Chief said to you. Maybe we'll work together again in the future.'

'I'd like that,' Angie said.

Simpson went to the bar to get her a glass of wine; she walked over to where Ross and Bridges were sitting, with pints in front of them.

'You look a picture,' Bridges said. 'Is this for our benefit or are you meeting someone else?'

'The latter,' Angie told him laughingly. She looked with surprise at Ross's smart blue suit and crisp white shirt.

'Just come from visiting my mother.'

'And he's got a dinner date with our friendly pathologist,' Bridges added, smiling into his beer.

Ross looked at Bridges accusingly, glad he hadn't confided in him he'd vacuumed the house and changed the bed clothes, fumbling his way through the buttons on the duvet cover. And that he'd transferred his remaining sausage rolls from the freezer to the bin.

Ross waited until Simpson came back and they were all seated. Then he told them about the phone call from the NCA Commander.

Simpson shook his head in disbelief, '1.6 tonnes of cocaine with a street value of £250 million! And our initial thought was that we were dealing with a botched carjacking!'

Ross stood up and raised his glass, 'In memory of Walter Price,' he said. 'Think of the misery that amount of cocaine would have caused, the lives it would have ruined.' He looked at Angie. 'It must be some consolation to know your headteacher didn't die in vain.' Angie nodded as they raised their glasses to Walter.

'And here's to us.' Ross raised his glass again, nodded at each one in turn. 'We got there in the end.'

And then Bridges stood up. 'A toast to DCI Ross on the successful conclusion of his final investigation.' He met Ross's eye. 'To happy memories.'

Ross held Bridges's gaze and smiled back, 'Yes,' he said. 'To happy memories.'

At twenty to eight, as Ross stood up to leave, Philip walked in. Angie introduced him to the others. They all shook his hand.

'We've been told about your contribution to our investigation,' Ross said. 'Giving up your time to drive DI Reeves around. And getting us the recording of that phone conversation.'

They insisted on buying him a drink before they left.

And then there was just the two of them, both with a glass of wine.

Raising their glasses, they drank a toast to their old headteacher. After that, they sat back and looked at each other uncertainly.

Angie took a deep breath, kept her voice level. 'I'm taking next week off. Going on holiday. It's a cancellation – a small cottage. One bedroom, one double bed.' She took another deep breath. 'I was wondering if you'd like to come with me.'

Philip took a moment, making his brain go over all he thought she'd just said.

'Yes. Very much. I'd like very much to come with you.' He'd seen her serious look, tried to keep the smile off his face.

'It's a three-hour drive from Birmingham.' She held up her cast. 'We'll have to go in your car.'

'No problem,' he said, failing this time to hold back the smile. 'Where is it?'

'Dawlish,' Angie said, and now she was smiling. 'Overlooking the beach.'

Chapter 47

Albert had chosen the one-star Michelin restaurant near Hyde Park for this evening's culinary adventure. He was increasingly curious to see if he could discern an appreciable difference between a one-star Michelin and a two-star Michelin. Would it be the food or the service? Or the wine pairings he was learning so much about?

He was determined not to let the news from Wales, Birmingham and Cornwall spoil his evening. It was a serious setback, no doubt about that. But there had been setbacks all his life, and he was wiser after each one. He had learnt there was no certainty except an eventual death. That the unexpected could always happen, as it had in Birmingham. So, it was prudent to hedge one's bets.

The Demerara had sailed from Trinidad thirty-two days ago. Four days earlier, the Mackenzie, a catamaran of the same size and with an identical cargo, had also sailed from Trinidad. And she had successfully unloaded in Aberdeen two days ago.

He would have to spend some time in Birmingham. He sighed at the thought of leaving London. Still, there were ten Michelin starred restaurants in Birmingham and the surrounding area. And he had only sampled three of them.

Albert smiled to himself, caught the eye of the hovering waiter and raised a finger to signal he was ready for his second course. He made the calculation again – 1.6 tonnes of cocaine with a street value over £250 million. There would be more than enough for Scotland. Some would make its way to Birmingham.

#

Acknowledgement

Lockdown gave me the opportunity to learn from the brilliant online writing courses run by The Novelry – thank you Louise Dean and Tash Barsby for your encouragement and advice.

My thanks to my fellow golfers: Terry Monnington for his helpful comments on an early draft, Richard Wheatley and Ian Barker for their encouragement.

My good friend, Chris Muirhead, has been involved throughout the writing of this novel. I have appreciated and valued his interest, encouragement and thoughtful feedback.

Reis Taylor Dixon, thank you too, for your interest and encouragement.

My family have been hugely supportive: thanks to my daughter, Ellie, for being such a willing sounding board and giving so generously of her time and expertise. And my sons Steve and Andy, and daughter-in-law Lisa, – your encouragement meant a lot. My granddaughters Nabila and Yasmin, – thank you for your help in the early stages of designing a cover.

Thanks also to Pat Jones (Lloydie), who will recognise the references to Majorca, gleaned through our many happy holidays visiting her.

And to the folk at New Generation Publishing – thank you for delivering what you promised.

Finally, this book would not have been written without the unswerving support of my wife, Rosemary. You are, indeed, a rare gem.

Made in the USA
Columbia, SC
18 May 2023

16908262R00236